KILLER OF ENEMIES

KILLER OF ENEMIES

Joseph Bruchac

Tu Books

AN IMPRINT OF
LEE & LOW BOOKS, INC.

New York

TU BOOKS, an imprint of LEE & LOW BOOKS Inc.
95 Madison Avenue, New York, NY 10016
leeandlow.com

Manufactured in the United States of America
by Worzalla Publishing Company, May 2015

Book design by Isaac Stewart
Book production by The Kids at Our House
The text is set in Adobe Garamond Pro

HC 10 9 8 7 6 5 4 3
PB 10 9 8 7 6 5 4 3 2 1
First Edition

Library of Congress Cataloging-in-Publication Data
Bruchac, Joseph, 1942-
Killer of enemies / Joseph Bruchac. — First edition.
pages cm
Summary: "In a world that has barely survived an apocalypse that leaves it with pre-twentieth century technology, Lozen is a monster hunter for four tyrants who are holding her family hostage"— Provided by publisher.
ISBN 978-1-62014-143-4 (hardcover : alk. paper) —
ISBN 978-1-62014-276-9 (paperback) — ISBN 978-1-62014-144-1 (e-book)
[1. Genetic engineering—Fiction. 2. Hunting—Fiction. 3. Survival—Fiction. 4. Extrasensory perception—Fiction. 5. Hostages—Fiction. 6. Chiricahua Indians--Fiction. 7. Indians of North America—Southwest, New—Fiction. 8. Southwest, New—Fiction. 9. Science fiction.] I. Title.
PZ7.B82816Kil 2013
[Fic]—dc23

2013023567

For my Grandmothers,
my Mother, and my Sisters,
the Warrior Women
who made me who I am.

CHAPTER ONE

Numero Uno

'm five miles away from the walls of my prison, up in the high country above the Sonoran Desert. Thus far, surprisingly, nothing has yet attempted to maim or devour me since I settled here a half hour ago. Despite the nearby presence that I sense of one of those "little problems" that I deal with out here in the wilds, I have met nothing to worry about . . . yet.

I'm sitting on my favorite ridgetop, leaning back against a standing stone. I checked first to make sure no big, hungry being with wide wings or sharp teeth was perched atop or behind said stone. I look back toward Haven, formerly known as Southwestern Penitentiary.

Even from this height and this distance, it is an impressive sight. Home sweet home. If you can call a place a "home" when it is where your family members are being held hostage against your good behavior. Sanctuary for some, but still fulfilling its steady old role as a prison for far more.

Haven's double row of walls makes it resemble the cross-section of a giant concrete truck tire. Although no truck tire was ever draped with miles of razor wire or topped with machine gun turrets. Of course, for the last decade, truck tires of any kind have been redundant aside from being used as fuel for watch fires.

I remember that time of motor vehicles, Mars rockets, and mag-levs. I was born in what used to be New America B.C.— Before the Cloud.

My hands start to tingle. I hold them up at elbow height, palms out, and turn until I am facing west. Yup, sure enough, something is moving up the hill through the thick stand of aspen and cottonwood trees below.

I can't see it yet. But from the motions of the branches it is big and coming my way. To be precise, it is coming for me. And for the thousandth time I say a little prayer of thanks for the unaffected workability of the heavy object I am now holding in my right hand.

Every application of electronics—from comtech, advanced weaponry, and computers to the tiny disease-purging nanobots that constantly healed our near-immortal leaders—totally ceased working with the advent of the Cloud. Even batteries.

However, our silvery visitor had no effect at all on the more basic technologies, such as those that use a mixture of sulphur, salt petre, and finely ground charcoal to propel a non-spherical projectile through a rifled barrel with explosive force.

Technology such as that of the .357 Magnum revolver clenched in my fist.

Safety off. Time to flow and go, girl. I head down into the forest to meet it halfway.

I don't have to go far before I see it lumbering up the slope, following the scent trail I was careful to leave. It's a gemod. I expected that, it being well into the afternoon. The regular critters tend to start their hunting early in the morning.

Gemods. Genetically modified beings, put together from the DNA of disparate critters. The pleasure parks of the most powerful Ones used to hold large numbers of such dangerous designer monsters. Until the creatures found themselves no longer confined by electric fences. And with their newfound freedom they also discovered they were on their own when it came to finding sufficient protein on which to survive—such as that of their former owners.

The bulky and bushy-tailed cat-like creature is now snuffling through the fallen aspen leaves. The leaves' silvery sheen is a nice contrast to the cat's golden coat. Its round body and that huge tail make it look awkward, sort of bumbly and harmless. Nowhere near as massive or threatening as some I've seen and survived—like the gigantic cave bear beast I was butchering the morning I was inducted into the service of my current benevolent overlords.

Not that I was a willing conscript. Especially after they

killed my dog. Despite their weapons, Lobo had lunged for the machine gun–toting mercenaries before I could stop him. As soon as they showed themselves, he'd known them to be enemies and leaped to his feet growling a warning. One quick blast of three shots cut him down right in front of me. Lobo's eyes were dimming as he tried to crawl back to me. And then the light in his eyes went out forever.

In that moment, I stood up with fire in my own eyes. All I wanted to do was kill them right then. And despite their guns, those AK-47 boys might have ended up dead then. But they were not pointing their guns at me. They had them trained on their three hostages. Although they had killed my father and my uncle, they'd brought with them my mother, my little brother Victor, and my sister Ana. They'd heard what I could do. They wanted me alive.

The little village my late father and my Uncle Chatto had set up in our hidden valley a few miles away had been the first stop on their recruiting tour. It was a place hidden so well that it was only found because of my father's kindness. He'd rescued two men from what seemed certain death when he found them lost in the desert a day's walk from our mountain stronghold. They were spies for Diablita Loca. They betrayed us, cut the throats of our sentinels, and led enemies into our small Shangri-la.

I shake my head, turn my mind away from my memories of Valley Where First Light Paints the Cliff, from the peach

4

trees that grew there in that ancient sheltered valley to the south, from the remembered faces of a father and an uncle I will never see again in this lifetime. No time at this moment for grief or regret. I need to focus on what is in front of me.

This critter is not a cave bear. But looks are not everything. If it's survived thus far, there has to be something lethal about it. It's not gigantic, but it is bigger than, say, a Siberian tiger. Its seeming neglect of my presence as I stand silently is the opposite of its true intent. It's been following my scent, planning to take me unawares. Members of the cat family tend to attack from ambush, hitting their prey from behind and stabbing their canines into the neck. Then all it takes is one determined shake to break the spine.

That is why, as the object of its affection, yours truly has now placed her back against a wide-trunked cottonwood tree. Somehow the tree survived the past century's clearing of the mountain forests. And right now, it is key to my survival.

I can feel my heartbeat quickening. Not a bad thing. It always does in moments like this. Speeds up reaction time.

Why have I not yet attempted to ventilate this critter? True, all I have is a handgun. A rifle would have been better, but this was all I was issued for my mission. One problem with being in the employ of crazy people: Rulers who find it amusing to expect me to succeed and unreasonably challenge me at the same time. But it's not my weaponry that is my reason for waiting. The big cat is only thirty yards away now, well within the range of my .357. And I am not unsure of my aim. At double this distance I can hole the bulls-eye in a target six times in four seconds. (It's possible to get off six shots faster, but for accuracy one needs half a second to adjust for recoil.)

No, my hesitation is due to two things.

Numero Uno, my stalker has its head down, hiding its eyes. A shot into the body mass would be easy, but some gemods have skin so thick and ribs so strong that even a Magnum round would pierce no more than an inch or two. Deep enough to tick it off. That is why I always aim for an eye shot. I have yet to encounter any beast with impervious retinas.

Numero Dos, this particular gemod is one I haven't seen before. Gemods were never made up as one-of-a-kinds, but in litters, batches, prides, mobs, gobs, or whatever you want to call them. And they were cooked up to be fertile, able to produce more of their kind. I might eventually run into another one like this. Thus, I'd be wise to observe as much of its behavior as possible—especially its method of attack—before sending it off to whatever afterlife a recombinant might experience.

Time to stir the pot and see what's cooking. I pull my motorcycle goggles back down over my eyes.

"Yoo-hoo," I call. "Over here, kitty-cat." Then I hurl the nice round rock I picked up from the ground, bouncing it off its skull.

AHR-REEEEEEK!

Its shriek as it rears up on its hind legs and spreads out

scimitar-sized claws is startling enough to make the hair stand up on my arms.

And at mid-point of that scream, it attacks, with a leap quicker and longer than most people with normal reflexes would expect. But not me. I had already dived back behind the cottonwood tree before it hit. And dropped to the ground.

WHOMP!

Quite an impact, that heavy blow which shakes the big tree. Delivered not merely with those big front paws, but also with that bushy tail. Quilled, of course. A handful of dislodged foot-long spikes fly over my head as the end of its tail whips partway around the trunk. Would have impaled me had I not dropped.

Part tiger and part porcupine? How nice!

Enough learning for one day. I rise to one knee. My gun is up and steady in both hands as it sticks its head around the tree expecting to behold a punctured corpse. Alas. It barely has time to look disappointed before—*ka-pow! ka-pow!*—I permanently dilate its left and right pupils with several ounces of lubricated lead alloy.

CHAPTER TWO

A Good Knife

There's nothing more comforting than the heft of a good knife in your hand. Especially one that's as heavy and perfectly balanced as the Tennessee Toothpick I've just pulled from its sheath at my waist. At fifteen full inches in length, it's bigger than the one Crocodile Dundee brandished in the ancient viddy that bore his name. Another item in my memory bank like such long-gone things as sound and pictures from hand-inserts and temp lenses. (Lucky for me, we never had credits or status enough to afford viddy-plants. Picture smoke curling out of overcooked corneas.)

I remember corny old Nick Dundee because my Dad loved that viddy so much. He was always slipping it into my queue of oldies. And—like that Croc guy—loving and knowing how to use a knife was part of who my father was. This blade I'm holding was his.

Was. Damn it. The week before he died, he gave me this beautiful bone-handled blade. His favorite knife.

I drag my right forearm across my face. Too much blood on my hands to use them to wipe the mist from my eyes. The warmth still rising up from the dead monster's body is wrapping a cloak of cloud around me as a cool wind blows across the clearing. That wind rattles dried leaves clinging to the tips of the branches of a small nearby aspen. Dead now, but green will once again glow from that tree. Spring will slowly return, its steps, as Dad always said, like those of a small bird. And with that season of renewal more shoots of trees will spring up from the soil. Dad used to point that out—that with the power gone, the forests will come back. Bad as the Silver Cloud was for most of humanity, it was a blessing for plants—and monsters. Too bad some of those monsters are humans.

I bend back to my butchering, a task made simpler by the fine implement in my hand. It is a more or less exact replica of the gift given way back in the mid-nineteenth century by Rezin P. Bowie (born 1793) to his older brother Jim (born 1796). With a guarded handle and a strong, weighty single edge blade, its back straight for most of its length before curving concavely to the tip, it was perfect for the frontier duels fought back then by such deadly dandies as Jim and Rezin. The lovely, lethal Bowie knife. More like a short sword. And when it's as razor sharp as I was taught to keep this one, it slices thick skin like butter.

I draw the blade down the length of the beast's belly, put the knife down. I use my hands to spread open the cut, exposing the beast's warm interior. Then I lean in, fingers spread wide, to lever out the stomach and other internal organs.

I have two reasons for my efficient, though bloody disemboweling. Numero Uno—investigate the stomach contents. I need to verify that this is the creature that claimed the lives of the three hunters and two couriers gone missing in this quadrant. Most recently only two days ago. That's when the decision was made to send me in.

A few minutes later I have the answer to part one of my pop quiz. Its gut held the masticated, partially digested remains of the second courier, identifiable by the numbered copper band (like the one I wear) on the gnawed left wrist. I prod with my fingers and extricate from the stinking colon a sturdy little metal case. I wipe it off on my thigh and then open it. It still contains the message that this courier risked—and lost—his life to carry. From Diablita Loca to the head of another settlement barricaded within the walls of a former automobile manufacturing plant a two days' run west of here.

I open the case and pull out the folded paper.

"Buenos días," it reads. "We must do lunch sometime."

And that's it. No requests for an alliance. No big strategic plans. Just a pointless message. I rest my forehead in my palm. This ironic, inane note and the ones I assume were just like it got how many people killed?

Five.

I stick the message case in my pouch, where it clinks against the shell casings from my two expended rounds. I have to account for not only every weapon but also every bullet when I check back in at the armory.

If I searched the few square miles around here, I would find what's left of the other four missing people. Their partly eaten corpses will likely be cached the way big solitary predators store their prey. They'll be covered with dirt, leaves and sticks pawed over them. Turkey buzzards are circling over a little range of hills a mile or so to the north. Probably above one of those half-buried bodies.

But I'm not going to check that out. That's not my work. Neither is interring human remains. But I still take the time to bury what's left of this courier. His name was Kyle. I used to nod at him in the food line. He had dark hair and a big nose. He didn't smile much. I can't recall anything in particular that he said, aside from a shy "Hey." Kyle was even taller than me. He had strong legs, a lean body. Running was his job. Different from mine.

Not many have my unique skill set. I am the best in Haven at my job. That's why I was sent out here today. I'm a monster hunter, a killer of enemies as my dad might have put it—partly tongue in cheek.

Dad was like that about most important things. Joking and serious at the same time.

But he was not joking when he gave me the name of our old time relative Lozen.

I t's a name to live up to. It inspires me and reminds me of all our ancestors. I try to hunt in their old way. First, I always show respect to the enemy. Not hate, not anger. Respect. Secondly, when I have made a kill, I speak to that creature's spirit. I ask forgiveness for taking its life.

Thinking of two things, I have not yet mentioned Numero Dos of my reasons for butchering every beast I kill. It, too, comes from the old traditions of my people and not the new, self-centered masters I must continue to serve if I wish to keep my mother and my Victor and Ana alive. It is a tradition to take into my own being some of a dead monster's power.

I cut out its heart. I hold it up and say a few old Chiricahua words. Then I eat it. Raw.

CHAPTER THREE

Little Food

I am two-thirds of the way back to Haven when I hear it. Or feel it.

Hello, Little Food.

Not again. I freeze at those breathless words that came right after the stabbing pain in the middle of my forehead, pain that is getting too familiar. It always happens when I am alone.

Hello, Little Food.

Those three words were not spoken out loud. Not carried on sound waves, but "heard" somehow, somewhere in whatever part of the brain can be touched mind to mind. I feel the hair standing up on the back of my neck.

My body is telling me to run. But I was trained too well to do that. My training started as soon as I could walk. Not just by my dad, but also by Uncle Chatto. Chatto, my Little Father, my mother's brother.

"Prey animals," Uncle Chatto said, "the hunted ones, are fooled by their fear. The mountain lion roars and the rabbit runs right into the paws of the one lying in wait for it."

And though I was only four years old when he said that to me, I nodded and understood.

So I do not run. Instead, I drop down to one knee. I slip the pack from my shoulder, heavy with all those pounds of meat I cut from the porcupine cat. Prime cuts to be eaten or salted and dried for later. My load weighs more than most men could easily carry. I'm deceptively thin, but few ordinary men are as strong as I am.

But this is not the time for strength. Getting low is the best tactic to employ right now. I'm out in the open, exposed. I've only crossed halfway across a wide field. It once was part of some giant automated agri-biz operation. No crops are planted here anymore. The soil is starved of the mix of chemicals that sustained its fertility, parched without the water drawn from deep wells that moistened it. It's now drier and more lifeless then the desert it was before it was artificially fed and irrigated. No rock or tree here to put my back against. Damn!

I'm just as exposed as I was the first time that self-amused voice spoke to me. The nearest shelter, a four-story-tall derelict robo-tractor, is hundreds of yards away, parked next to the burnt-out hangar that once housed it.

I do just as I did a month ago when I first heard that breathless voice. I sweep my gaze slowly in a circle, heavy gun in one hand, heavier knife in the other. Nada. Nothing moving. No shape resolving itself into an enemy.

I don't know how near this someone else—or something else—needs to be for its telepathy to work. Feet? Yards? Miles? Does it have to see me? I am fairly certain, though I can't say why, that it does see me. I am even more certain that its addressing me as "Little Food" is not a positive sign for my continued health, even though the deep voice echoing through my brain has what I can only describe as a mellow, friendly tone.

I wait. That's all I can do. Breathe in and out. Count. *One and one pony. Two and one pony.*

I get up to sixty before the voice touches me again. It's fainter. Whatever is communicating is moving away.

Not yet, it says. ***Not yet.***

Then it's gone.

Somehow, again I'm not sure why, I believe that voice to be telling the truth. Not yet. Still, I wait long enough to be fairly certain that an attack really is not coming. Then I shrug the pack back up onto my back. I trudge across the sere plain where little winds spin dust devils in front of me. Half a league, half a league, half a league onward. I climb up the small familiar hill where pines are reclaiming a once bare ridge top. Not as good a view of Haven from up here as on the peak four miles back where I encountered the porci-cat, but high enough to take it all in. I sit and watch the swirling patterns of smoke in the sky above Haven, smoke rising from the fires kept burning for protection atop the walls.

One more mile to go. Part of me can't wait to get there. That's the part that is worried about my mom and Ana and Victor. They're the reason I have to survive. My worries about them make me have nightmares about dying almost every night. What bothers me about those dreams is not my own dying, but that my getting killed will leave them with no one to watch over them. I have to protect them and keep trying to work out some way to get them out of there. So far all I have are vague ideas, plans thwarted by the security of Haven. I've already figured out one escape route that I could take at night and get away for sure. My scouting trips have always served a double purpose. Numero Uno for the Ones: Kill their enemies.

Numero Dos for me: Plan our escape. Each time I've gone out I've taken note of safe sheltering places and have stored piles of firewood there. I've stashed dried food—and a few other things—in various places along potential getaway routes. I've located sources of the precious water so vital for survival. Here in the southwest your body loses a pound of it every day through sweating alone. Our ancestors managed to survive for so long with thousands of white and black soldiers pursuing them because they knew all the springs and seeps. My name-sake, Lozen, was a water finder, a gift as important as being able to locate the direction of her enemies before they could reach her.

Enemies. That's another obstacle at least as big as Haven's walls.

After getting over the wall, any nighttime getaway would only be relatively easy if I was alone, not with three other people. Things wait outside Haven at night. Every night. Welcoming, but not in any way that would be easy for us to survive. By myself I could elude, outrun, or outfight them. But my family couldn't do that. Without access to the armory, we wouldn't have the weaponry needed to protect ourselves at night. While I am pretty sure Guy—who runs the armory—is my ally, that's one problem I haven't quite solved.

Not that I would actually be able to get my family to that escape route yet. It's no accident that every time I'm sent out on a mission the Ones make sure that my family is tightly secured somewhere. We're allowed to get together only for brief visits. Since being brought to Haven we've never been able to spend even a single night together. But I'm not going to give up until I find a way. No prison is escape-proof. There must be a way. There has to be.

Just thinking of them makes it seem for a moment as if they're here with me. I can smell the comforting odor of the herbal soap that Mom makes coming from her hair. I can feel Ana's soft palm on my arm as she looks up at me with her beautiful eyes. Too beautiful. It worries me about the way some of the worst men here have started to notice her. "Lozen," she'll say as she always does, "I'm so glad you're back." And I can see tough little Victor pretending he's not all that excited to see me, but making sure that he sits down close enough to lean his back against me. He wishes he were old enough to be trained to do the kind of work I do. I thank all the saints in heaven that he is not. I already have enough to worry about.

I'm glad he's only eight. If he was older, he'd be forced to use his hunting skills in service to the Ones, not our people.

If it weren't for my family, I would turn around and start running, not stopping till I'd put at least fifty miles between me and this place. Eager as I am to see them, to make sure they're all right, I need to prolong my return to Haven's tight security and tighter bonds just a little bit longer. Breathe the air of something that is almost freedom for just a little bit longer.

In a funny way, I am glad I heard that voice again, even if whatever communicated seems to view me as a midnight snack. It means I am not imagining my new ability.

That ability: reading other people's minds. Not exactly like in some old sci-fi story. I just hear bits of speech, sometimes not even words but just scenes from the brains of people around me. And usually I have to really focus to do it, though sometimes it just pops up on me. And when I do, I feel as if there is a needle, getting hotter and hotter, right in the middle of my forehead.

There have been rumors about other people being able to do it. Just rumors. And I've told no one about my own experience. It started not too long after the cloud settled in. Which

18

makes me speculate about a few possibilities. One is that telepathy, speaking mind to mind, may be something latent in all human beings. Maybe it is something genetic—better developed, more common—in certain people, certain families. My nineteenth-century namesake, the first Lozen, was able to do things others could not. She could perceive danger coming from farther away than eyes could see. When she spoke with the spirits, they told her about things that had not yet happened. Maybe mind-reading was one of her skills.

A second speculation is about why I was never able to experience this before. My theory is that all the now-vanished modern communication activities in the world—telephones, short-wave, video and audio broadcasts, computers, the Internet—acted as a damper on paranormal abilities. Then the Cloud overthrew humanity's fragile electronic empire. It also released a whole passel of craziness from the minds of the human survivors. Cults and their accompanying armies sprang up overnight—like the Know Nots who rose after New America fell. They believed that knowledge was the cause of humanity's downfall and went around burning libraries and every form of printed matter they could find.

I can't stay here long. I sigh, stand up, start walking again. Down one hill, up another, and so on until I am only one ridge away from Haven. One ridge away from its walls that surround you like a giant's fist, holding you so tight that you have to struggle to breathe. But those I love are there, too. I have no choice but to return.

However, I don't have to hurry. I sit down again, this time next to a stone with petroglyphs on it that look like bird-winged beings. I raise my gaze to watch a golden eagle circling overhead through the shimmering air. I wish I could join it. That big bird is free. Its power was undiminished by that subtle effulgence that has silvered Earth's sky since it all ended.

It happened so fast. I am sure some people thought it was a dream, even though we all watched the start of it on handhelds and implants and city center com-screens. A shimmering silver cloud far out in interplanetary space. First spotted by one of New America's dozen Mars satellites. Heading toward Earth from beyond Jupiter, first concealed by that giant planet's mass until it was well past it. Moving at a speed just slow enough for images of it to continue to be flashed for a full day on all the public personal viewers, such as those imprinted inside the eyelids of the Ones and the cheaper mass-produced temp-screens leased to the ordinaries at reasonable rates. One very full day. Time enough for it to be seen and discussed all over our planet before it reached us. A magnetic phenomenon? A sentient entity?

At the speed it was approaching, over a hundred thousand miles per hour, there was not much time for anything much to be done to prepare for it. Not that anything much would have worked. The fifty or so thermonuclear asteroid buster warheads deployed against it did not explode. They might have disinte-grated any oncoming space rock into dust, but not this threat. No big atomic explosions. Just a cessation of transmission as that cloud, now estimated to be twice the size of Earth's moon, kept coming. It quietly settled into the atmosphere, adding a gentle glaze to the sky through which the sunlight streamed and the night stars remained visible. More visible than before when all the lights of the cities went out.

And countless billions of screens went blank forever.

The results of the permanent silencing of every bit of electronic technology from Marconi on were notably noisy in many instances, such as in the rapid unpowered return of all aircrafts to the unforgiving surfaces of our planet's lands and waters. Or the screaming of ordinaries trapped a thousand miles from the nearest station inside subterranean trains that stopped speeding through the tunnels bored deep in the earth to link the continents.

Countless scenarios of disaster played out during that time, among them those hooked up to life-saving machines now permanently obsolete. Or—alas for nearly all of the elite—the disastrous consequences visited upon those now more than half-machine themselves because of their numerous transplants, upgrades, and enhancements. The most important men and women who chaired the three great corporate nation-states of New America, Euro-Russia, and Afro-Asia all perished painfully, quickly, and dramatically.

Luckily for my family, we were what was once called lower class. We had nothing attached to us other than by external mag strips.

It was lucky for me in particular that my youthful skills

included such (pre-cloud) anachronistically useless pursuits as hand-to-hand combat, marksmanship, tracking, and wilderness survival at a time when the wilderness itself was barely surviving. Those esoteric and (pre-C) outdated interests can be blamed on or credited to my family, especially my uncle and my dad—stubborn descendants of a nation that had been targeted for destruction in more than one century yet still survived.

Not all of the Ones, our planetary elite, perished with the coming of the Cloud. Those with plenty of lust for power but not enough status for full modification—they survived. And the more basic weapons held by what was left of their armies still worked. That was when they began to bring "order" out of the ensuing chaos. Order meaning the establishment of little dictatorships like the one we have at Haven.

That struggle for order is still underway around this continent and in what's left of the other great corporate states as well. But the reestablishment of anything resembling nations has been held back by a bunch of things. Limited communication, for example—aside from runners and carrier birds. No means of rapid transportation with the demise of internal combustion engines.

That didn't stop people way back in the day, but then there are the gemods and the various other non-human or semi-human monsters that were released from their electrified cells, cages, and other enclosures. The presence of those beings quickly made the cities death traps. Predators know that the best places to hunt are the water holes. For water holes, substitute supply marts where cred machines no longer worked and windows and autolock doors have been broken or pried open by looters looking for packaged food and drink. And now imagine various critters of different shapes and sizes with interesting combinations of fangs and claws leaping out from the concealment of counters or dropping from the ceilings.

The cities were not places to survive. Nor was life under the rule of petty warlords that much better. That's why some of us—like my family—retreated from the craziness. Rather than fighting with each other, we tried to cooperate. We created a little tribal community where our knowledge of the land and old ways of sustaining ourselves could be put to good use. We had two dozen peaceful people living together in our valley before the scouts from Haven found us. Only four of us are still alive.

I shade my eyes with one hand and squint down at Haven. While I've been sitting here musing about a vanished past that is not coming back, the sun has moved across the sky. It's shining so brightly that my eyes have started watering. I wipe the corner of them with one knuckle. I look up at the sky. No sign of the eagle anymore. It's flown as far out of sight as any futile dreams of freedom.

I stand up and brush the sand off my knees. I sling my bag over my shoulder. Time to return to my home sweet prison.

CHAPTER FOUR

Password

I am welcomed by adoring crowds strewing my path with blossoms as they chant my name.

Lo siento, senorita. That would make life a lot nicer, wouldn't it?

Instead, after I have pounded on the small metal door in the middle of the big metal door that is the main entrance to Haven, I stand out in the hot sun mentally counting to myself.

One and one pony. Two and one pony.

At one hundred and one pony I bang again. The prescribed six times that comprise today's password. Or pass-pound, I suppose.

Nothing. They could put a bench out here for scouts and couriers to sit on while they wait. But, no. That would be too easy.

I sigh and start counting again.

I get up to five hundred before anyone answers.

"Friend or foe," a high, hostile voice calls down from the gun tower above the gate.

I look up, showing my face to the person who just spoke and remains hidden, aside from the metal eyes of his double-barrel protruding from the gun slot. He knows who I am. Probably recognized me when I was still half a mile away, crossing the wide expanse around Haven that is kept free of anything other than gravel.

"It's me, Edwin," I reply, trying not to sound exasperated. Which I am, as well as tired and feeling an ache in my back.

"Friend or foe?"

Edwin, who believes he is at least the second toughest guy in Haven, saw far too many war movies in his pre-C life.

"How about neither?" I reply, thinking, *do your damn job and unlock the frigging door!*

A bee-sting sized pain stabs the middle of my forehead. And I hear Edwin's thought in my mind.

How about waiting, bitch?

Those words in his head are mixed with a very unpleasant image that features me in a most uncomfortable position while Edwin—twice as muscular as in real life—stands over me. The creep tried hitting on me half a dozen times before I finally snapped and swept his feet out from under him as he accidentally (for the fourth time) groped me in the mess hall. Of course he hopped right up again, red-faced. Made it look like he slipped on something. I didn't argue with him then, nor do I now.

Never argue with a man who has the drop on you from twenty feet overhead. True, I could shoot him, put one round right through that gun slot into his narrow little forehead. But then what? I would still be stuck out here. Plus homicide is—depending on whether or not you are either one of the Ones or one of their minions—illegal.

Time to take a deep breath and keep my temper.

My tormentor, Edwin, is the day's Keeper of the Keys. Scarlet Red today. Jet Black tomorrow. White, the next day and Forest Green the fourth before it goes back to Scarlet again.

Edwin's in charge. So I have to follow his silly, useless rules.

"Friend," I say, making my voice not just friendly, but a little sultry—as if his show of masculine power has impressed and even turned me on. That should help. Edwin likes to think he is irresistible, when as far as I am concerned he is the polar opposite. Not this Neanderthal nitwit. If I ever thought of any man in a romantic way it would be someone like Hussein. Someone who's quiet and gentle, someone who covers his strength with grace and politeness. As if there's any chance in the world for romance in Haven. Or any chance of Hussein ever seeing me as anything other than someone to greet politely as we pass.

"Ah," Edwin says, his tone more businesslike. "Excellent. Now what is the password?"

I do not say what I am thinking, even though it begins with the first letter of today's chosen phrase.

"First light."

"Good. Absolutely correct. You may enter."

I raise one eyebrow and then look pointedly at the still-unlocked door.

"Oh, right. I'll be right down."

This time I only get to fifty and one pony before I hear the jangling of his keys and the slap of his feet reach the other side of the door.

"Now which key is it? This one. No. Not this one. Ah, this one? Nope. Here it is."

Click of light. Old-spooky-house creak of metal door as it swings slightly open. How wonderful. I am finally free to enter the prison that is all the home I may ever know.

"How nice to see nothing has eaten you yet," Edwin says, his foot still blocking the door from opening more than a crack. At moments like this I am not feeling blessed about how much sharper my senses seem to be than most ordinary people, especially my olfactory nerve. With my eyes closed, I can recognize the people I know from yards away. Hussein, for example, smells like the leaves of the tomatoes in the garden he oversees. And why am I thinking of him again? Probably just because of the contrast offered by the human obstacle before me.

Edwin's scent is far from heaven-sent. I'm not sure if he ever brushes his teeth. His breath makes me think of rotten meat—probably because he has a bad tooth or two in that nasty mouth of his. Dentists do not exist in Haven. Then there is his rank body odor. True, none of us ordinaries are able to take regular showers, with water being such a rare and precious commodity. But his rank is above ours and thus his water ration is greater. You'd think he could at least sponge off his pits and change his underwear now and then.

His scent is also a giveaway that he's on Chain. Once on Chain, you need the drug at least twice a week or you go into hard withdrawal. Diablita keeps certain of her men hooked on it. I hadn't known that Edwin was one of them. Last run-in I had with him, his B.O. hadn't been nearly this bad.

Not only does Chain make its users dependent and desperate for the drug—like the two men who betrayed us and led Diabilita's men to Valley Where First Light Paints the Cliff—it also makes those persons much stronger and turns them into berserkers when they go into battle. Chain really kicks in under stress. It deadens them to pain and makes them keep on coming even when they are badly wounded. Ready to beat you to death with their own severed limbs.

So it's best not to upset Edwin.

Despite the fact that his delightful odor de disgusting is filling the air between us, about all I can see of him right now is his blood-red armband—the mark of one of Diablita Loca's minions—and his nasty eyes moving up and down my body.

"Happy to see me?" he asks.

Not a trace of sarcasm in his nasal voice—unless you count every word he just said and the haughty tone he spoke it in, as if he were a One. Hah. As if a rat could become a cat!

I don't take the bait. If I spit a clever putdown back at him, it'll just mean having to wait longer the next time I need to have him open the door for me. And that next time might be late at night with something large and hungry close at my heels.

"Yes," I say, keeping my voice as friendly as I can manage, even though I imagine the toe of my boot making contact you know where. I show no emotion on my face. I keep it as calm as the surface of a pond. That calm—some might say stupid—face is what I always show to the world. No anger, no sorrow. No laughter, no tears. I will never let them see me crying, no matter how much my heart may be torn.

Never let your enemies see your weakness is what Uncle Chatto said.

"Enter," Edwin intones. He steps aside just enough that I have to brush against him as I enter before he slams the door shut again. While he is locking it I walk away before he can say or do anything further.

Not alone, of course. I am closely tailed by two blasé guards, both with red armbands, whose job it is to escort me. They seem bored by their job, but armed as I am I have to be escorted. That's the rule. They're not authorized to take my weapons themselves. Yet another rule. Only one person is allowed to disarm a scout when said gun-toter gets back.

Disarm, log in, and lock up all lethal items carried on that scout's person. The armorer's job.

Thus, the well-guarded armory fifty yards further on is my first destination. As I approach it I hear the sound of hammers striking steel and catch the whiff of molten metal from the workshop buildings and labs to my left.

Metal workers and smiths are among those constantly being sought out (hunted down, more like) by the Ones as they build their various fiefdoms. Such skilled people have the knowledge and manual skills to manufacture things that the Ones desire. Electricity, like Buffalo Bill, is defunct. But not combustion.

Here in Haven, the amount of gasoline and oil that is available is limited. But the pine and aspen forests on the mountains that rise above the desert only a few miles away can provide more than enough wood for fuel. Hence making use of wheeled devices powered by steam is a major priority of the Ones. Reverse engineering vehicles so that no electricity is involved in their running is, to say the least, a challenge. Thus far their successes have been minimal. The thought of a new age of wheeled vehicles, including such lovely devices as tanks and armored personnel carriers powered by combustion sans electricity, makes my flesh crawl.

My escorts relinquish me to two other guards stationed in front of the armory door. One wears the green armband of the Jester, the other the white of Lady Time. Although they are hired thugs like all their kind, these guards are not total dicks like Edwin, nor do they have the little facial tics that Chainers get. Not all guards are on that drug. The supplies looted from abandoned pharmacies are limited and the Ones have yet to find a chemist who knows how to make more.

The two guards look at each other. Their faces are almost as emotionless as mine. Then they nod and step to either side to let me enter.

One-eyed Guy greets me with a grin as I come through the door. He's not one-eyed because he had one of those failed sub-retinal devices transplanted in his right socket. His missing eye is the result of a narrow escape from an indeterminate critter whose claw made that long double line of scars down his cheek and forehead. He was Haven's Killer of Enemies before that encounter. I was recruited to take his place.

He doesn't resent me for that. In fact, though he never mentions it any more, he is regretful about all that happened to me and my family as a result of Haven's need of a new monster slayer. Without saying it in so many words, I know I can count on Guy. I know that he knows I have hopes of escaping. And he knows that I know he will help me however he can. Just as we both know how cautious we have to be. Harsh punishments are meted out for anything, even a careless word, that might remotely suggest rebellion against the Ones.

Like me, Guy wears no colors other than the muted brown of his khaki pants and short-sleeved shirt. He smells of gunpowder. I love that smell. His job now is to keep and care for our deadliest armaments. There's no way that the Four who rule our lives would allow someone in his position to be in the service of any single One. It's why the armory is always guarded by one man from each of their retinues. Two in front, two in back at all hours of the day.

"Good t' see you, lass."

His Scottish accent is as real as the warm sincerity with which he greets me. Guy is a former middleweight boxer from Glasgow, whose long-shot quest for a world title in Vegas fell apart with the rest of our modern world ten minutes after he left the airport. None of the jets that plummeted from the sky landed on the stretch of roadway where his cab stalled. The tale of how he made his way across three disintegrating southwestern states to end up here several years ago might seem remarkable—if his story was not matched by so many others who survived against odds greater than those in any casino.

"Guy," I say.

He grasps my right wrist and my elbow. I grab his and we bump our shoulders together. Though he's fifty—one of the oldest people here in Haven—he's still stronger and fitter than most men half his age. And twice as useful. It would be hard to find anyone who knows as much as he does about weaponry. His father was a racetrack blacksmith, one of his uncles a gunshop owner and professional bodyguard, and another the author of *The British Guide to Nineteenth Century Firearms*.

Guy steps back and holds out his right hand. I slip my .357 from the holster and offer it to him butt first.

He sighs. "Just get it over with, lass."

I do the little twist of my wrist that spins the gun's grip back into my palm with the barrel pointing straight at Guy's forehead.

"Bang," I say.

"Nah!" Guy replies. His hands move so fast they are blurred as he twists the gun from my grip, points it an inch above my head and pulls the trigger.

Click.

The sound of the hammer falling on an empty cylinder. As always. Just as always, I have emptied the gun before passing through the armory door.

I hold out my left hand and drop the bullets into Guy's already outstretched palm.

He twitches the corner of his mouth into the shadow of a smile as press my lips a little closer together and give him the hint of another nod. It's as close as we ever come to laughing over this grim joke we always share.

We could kill each other, but we won't.

CHAPTER FIVE

The Jester

Guy is my immediate superior in the chain of command that is so important to our benevolent overlords. He already knows, as do our rulers, that my mission succeeded. That is evident from the fact that I returned in one piece.

But rules, no matter how capricious and unnecessary they may be, are meant to be followed here in Haven. They insure discipline . . . and obedience. So we have to go through the usual debriefing rigamarole. Which is always as brief as I can make it.

All of my registered weapons now locked away—even my father's Bowie knife—I follow Guy into the interview room adjacent to the armory. He locks the door, takes a clipboard from the wall. We both sit at the table next to the big mirror.

As we go through the interview I did not look over his

shoulder toward that mirror, behind which listeners are stationed. Just as there were listeners observing us in the armory through the peepholes drilled into the wall. Guy interviews me after each kill, but that doesn't mean that he's actually trusted by the higher-ups. In fact, the higher up it goes, the less trust there is. Thus, his interviews are always observed by several eavesdroppers behind that mirror. They watch and listen and report back to their various overlords. Their identities are secret. You never know when someone who is pretending to be your friend might be one whose main mission is to inform.

Even Guy has no idea who the people behind that mirror are. In the small world of Haven, where information is as deadly as the guns we use, he's seen as nothing more than an ignorant gun hand. Which is a good thing. Being underestimated here means you are less likely to be seen as a real risk, a danger to the establishment.

That's why I will act dumb during this interview. Why Guy and I both find our little charade of stupidity amusing.

"So," Guy begins, "you got it?" There's a twinkle in his eye.

I nod and stay serious, covering up a chuckle by disguising it as a cough.

"Was it the one responsible for the disappearance of our couriers?"

I grunt and reach down into my pack. I extricate the bent copper bracelet and the message case and drop them clattering on the table.

"That is a yes," Guy says, making a check on his pad. "Gemod?"

I nod again. Guy checks another box.

"Type?"

I think a moment before answering, picturing the critter in my mind. "Uhhh, Porcupine? Tiger?"

"Hmmm," Guy says. He lifts his right hand to his chin as if pondering the thought. But as he does so, he places his left hand across his chest and begins to sign.

In our post-electronic world it's no longer possible to eavesdrop unless you are within earshot. That is why those with the best hearing get drafted into service as listeners. It also means that things may only be seen from certain angles—even through peepholes or two-way glass.

"The new bullets worked well?" Guy asks—at the same time that his hands convey the message that sends a chill down my back. *Your mother and sister and brother were moved.*

"Uh-huh," I reply, keeping my face as expressionless as my voice.

Guy motions at my pack, which has made a bloody mark on his cement floor. "Salt some, smoke some?" he asks.

"Sure," I say. Without refrigeration, another casualty of the Cloud, the only way to keep meat from going bad is by using the oldest methods. Salting, smoking, drying into jerky. I push the pack over to him with my foot. He pulls out everything except the tenderest cuts. I'll cook those up later. He slides the pack back to me.

"Ten percent?" he asks. His usual cut for preparing any meat I bring in from a kill.

Expect them to come get you, his hands say.

"Sure." I put both hands flat on the table as if to lean on them to help me rise, but actually to hide the fact that they are trembling. A mix of anxiety, anger, and fear. "Done?"

"Done," Guy says. He stands up, a broad nearly idiotic grin on his face. "Good eats, eh lass?"

I smile back, maybe even more moronically. "Yeah!"

Unless I get eaten first.

W hen I leave the armory I am, of course when within Haven's "safe" environment, disarmed. Or at least that is how I appear. My guns and my Bowie knife have both been left, as always, in Guy's safekeeping. The only thing he's given me are the words he always speaks when we part.

"May the road keep you safe."

But I do have a few other little tricks up my sleeve just in case my journey runs into any dangerous roadblocks. More accurately, I have one in my belt, which has a flexible blade hidden inside that can be whipped out with one twist of an ornamental stud. And I have another four-inch-long needle of a knife inside the heel and sole of my shoe.

So I do not feel totally naked as I cross the yard—even though I feel Edwin's beady little eyes on my back and catch enough of his thought to know that he is mentally stripping me yet again. Sadly, though I wear clothes that are as bulky as I can possibly wear without slowing myself down, they do not hide enough of my figure to disguise the fact that I am not at all shaped like a boy.

I don't swing by the washrooms to get the half cup of water and moist cloth that ordinaries like me are allowed to bathe with. My dark hair is sticky with sweat, my face and arms are smudged with red dirt. My fingernails have dried blood under them. If they are coming for me, I'd rather have them find me dirty.

I do take a detour to the western wall through the vegetable gardens. My mother works in the gardens, and I have a faint hope I might see her briefly. The Ones rarely let her or my siblings out of the family quarters when I am in from a hunt, but perhaps they forgot.

The gardens remind me of her even though I don't see her working. They are an oasis of green, one of the few calming places here in Haven. We grow over two dozen different vegetables and fruits from seeds and cuttings that Haven's foragers have gathered on their trips outside the walls, and the garden is carefully irrigated from the spring that everyone here in Haven depends on.

I shake my head at the thought of how people in the past used precious water to carry away their human bodily wastes instead of just carrying your night soil bucket to the compost pile, which is just on the other side of the gardens from where I stand.

Mom's not there. But Hussein is. He's there all alone, working in a patch of potatoes, singing. He is the head gardener here. Even though he's only nineteen years old, he has a green thumb. No one complains about his youth or the fact that he talks to his plants.

He notices me watching him and lifts his head, a little smile on his face. Is that smile for me? Probably just left over from whatever conversation he was having with those potato blossoms. But it's such a nice smile that I almost smile back at him before I remember the importance of keeping my emotions to myself whenever I'm out in public view. I do raise my hand in greeting to him. And he waves back at me.

Dormitory A—which used to be Cell Bloc A—is where I sleep. It's the single female ordinaries wing. B is single male ordinary. C is for ordinary parents with small children, which means I may be allowed to visit my family but cannot stay with them. I start toward C, where the guard stationed at the entrance recognizes me. He looks down at the sheet on his desk for confirmation, nods to himself. Then he shakes his head and jerks a thumb toward A. I don't ask why. I don't protest. I just do as I am told. But the thoughts going through my head are all silent screams. Where have they been taken? What is happening to them? And why?

There are fifty women and girls in A Bloc. A few of them say hello or wave a hand at me. Most just ignore me, used to my indifferent silence. Aside from Guy, no one in Haven is my friend. Making friends is dangerous enough as it is without trying to befriend someone whose life expectancy—mine more than theirs—is about equal to that of a fly. Also, friends, like family, can be used as leverage against you. Better not to have any.

I reach the door to my house. My cell. I'm pleased to see it hasn't been opened. The bicycle chain I have wrapped around the bars to keep the door shut is still doing its job, the combination lock that holds the ends of the chain still in place. Not that it would deter those in charge here. Every guard station has its own set of bolt cutters. But at least I know that none of my fellow prisoners—I mean residents—have gotten into my stuff.

I work the lock, unwind the chain, slide open the heavy door with one hand (most of the male guards take two hands to do that), go inside, slam it back shut, rewind the chain. But I don't bother to click the combination lock shut. Nor do I settle myself down to whatever sleep is possible in this place where too many sorrowing people are caged together. Where despite the rules requiring silence after lights out, the sounds of women screaming as they wake from nightmares punctuate every night.

No way to get the meat to my family right now. It would have been great to sit and talk with them as Mom cooked some of the meat I brought back. But they had already been escorted back to their bloc by the time I got back. I was too late for when people are allowed to either go to the mess hall or cook on their own in the outdoor cooking area. No fires are allowed inside the residential blocs. But I have to eat.

I take one of the tenderloin strips from my pack and put it into my mouth. Raw meat isn't that bad when it's already salted and you chew it thoroughly as I'm now doing. I do have a drying rack here in my cell. I hang up the rest of the salted tenderloin I'd cut into strips before returning to Haven. Planning ahead is a requirement here—my knife is back in the armory. And I am not about to pull out either of my two hidden blades. Even when you are in your own home—cell, rather—you might still be under surveillance from peepholes in the walls.

I lay down on my cot. Rest while you can is my rule.

They will be coming for me. Probably at dawn. I close my eyes and let sleep take me.

When I open them again the first light is coming through my window. But it's not the new day that wakened me. It's the tingling in my palms and the thud of heavy boots down the hall. Heading my way, of course.

Four guards with green armbands. They take me through a succession of doors. Thirteen in all. Each one is clanged shut and locked behind us as we pass.

Then up one flight of stairs. We are now in the secure area at the heart of the prison.

It used to be the education wing. Now it is divided into the four separate and equally-sized areas that lodge our leaders.

Though I am only about to see one of them, an elite quartet

rule here in Haven. The Ones. Two men, two women. All of them are much older than they look. Their tall bodies are perfect—aside from the disfigurement caused by the tearing out or burning out of optical and auditory enhancements. All of them are one-eyed and one-eared as a result of that. They wear masks to conceal that, but everyone knows they must be terribly scarred. However, despite their disfigurement, the gene modification that slowed and reversed their aging was unaffected by the Cloud.

That anti-aging therapy was only available to the more wealthy and powerful. Not ordinaries like me. Though none of the four are young in age, they're beautifully shaped, as youthful and strong as idealized statues of Greek gods. Luckily for them, when the Cloud came they were only in the lower tier of the wealthy and powerful. They hadn't yet risen to the level where they could afford the microscopic nanobots that flowed through the blood streams of the very, very few who controlled the entire planet. Those few had hundreds of enhancements meant to enable them to live forever as cyborgs. Part human, part machine, they were able to see everything, to kill with a glance, to wave a hand and bring thunder. Gods, it seemed.

And all of them met their Ragnorak when the Cloud descended.

I'm stripped down to my underwear at the next gate, something the Ones liked to do because they are rightly paranoid that their followers could turn on them. So much for my hidden weapons.

I'm escorted to stand in front of a large green door with a yellow smiley face painted in its center. Since the mouth of that face is both crooked and decorated with a pair of fangs, the effect is less than warm and fuzzy. More ironic and insane.

The largest of the four guards steps up to the door and raps on it three times.

"En-terrrrr."

The guard opens the door and steps aside. A rough hand is thrust against my back and I stumble over the threshold.

There, in the center of the round room, lounging crossways in a huge overstuffed chair, is the One who has summoned me. His spiky thatch sticks up straight from the top of his head like a jaybird's crest—if jays had green hair. His long naked legs end at feet with toenails painted as green as the silk robe he has wrapped around himself. The Jester.

He swings up to his feet with a graceful turn—all of the Ones are as lithe and nimble as dancers. It ends in an exaggeratedly comic little shuffle and stomp of his feet on the wooden floor with his hands spread out like an actor in one of those long-forgotten musicals. The mask he wears is that of a green-skinned joker, face distorted in a wide grin.

I do not applaud. Unlike the four guards behind me who are clapping their hands in a well-rehearsed gesture of appreciation.

"Sooooo," the Jester drawls. He thrusts the index finger of his right hand high above his head and the applause stops instantly.

He sweeps that upraised hand down to point at my chest. He leans forward at the waist and thrusts his long-jawed head so close to mine that I can smell his breath. Minty and rank at the same time.

His single mad green eye stares at me through a star-shaped eyehole in the mask. He straightens up and holds his hands out, palm up. A noble king bestowing a boon on an unworthy subject.

"I have a looooov-e-ly new assignment for you."

No attagirls. No "Good job. Take a week off."

"I'm sure you are quite deeee-lighted to hear this."

Sardonic? Sarcastic? No, both.

I nod, keep my face as blank as a piece of slate. I'm safer if I appear too stupid to know I am being made the butt of his irony.

"Hmmmm-ummmm . . ."

His masked face moves up and down as he surveys my nearly nude body.

Pain shoots in my forehead as his thoughts crawl across me like a slug.

So stupid, yet useful, this one. Not much real intelligence, but the ability to take orders, to memorize . . . yessss, and kill. Savage little creature. One wonders what her brain might look like. Yesss.

44

The image that comes to me then from his slimy mind is so disgusting, so graphic that it turns my stomach. I swallow hard.

Stay in control, Lozen.

I keep my hands steady. I do not allow them to curl into claws that could rip out his throat. He might be taller and look stronger than me, but I could kill him twice before any of the three guards around him could move.

"You are to scout the western road. Twenty miles east. Clear it as needed."

Another nod.

"You'll see your mother and—how many?" He turns to the guard nearest him who quickly holds out one index finger on each hand. "Your two siblings, when you return from your scout."

Nod number four. And a small feeling of relief at this minimal reassurance that my family has been taken into tighter custody for the simple purpose of putting more pressure on me.

"Tooo-mor-rrr-ow, tooo-morr-row," he croons. "Now goooo."

A dismissive wave of his hand as he turns his back.

That's it. Interview done.

I nod again, begin to start toward the door.

"One more thing," the Jester's voice stops me halfway through my turn. He is posed in front of his chair, bent to the side with his arms out, one palm facing the ceiling, the other

45

almost touching the floor. He cocks his head in clear expectation of a verbal reply.

"Yes," I say. It's the first word I've spoken since being ushered into his chambers.

He nods, straightens and puts his hands on his hips.

"Do have fun!"

CHAPTER SIX

On the Road

The highway west. Great. Now I know where I am going to die.

As I am escorted down through the thirteenth door, I look calm. But my heart is thudding so hard and fast in my chest that I feel like a walking drum.

Despite the defunct motor vehicles that have littered the interstate highways since the day the Cloud arrived, those roads are still passable, especially by a light, human-powered machine. Bicycles—the one form of wheeled transportation unaffected by the Cloud. But bikes and broad highways are no longer being used around Haven.

Why are we no longer using bikes? And why do we not use the highways instead of traveling on foot on the narrow trails over the hills and through the mountain forests?

It's because the people who ran errands for the Ones on

bikes along those highways never came back. It seems there were certain problems about bikes and highways.

Problem Numero Uno was visibility. A person on a road on a bike is highly visible, especially here in the Southwest where the roads go on for miles without hardly a bend. Visible to enemies.

Problem Numero Dos, especially along the highway west, was the Birds. Birds with a capital B for *big*. As big, I suppose, as the Monster Birds that were wiped out in the time of our First People by Killer of Enemies and his brother Child of Water. My target on this trip, though the Jester never said it aloud, is to neutralize that threat.

As I leave the main building and cross the courtyard, the warm morning sun touches my face. That same sun on hot, dark pavement causes thermals, masses of heated air that rise high into the sky. That's why large flying creatures such as vultures and eagles—and their even bigger mutated cousins— have a special fondness for roads. Those thermals help wide wings stay aloft.

Those monster birds also seemed to be especially attracted to bicycles. Maybe it was something about the sound of the wheels on the road or the gentle noise of the pedals being worked. Whatever the reason, getting on a bicycle anywhere outside of Haven was an invitation to, so to speak, come fly with me.

The rocks far below the high cliff where they nest are said

to be littered with broken human skeletons and smashed bicycle parts.

How do you kill a creature that can just fly out of reach of your weapons—a creature that is as big as a plane?

I've barely managed to calm my breathing by the time I reach the armory door. Guy is standing there. Even though it is just after sunrise, he's already waiting for me. As usual, he got the word about my assignment. I say a silent prayer of thanks once again that he is on my side.

He's smiling as he holds out something no bigger than a medium-sized backpack.

"A wee present for you, lass."

"You're kidding," I say. I take it in my hands and heft it. The words ACE BASE JUMP SPECIAL are stitched on it in red thread.

"Strap it on tight," he says. He taps the looped cord near the bottom. "This is what you pull."

"How old is this?"

"Like new, lass. The chute is made of the finest neo-silk. I know it well, having been a paratrooper meself. Plus I spent a good hour before dawn repacking it. Should work well." He chuckles. "If not, just ask for your money back."

"Hah."

Of course that is not all he has for me. From his seemingly endless collection of combat gear—just about all of it no longer replicable with what technology is left to us, but all of it still carrying a lifetime (ho-ho) guarantee—he has amassed a rather sizable pile of items for me.

Numero Uno, close to my skin, a layer of body armor. It weighs less than a medium-sized book, is soft and flexible to the touch, but harder than carbon steel when something tries to pierce it at any velocity faster than a gentle nudge. It is so light, conforming to me like a second skin, that I'll hardly feel as if I am wearing it.

As I slip it on, Guy starts a little monologue, reviewing what we both already know.

"Our big feathered friends are hard to kill. Bullets seem to bounce off."

I nod. I remember the story that the two surviving scouts told about their encounter. They emptied their AK-47s at the attacking birds. Even panicked as they were, some of those rounds must have hit home. No effect. Although I would bet my life—and probably am betting my life—that they missed my favorite targets, the eyes.

Numero Dos, Guy puts into my hands what looks like an old-fashioned hoodie made of that same deceptively strong material. When I pull it up the vulnerable back of my neck is protected. The only part left uncovered is my face after I've put it on.

"We also know," Guy continues, "their preferred method of dispatching their prey. Grab, peck, fly high, and drop."

Another nod. The two survivors, who'd taken refuge in a

50

narrow cave, had watched in horror as their four comrades were dispatched. Sharp piercing claws were wrapped around their screaming bodies, scimitar beaks stabbed at the backs of their necks, then they were taken for one final ride up a few thousand feet before being dropped. I suppress a shudder.

I'm all dressed save for one final thing. Guy's wee present. He helps me fasten the Base Jump Special to the front of my body, double checks the straps.

"Now," he says. "Weaponry."

No rifles. Too cumbersome, and no more effective at close range than the handguns I'm taking with me. My favorite .357 and one other smaller sidearm, a Glock, for back-up. Both loaded. The Glock with only twelve rounds rather than the thirteen possible with one in the chamber. Glocks don't have safeties, so it's better to jack one into the chamber just before you're ready for action. Carefully counted out additional rounds for the .357 and two spare clips for the Glock. My trusty Bowie knife and three other blades of various shapes and sizes. Then one last thing, which looks like one of those billy clubs that policemen (another extinct species) used to carry.

"Watch this, lass."

Guy twists the handle and it elongates, each section clicking tightly into place, into a six-foot staff.

"And this."

He presses a red dot on the handle. A foot-long, razor-sharp, double-edged blade emerges from the end.

"Here." I say.

Guy slaps it into my hand. I press the dot with my thumb, collapse it. Press the button, open it again. Smooth and easy. Once, twice, three times. Try to bend it when fully extended. Nope, light as it is, it's as unyielding as steel. I stab its blade against the concrete wall of the weapon shed. The blade doesn't bend or break, but it does gouge out a piece of the wall.

"Sold," I say, as I collapse it back down and slip it into the sheath that will attach to my belt, securing the Velcro strap that will hold it in place.

"Ready?" Guy asks.

"Born ready," I reply.

It's a corny thing to say, I know. But it's become a mantra for us every time I head out on one of my suicidal assignments.

Guy slaps me on the shoulder, hard enough for that palm-sized section of my body armor to stiffen to absorb the blow. It's not any power source that causes that, just the sudden shock of impact that makes the molecular structure alter to absorb the blow. Something to do with surface tension.

But he's not done. He holds up a hand, gesturing for me to wait. He disappears into the back of the armory and comes back out with one final thing that he wheels up to me. I bite my lip at the sight of it. I'd been expecting it, but it reminds me that I am setting out on this errand as a human decoy. I'm both the goat tied to a stake to lure in the tiger and the hunter.

"Crap," I say, letting my breath out as I do so.

"Nah," Guy replies. "It's a fine machine. Now just try to bring it back in one piece."

What about bringing me *back in one piece?* I think. But I don't say it. I grab the handlebars of one of the last surviving trail bikes on the continent and start to push it out the door.

"May the road rise up to greet you and keep you safe, lass," Guy says to my back.

I don't turn around. I just nod and keep going.

've been pedaling for most of the morning along the western road. Haven is far behind me now. I've only paused once. That was perhaps an hour ago when I stopped to survey the peaks, which were looming closer. I'd also taken the time to eat some of the venison jerky Guy had packed for me and drink from one of my canteens.

It's a beautiful day. Or so some would say. The only clouds in the sky are those that hover around the further peaks. I look up in fascination at the clouds. Our family is mixed. There is Navajo and Pueblo in us, too. Dad told me that the old people, our Pueblo ancestors, believed those clouds were beings who lived there in the shape of rain clouds. When those old people sang and danced in the right way, at the time of spring planting, those sacred and powerful beings would return to the skies overhead and bring the rain.

My thought about it, though, is that on a clear day like this in the desert when you can see for a hundred miles or more, you can be seen from just as far away. A little shiver goes down my back—and it is not from feeling cold. Something, somewhere, with far better eyesight than mine is watching me.

I think about being Apache, about how it inspires me to be brave. I think about that heritage even more because of my namesake, about being a warrior woman in our old way like Lozen was. And with those thoughts, my hidden doubts come back like dark shadows to haunt me. I'm not afraid of dying. Well, not that afraid. But I do fear failing. I find myself wondering once again about whether I'll be able to live up to that responsibility, that legacy.

I push my goggles up onto my forehead, then take out my collapsible scope. I scan in all directions. The small panicky herd of deer that I spooked off the road is still hunkered down under the overhanging wall of an arroyo a mile back. If I wasn't out searching for a monster, I could have easily taken one of them. I felt that one of them—the fat three- or four-year-old doe with no fawn—was ready to offer its body to be food for my family. Then I would have offered pollen to thank its spirit from the pouch that always hangs at my belt. But not now. What I need to hunt today has wings, not hooves.

I'm not worried about any other kind of predator in this territory, gemod or human. Not during the day. Anything and anyone crazy enough to show itself in the daylight would be potential prey for those feathered horrors. That's the reason those deer were so spooked before my bike ever arrived on the scene.

But there is nothing flying. Not even a small bird circling.

The midday sun is beating down on the dark, cracked pavement, overgrown here and there with dried grasses and brittle shrubs. The pavement's reflection of the heat makes it even hotter than the hundred degrees it must be off the road. I cannot stand still long without being cooked. I lower the scope and push off again.

The wind in my face feels good as I pedal faster. It brings back the memory of riding a bike with my dog Lobo loping along beside me. He loved it when I was on wheels because then he could run his fastest and I could still keep up with him. He was half wolf—running with the pack was in his blood. And I was his pack.

I feel free, almost to the point of being carefree. But not quite. Acting carefree is the first step to being dead. And thinking about Lobo does me no good at all. It just reminds me of one more thing I've lost. Better to think about what I do have.

I take one hand off the handlebars and pat my vest. I slide my palm down to shift the comforting weight of the gun belt further back on my right hip. I touch the Glock in its shoulder holster, then I reach across to my left hip where the handle of the extendable club is sheathed, just in front of the hilt of my Bowie knife. Each weapon is in place, each easy to reach.

The soft whirring of the bicycle chain, the hum and bump of the wheels on the road, they're almost hypnotic. It has been years since I've ridden a bike. That thought takes me back to another memory, of Mom and Dad as they helped me ride back and forth between them on my first two-wheeler. I pedaled a little too hard and ran into Dad. I knocked him flat on his back. His big arms embraced me and the little bike and my mom as she ran up to us to make sure we weren't hurt. Then all three of us were laughing and laughing, laughing like idiots.

I quickly stuff that image. No time for even the memory of laughter now. I reach up to wipe the moisture out of my eyes—darn dust. Forgot to lower my goggles. I pull them down over my eyes.

I need to concentrate all my senses on the danger right here. I can feel it, but I can't yet see it. I pedal slower. I've covered another four miles now. No visible sign of anything threatening around me. I've been scanning the sky above me as best as anyone can when they are pedaling a bike and trying to stay on the road, which has now begun to climb. The highway here has been cut into a lava slope. It's winding up and around a mesa. The rusted road sign right next to me reads WATCH OUT FOR FALLING ROCKS.

And as I read that sign, it comes to me. It is more than a tingle in my palms. It is like a current, shot through my whole body. I turn my head and see a big shape rising over the mesa, which had blocked my view of what was circling up from the canyon behind it. The giant bird heading my way has something in its talons.

Oh crap!

I swerve off the road hard, ditching the bike on its side, dive and roll toward a rocky outcrop that juts out like a shelf.

THWOMP!

The first boulder that has come plummeting down out of the sky cracks the thick pavement right where I was. It bounces once, flattening that all-too-accurate road sign, before it goes rolling off down the road. The second dropped boulder hits a split second later. It clips the edge of the rock overhang that has given me life-saving shelter, spraying me with sharp little shards of stone. Thudding into the ground, it wedges into the opening I just rolled through. It blocks the mouth of the shallow cave like a cork in a bottle.

I wipe blood out of my eyes from a thin cut on my forehead where a razor-sharp piece of flying stone sliced me. I can see light around the edges, but the heavy boulder seems to be stuck. I manage to get my legs under me and push against the stone. It doesn't move. I can reach my arm through the widest space between the boulder and the stone of the cave mouth. But that's all. I'm trapped.

I've chosen being buried alive as the best alternative to being flattened like a bug.

CHAPTER SEVEN

TRAPPED

One nice thing about being entombed when you are not yet a corpse is that it gives you plenty of time for thinking. That is also one of the worst things about being in a situation like this. It seems as if no matter what you think about, it all comes down to: *Crap, I'm trapped!*

I've been in here for a while. Long enough to try every possible approach to moving this frigging stone. The space in here is so small that there's just room to reach my elbows back and shift my body around. Pushing—not even an inch of give. Digging around it—lots of luck on that front with nothing but stone against stone. Prying with the extendable lance, which is strong enough to neither break nor bend, doesn't work either. Not room for me to get enough leverage. I've produced no visible result other than skinned knuckles.

Not that getting out would have been such a great thing.

Only a few heartbeats after I realized I was trapped, I had a friendly visitor.

Whomp, whomp, whomp of leathery wings. *Thud* of a heavy body landing. Skitter of claws on the stone outside.

I peered out through the widest crack to see what the critter looked like that had such a crush on me. An angry red eye the size of a dinner plate stared in at me. I grabbed for my lance. But the space was so constricted that by the time I got it out and extended, that eye had been pulled back and replaced by a big hooked beak.

However, the space was so small that all my big Tweety-Bird buddy could do was reach halfway through before the width of its beak prevented it from thrusting further.

Far enough for me to stab at the nib, the softest part of Big Bird's bill, with the blade end of my lance. That provoked a loud, displeased protest.

SCREEEE!

It hurt my ears more than my lance injured it. But it did not try poking in again. Instead, it began clawing at the stone with its talons, trying to dislodge it like a bear digging for grubs in a tree trunk. But each time it poked one of its toes in far enough to reach through a crack and start to grasp the lodged-in stone, I jabbed at it with my lance.

SCREEE!

Turned out its feet were a little more vulnerable than its beak. Though I was never able to dig in deep, I did draw blood each time I stabbed at it. And I began to think if I did survive this, it would be with significant hearing loss.

Well, actually, I wasn't *quite* thinking that. My actual thoughts at the time were more abbreviated, profane, and monosyllabic.

And before long, the monster bird stopped trying that approach. And it sat there thinking.

I could hear its thoughts.

They weren't in words like the thoughts of people—or even the thoughts of whatever species my unidentified watcher might be. It was more like images and emotions.

To translate it into human speech would be something along the lines of a mixture of rapacious hunger and infuriated disbelief that its attack had failed. Not only had its potential meal not been turned into a juicy pancake (pleasing mental picture of crushed flesh and protruding broken bones), it was beyond the big bird's reach. And it had the nerve to fight back (unhappy image of sharp shiny tooth stabbing into its toes).

Unfair, unfair!

I leaned my face against that wide crack. Big Bird was perched on the road's edge about thirty feet back from my stone sarcophagus. Far enough for me to see it, but so big that I could only lay eyes on part of it. Cross an outsized condor with an overgrown komodo dragon and you might be able to imagine the drooling, ebony-feathered monster I was observing.

Its wingspan had to be at least eighty feet. The four claws on its huge feet were each the size and length of a man's arm. Its beak, which was gaping open, was ridged with dozens of shark-like teeth that hooked backward. It was so clearly an apex predator, so perfectly designed for its task of being death from the air, that it was almost beautiful.

But not quite. What would be beautiful to me would be seeing it in exactly the same condition it had tried to place me—deceased, defunct, and dead!

I raised the .357. The crack between the overhang and the well-wedged stone was just big enough for me to be able to squint over the front sight and get a bead on Big Bird's body.

But only its body. Its head was held up too high and was also turned away from me. I couldn't see either of its vulnerable eyes. And worse, beneath its feathers were scales. Thick enough to probably bounce a bullet off them. Still, if it just angled its head down and peered back over its shoulder, I could probably pierce one of its peepers.

Turn around, I thought. *Look at me.*

TURN AROUND, LOOK AT ME!

But instead it made a different decision. I read the exasperated emotion that passed through its primitive mind. Translated into human speech it was:

Aw, screw it.

It leaped up, flapped its wings—*whomp, whomp*—and vanished from my view.

CHAPTER EIGHT

More Time to Think

There's not a lot to do inside a shallow stone sarcophagus that is just big enough for you to turn around in. I wait for a while to see if my wide-winged nemesis is coming back. Nope.

If I had a watch, I'd check the time. But the only clocks and watches—old-fashioned spring-powered wind-up ones, of course—in Haven belong to our benevolent overlords and their most loyal lackeys. Everyone else just uses the cycles of the day and night when they are on their own outside the walls. Inside the walls, their lives are run by the hourly bells and bugle calls that tell them when they are to work, eat, and sleep—at the command of the Ones.

A small slant of light from the autumn sun touches the back wall of the cave. I slouch back and watch it move, counting to myself.

One and one pony, two and one pony . . .

When I hit sixty, which is equivalent to a minute, I make a mark on the spot the edge of that sunbeam has reached. Then I make another at one hundred and twenty. Two minutes.

When what I estimate to be two hours has passed, I unsling my canteen and take a small sip. Aside from the air we breathe, nothing is more precious—or used to be more taken for granted—than water. It's not taken for granted now. Water is painfully scarce in this arid land. The electric-powered pumps that brought up that liquid of life from deep aquifers lie rusted in silence. Natural springs and rivers are much harder to come by.

I have two canteens. If I use them with care while I am trapped here I can make them last for two days. And then . . .

If I was not in this stone rat trap, I could find water. I inherited that gift of Lozen's, too. Water calls to me. I can hear its voice whispering that promise of quenching my thirst from miles away. Two centuries ago, when white and black cavalrymen hunted my ancestors, the soldiers often had to give up the chase and turn back because they ran out of water.

But not us Apaches.

Thinking about water makes me feel thirsty, even though I have just taken a sip from the canteen. I need to turn my thoughts to something else.

Food? I could take out some of the jerky I've brought with me, or the corn meal or fruit that has been pounded into flat strips and then rolled up. But I'm not hungry. You can go for days without food, and I'm not going to eat just because there's nothing else to do.

I open the pack I've taken off my back and spread out the contents. Fire making kit, knives, rope, ground cloth, cooking pot, cup, spoon. I arrange them in front of me. Then, one by one, methodically, I put them back in the pack.

Look at the line of light on the wall.

Another hour passed. I lean forward to peer outside through the crack. Nada. Zilch. Zero. Bupkis.

No one coming to my rescue, no thing attempting to pry me out and eat me. Though I knew all that, sensed it with my powers before I looked.

I've tried pushing before. But have I tried my hardest? Just one way to find out.

I flex my muscles. Stretch as best I can in these narrow quarters. Pull one knee and then the other up to my chest. Then I put my back against the wall and my feet against the stone. Take a deep breath. Push. Push harder.

I am stronger than anyone else in Haven, even those who, unlike me, were bred and enhanced for strength. No one, outside my immediate family, knows just how strong. Dad used to joke about how I could have been an Olympic weight lifter—if the Olympics hadn't become a thing of the past before I was born.

Sweat beads on my brow and the uneven rock wall digs into my back as I thrust again and again. But, powerful as I am, I can't make this damn boulder budge.

I lean back with the pack under my head, close my eyes. I do not sleep. I can do that when night comes if I'm still stuck in here. Instead I turn my mind to the never-to-be-forgotten sound of my father's voice telling me a story. Although we were poor as far as money went, back pre-C we were rich with stories.

"Dad, tell me a story," I whisper.

And his voice comes to me.

The giant eagles were among the worst of the monsters in those days long ago. They built their nest on a high bluff in the top of a great tree. The mother eagle would sit on a rock on one side of the nest and the father eagle would sit on a rock on the other side. Whenever it saw smoke from a cooking fire, one of those great birds would swoop down and grab the human being who made that smoke. It would carry that person back to the nest in the big tree and feed that person to the young eagles, who were always hungry.

Child of the Water saw this. So he made a stone club. Then he killed a deer. He pulled out its intestines. Then he cut the throat of the deer and filled the intestines with that blood, tying them at either end. Holding on to his club, he wrapped those intestines all around himself and waited.

The father eagle saw Child of the Water lying there, not moving. That eagle flew down and picked him up. Because blood was leaking out of those deer entrails, that eagle thought Child of the Water was dead. It carried him up to the nest and dropped him in among the young eagles.

But Child of the Water was not dead. Using his stone club, he knocked the father eagle over the head and killed it. He killed the mother eagle the same way and all of their little ones. Then he used their feathers to make good eagles and other birds.

'm smiling as I listen to my father's voice finish that story in my memory.

As long as we can remember them, our families will always be with us. That is what my mother always says. Perhaps not in the same way, not so we can reach out and touch them with our hands. But we can touch them with our hearts.

Something touches me. Not in my heart, but in my mind. It's as if a strand of a spider's web has just blown across my face and then rooted itself in my forehead.

My hands are tingling.

A heavy foot scuffs against the loose gravel on the other side of the big stone.

Little Food, says an amused voice in my head, ***You are really caught now.***

CHAPTER NINE

Rescue

You want out?

Duh.

Move back.

There's barely time for me to do so before something is rammed into that crack through which the Monster Bird had tried to thrust its beak.

Ka-chunk!

This something is longer, thinner, made of metal, and it just misses me as it is pushed all the way through to bounce off the wall of rock next to my head. It takes me half a second to recognize it as the end of a heavy steel pry bar. Rusted, but still strong.

What kind of monster carries around an antique wrecking bar?

The bar slides back until it is in just the right spot. Whoever or whatever is outside is manipulating this thing as if it was as light as a splinter of wood.

Thunk-thunk.

The stone begins to move and I ready myself for whatever is about to happen. The image is going through my mind of a lid being pried off a jar of fruit and a hand reaching in to grab the sweet contents. Is it my image, or that of the extremely strong being outside who is helping—so to speak—me get out of here?

Out of the frying pan and into the fire.

That is my own thought for sure. How many times did I hear Uncle Chatto say that? Usually when talking about our history back in the last free days of our people when we alternated between trying to live in peace, fighting, and fleeing.

Thunk-thunk!

The big stone moves back a few more inches. And for half a second I see what is holding that pry bar. It's a huge, hairy shape. But I can make out no more than its broad-shouldered, hulking outline before sunlight floods in and blinds me, and then the stone rocks back into place. One more pry with that bar and it will roll away.

I cross both arms in front of my face to shield my eyes from the light. My .357 is in my right hand, my Bowie knife in my left. My back is against the wall. Whatever reaches in for me will find I am far from a piece of preserved peach!

THUNK!

So much force is put into the last pry of the bar that small pieces of rock are broken free and sparks fly between the steel and the stone. Like a living thing, the big rock leaps away, freed from the ledge that held it in place, and goes rolling down the slope. I stay crouched where I am.

Ready, I hope, for whatever happens next.

But nothing attacks me. No huge claws reach for my body, no teeth try to tear out my throat. What kind of half-assed monster is this? Doesn't it know the rules? I have so much adrenalin pumping through me that my own teeth are bared and my knees are shaking.

Come and get me, Bozo!

A long-fingered, wide, furry hand appears, reaching down from the ledge where my rescuer and potential devourer must be crouched. It waggles its fingers at me.

Bye-bye for now, Little Food. Play nice with the birdies.

Then the hand is pulled back up out of sight.

What the . . .

I fight the impulse to roll out of my former slammer to get a glimpse or a shot at the sarcastic son of a bitch messing with my head. Maybe leaping out is just what it wants me to do. Is it enemy or ally? Playing cat and mouse?

Whatever. Just wait, girl. Slow your breathing down the way your father taught you. Count.

One and one pony . . .

When I get to one hundred, I crawl slowly out. No sign of

my furry friend or foe. Or its pry bar. Maybe it has gone back to working on the railroad. Why hasn't it attacked me? Why did it help me?

I'm not going to find the answer to that riddle right now. I have bigger fish to fry first. Or should I say fowls?

I pick up the trail bike. It has a few scratches on it, but is otherwise unharmed. Guy will be happy about that if I keep breathing long enough to return it to him. But I am not about to use it now or get back into plain sight on the road yet.

I stow the bike in my previous sarcophagus, then make my way stealthily toward the arroyo to the east.

Deer hunting time.

CHAPTER TEN

Bait

I look up from my bloody work. Nothing overhead yet within my vision. But it does not mean I'm not being watched from farther overhead than I can see.

The deer were just where I knew they would be. It took only one shot to bring the doe down, made easier by the way she turned her side to me, giving herself. That was good. I am moving fast, but not so fast that I have neglected to give thanks properly, to gut her out and then to hang her carcass up from a cottonwood limb in a cool shady spot in the arroyo so that the meat will not spoil while I am gone. I pray that I will be able to come back to this place and take her meat to my family.

Hanging the deer's body also made it easier to drain her blood into the intestines, slick and rubbery as an endless white inner tube.

I sling the guts across my shoulders, smearing more blood all over myself in the process. It stinks.

Good.

I crawl up from the arroyo and out onto the wide stretch of road above it. The deer's guts are wrapped around me like a bloody pale python. I drop to my knees, reach back to make sure my neck is covered by my hood, make sure the intestines don't cover the parachute—just in case—check that all my weapons are secure, and then lay down. Quiet as roadkill, and hoping I will not have to wait long. Otherwise I might end up baked instead of bait.

Or choked by the smell of the deer's innards, a thick miasma that gets worse as they get hotter, making me want to vomit.

But I don't. I stay where I am. I wait and I count.

I'm up to five hundred and about ready to get up when I hear it: the whistle of wings as a huge body dives down, and then its cry.

SCREEEE!

THWOMP!

Most of the air in my lungs is knocked out of me by the impact. It has just thudded down over me so hard that even though most of its weight fell on the road surface, my back would have been broken had I not been protected by the body armor. One claw is dug a foot deep into the road next to my face. It came so close that it grazed my cheek. I feel warm blood flowing down my cheek, wonder if the gash it made will leave a scar. Assuming I live long enough to heal.

Its beak taps the back of my neck. Not that hard. Just probing to see if I am really dead.

72

Then it strikes three more times. Each time harder than the last.

I now have the worst headache in history. But the armoring fabric hardened with each blow. It prevented the beak from piercing my neck and separating my vertebrae. I am still more or less conscious. And aware of what is going through the Monster Bird's brain. It is frustrated, puzzled that it hasn't been able to cut into my flesh. It reaches back, tears at the deer intestines wrapped around me.

Ah, blood. Good.

And now it has made a decision.

Take prey to nest.

The claws tighten around me. Out of the corner of my eye I see the wings spread out so wide that they seem to go on forever.

Flap.

Up, up, and away we go.

My arms are pinned to my body by the claws wrapped around me. No way to get at my weapons. That's not good.

However, I am face down and thus have a lovely view of the land below and of where we are headed, right toward that highest cliff face where a nest as big as a boxing ring has been built on a boulder-strewn ledge.

Little birdies (if you could call pin-feathered horrors the size of hippos "little") are thrusting their eager heads into the air and cheeping with delight.

PAPA BROUGHT DINNER!

73

How nice it is to be wanted.

Papa doesn't bother to land. He just opens his claws as he swoops over the nest. Luckily for me, his aim is good and I slam-dunk between my new nest-mates.

All I can do is pull myself into a ball to keep my face and hands out of reach as the four baby monsters hop eagerly in. My legs are caught, though.

They shove each other back and forth, each one trying to be the first to tear at what they think to be my flesh. In no time at all they have stripped the bloody deer guts off me, swallowed every bit, and inflicted even more bruises on my body—which is going to look like I have been run over by a herd of elephants after all this. But I think nothing is broken, neither bones nor internal organs. And though I've been brutally banged around, I still have my strength and my wits about me. The melee has freed my leg from between those woven saplings. And as the four nestlings settle back, swallowing, I scuttle out from between them and get my back against one side of the deep nest.

No sign of Papa Bird now, who circled once, then soared away over the peak to the left of the nest after dropping me. My guess is that he's gone back to hunting, like his yet-unseen mate, for more food for their ravenous little ones. I could use my gun, but the sound of its shots would surely bring him back. I have my belt knife, but I don't want to get within range of those sharp beaks. I unsheathe my staff, pull it out to its full length, each of its segments clicking tightly into place. I twist the handle and the blade pokes out of the end and locks.

Four sets of big, hungry eyes have fixed themselves on me in response to my movements. They don't see me as a threat but as an entrée. Once again they come swarming in, flapping their unfledged wings, each trying to shoulder aside the other and get this last morsel.

They are scaled like their father, but the spaces between those scales have not yet closed up. Feathers haven't grown into the gaps. I aim quickly and carefully to thrust up at the first one as it strikes down at me with a beak half as big as my upper body. My sharp blade pierces between the scales on its exposed throat. As its head still presses down, trying to strike me with its beak, the blade pierces its brain. The monster chick quivers, stiffens, falls off to the side as I wrench my weapon free. I'm just in time to catch the second chick in its throat in almost exactly the same way. But as it falls, it pulls me off to the side and its two nest mates are on top of me.

Kawk! KAWK KAWK!

Anger and fear. Calling for help.

Their wings and beaks and claws are striking at me. The body armor is absorbing most of the impact, but I am being whipped around like a willow branch in a storm. I wrap my left arm partly around the beak of one of the chicks. I am still holding my staff with my right hand. I pull it back, stab it deep into the center of an angry red eye.

The bird drops on top of me. I am trapped under the weight of its body. Yellow ocular fluid and blood ooze out from the blade buried in its eye. My other arm is pinned under my body, my face exposed. If the final chick attacks now I'm a goner. But I don't see it.

I manage to pull myself out from under the limp, heavy body.

It is made easier, unpleasant as it is, by the fact that the nest and everything in it is now slimy. As they attacked and died the chicks were voiding themselves and there is yellow monster bird crap everywhere. And I thought the deer guts stunk!

I climb up the side of the nest and peer over the edge.

Ooops! There, far below, splattered on the sharp stones of the valley is the last of the four chicks, which saw how the battle was going and chose flight as its option—before it was ready to soar.

Somehow I have won.

SKREEEE!

The whole nest shakes and the air is shattered by the scream of Papa Monster Bird as it lands.

Too late to save its young, but way too soon for yours truly.

CHAPTER ELEVEN

The Female of the Species

My spear is still stuck in the scaly throat of baby bird number three. There is a three thousand foot cliff behind me, and a forty-foot-tall horror staring down at me.

Can I call a time out?

As the Monster Bird leans down over me, one foot raised to crush me with its claws, its beak poised to drive down at my face, the words of a poem by Kipling or Stevenson or one of those old poets Dad used to quote come to my mind: *The female of the species is deadlier than the male.*

Namely me. The few seconds' pause has given me time to unclip the strap and pull my gun from its holster. I raise the .357, hold it firmly in both hands and fire it three times.

Ka-pow! Ka-pow!

Maybe one shot would have been enough, but a girl can't

be too careful in moments like this. And I have always preferred a double tap. At this close range, it is not much of a compliment to my marksmanship to say that my aim was true. I hit the bull's eye—or rather the bird's eye—twice in the exact center. And, with that many ounces of lead outbalancing its ability to keep breathing, Papa Bird immediately perishes.

And still might kill me. I scramble aside as it falls. Its enormous slack-winged body thuds down, filling most of the nest aside from the one corner where I was crouched.

And now what? I climb over its body to the top of the woven branches of the aerie and survey my surroundings. There's nothing but sheer cliff behind me. I am not equipped to scale that. And in front, there's just a straight drop from this jutting-out ledge.

I look around and weigh my options. They're limited. Despite the crappy accommodations, I do have shelter and enough poultry to feed an army. But the only water is in my two canteens. At most I can survive here for a week or two. And no one will be coming to rescue me in this world without helicopters. Aside from Mama Bird, nothing is flying here.

I study the sky as I hold up my palms. No sign of her yet, and no tingling to tell me she's nearby. But she'll be back eventually. I'd rather not encounter her—or the big stones she might drop on me—here on this little point of rock.

No point in putting off the inevitable. Jump time. I reload the chambers of the .357 and seat it firmly in its holster, fasten the strap. It takes a bit of effort to get my spear out of the throat of the dead chick—which Daddy Bird crushed, but I could still reach at an angle. By working it back and forth I manage to pry it loose.

I heft the lance in my hand. It feels as if it belongs there. It's perfectly balanced and just the right weight. This is a weapon my namesake would have loved. Maybe even named.

But I'm not that imaginative.

"Thank you," I say.

I collapse my unnamed lance down and resheathe it.

I climb to the top edge of the cliff over the deepest drop. I recheck the security of the straps, pat the pack on my chest, and spread out my arms. As I do so, I find myself remembering a corny joke my father made.

It's about what the Apache paratrooper did when he leapt out of the plane. "He didn't yell 'Geronimo,'" Dad said with a straight face. "He just shouted 'ME!'"

I'm smiling as I bend my knees, jump and yell, "Meeeee!"

The wind whistles past my face as the ground rushes up toward me. There's a feeling of exhilaration and plain old dread as I plummet down like a rock. Or maybe an egg about to be scrambled is a better comparison. Despite my body armor, there would be no way to survive this high a drop. The mangled remnants of the monster chick far below me bears witness to that.

I yank the rip cord. The parachute streams out, a red and

white ripple in the wind. Then it opens and I feel as if I've been caught by a giant hand and jerked upward as the chute cups the wind. I begin gliding along like a hawk above the canyon. I reach up with both hands to grasp the lines that fasten the chute to my body. I pull on the left line and I change direction. Pull on the right and turn the other way. It's just as Guy said it would be. I can fly this thing like a glider and choose my landing spot.

Is this how an eagle feels when it is soaring? I love it!

"HIIII-YAAAHHHHH!" I yell, my triumphant voice echoing off the walls of the canyon.

I felt so happy and free for that one brief moment. I just had to shout! I couldn't help it.

But maybe that was not such a good idea. A familiar feeling makes my hands tremble.

By the twitching of my thumbs, something wicked this way comes.

I pull on the right line and turn in the direction in which I know I am going to see it. And Judas Priest! There she is. Diving right at me with outstretched claws—and even bigger than her mate. Her angry cry tears the fabric of the sky.

SCREEEEEEEE!

Hello, Mama Bird!

There's no time to pull out a weapon or take aim. Just one tactic that might work. In the second before its claws strike home, I yank hard on the left line and pull up my legs so I change direction and become a much smaller target at the same time.

I'm buffeted by the wind from her passing, but her claws miss me. Unfortunately, my parachute is even more affected by her dive. It folds up and I start to fall again.

Luckily for me, the parachute flutters, straightens and grasps the air once more. I'm back to a more or less controlled glide. And I'm much closer to the ground. No more than maybe two hundred feet below.

Not so luckily, however, here comes my feathered nemesis back to resume our *pas de deux*. Or *pas de trois*, if you count the parachute. As she comes in for a killing strike, the combination of my frantic pulling on the lines and the vortex created by her own body results in something unexpected. Not only does she miss me, but the parachute lines tangle around her legs and the chute itself goes over her head, covering her eyes.

If I weren't still connected to those lines, that parachute, and a monster bird flying blind, it might be funny. She rises, climbing out of the canyon, and pulls me along with her. We glide over one ridge after another.

Can't just hang here. Trailing behind her like the tail of a kite, I'm likely to be smashed like a bug on one of the sharp canyon spires we're whipping past. I pull myself up hand over hand. I want to get close enough to get on her back. The muscles in my arms burn, but I keep going, a foot at a time.

I'm close enough to grasp at the huge feathers that ridge her neck. But we're losing altitude. I see around her shrouded head that we are heading down at an angle into a narrow canyon. I brace myself as best I can for a hard landing.

Thud-a-thud-thud. I'm bounced along the bony spine of a sprawled-out, somewhat stunned, but certainly pissed-off raptor as big as a bomber. At least we've stopped moving. The chute lines have tangled around me so much that I am trussed tight to her back. Shifting myself, I manage to work one arm free. Now there's enough slack for me to roll to my side. I pull out my Bowie knife and begin to slice through the nylon lines.

Something wiggles against my leg. Then I feel a sharp stabbing pain.

I look down to see what has bitten into me where the body armor has shifted to expose bare skin. It's one of a dozen pale eight-legged critters, each one the size of a marmot. They chitter as more of them swarm toward my legs.

Bird lice? That has to be what they are. Giant bird lice on a giant bird. Wouldn't that be an irony to be eaten by parasites after bringing down their host? I kick at their fleshy bodies but they keep coming. Then one of them bursts like a fleshy water balloon as the heavy heel of my boot comes down hard on the center of its body. Green goo oozes out. It stinks even worse than the bird crap I am coated with. The other lice, obviously discomfited by their sibling's demise, scuttle away back under the feathers on Mama Big Bird's back.

I slice through the last line, push myself up. I roll, crawl, stumble, and slide as I try to get off. The feathers are slippery and so am I. But I can't stop. Mama Big Bird is also starting to move, trying to push herself up to her feet. I tumble, roll, hit my feet running.

Good thing that I do.

CHUNK!

Her beak hits the ground where I would have been if I'd stopped to survey my surroundings.

Keep running, girl. Don't look back yet.

CHUNK!

Another beak strike, but not as close as the first. I leap over one boulder after another, cover perhaps a hundred yards before I dare to take a quick glance back over my shoulder.

I'm not being pursued. From this distance I can see that my winged attacker is not going to be coming after me or anything else. Not with a wing that is so visibly broken, blood dripping around the exposed bone halfway to her shoulder. She is trying to right herself, but she is stuck on her side, wedged between the sharp-angled rocks that broke her wing. Her weakly kicking feet are digging grooves in the sand. Her struggling is getting her nowhere.

Part of me feels sorry for her. I can't help but admire the beauty of something so perfectly made to be a predator, to rule the air like no other winged or feathered creature that has ever lived on this planet. And now the cloudland is lost to her, her mate dead, her little ones no longer destined to be part of an empire of death from above.

Yup. Too bad for you, honey.

I make my way close enough to be able to see her eyes and take aim. As I do so, she raises her head and stares at me.

I'm ready. Send me back to the sky.

I raise my arm to wipe the dust that has blown into my eyes and is making them water.

Bye-bye, birdy.

CHAPTER TWELVE

The Spring

What do you do when you've just killed a monster? Well, you could do what I am doing right now. Calmly holster your gun, then turn around and puke your guts out.

I manage to walk over to a rock that is shaded by the cliff and shaped like a seat, put my hands on it and gently lower myself down. I am feeling as weak as a day-old wolf pup. (No way, even now, am I going to compare myself to a kitten.) I am bruised, bloody, and I smell like the delightful mixture of monster bird crap all over my body and the bird louse goo that coats my left leg. If there is any other deadly critter anywhere near here I suspect they will be repelled by my smell as if I were a skunk.

I am equally disgusted with my odiferous self. It's hard to keep my gorge down. But if I vomit one more time, lose any more liquid from my body, I may be too weak to walk.

I reach down to my side. One of my canteens was torn loose somehow during my wild ride. But the other one, more than half full, is still there. I uncap it and take a small sip through my cracked lips, enough to get rid of the dryness in my mouth and the tightness at the back of my throat.

However, the nausea, like an old faithful friend, does not desert me.

I shake my head and am relieved when it doesn't dislodge itself from my neck and go rolling away. Every part of my body is in agony right now, from my hair down to my toes. My cheek where I was slashed by Papa Bird's claw is throbbing like a second heart. Even thinking about standing up hurts. Plus it is now night, the normal time to give my body up to sleep even when it hasn't been through a twelve-round battle with a flock of avian horrors.

But I can't rest now. Not if I want to survive. It's going to be bitterly cold now that the sun is gone. I need shelter. I force myself to my feet.

Take one step, girl. Good. Now another one.

Soon I am walking, slowly to be sure, but steadily. Luckily, the moonlight is bright enough for me to easily see where I'm going. And as I walk I am studying my surroundings. I know where I am. The monster bird's last flight took me another four miles further west from its aerie. This canyon, if I am right and not hallucinating—which might be possible considering how everything around me is blurry at the edges—opens up around the next bend.

I can also feel myself being drawn by my power, which has come back to guide me to this place I've never visited before, even though it was described to me by both my father and my uncle. It's a place of refuge that was known long ago by my namesake.

Just a little further, Lozen. Keep going.

I pass a spiral shaped petroglyph chipped long ago into the surface of a great round boulder. And there it is, above me—a little clump of dark vegetation growing thickly around the base of a red hill.

I make my way carefully through the cholla cactus and old saguaros that cover the slope. I reach that clump of shadowy green and hear a sound that every creature in the desert knows and loves. The soft echo of dripping water. I kneel, my head spinning as I do so, and crawl through the narrow, hidden opening between the stones.

And I am in another world. This hollow in the hill is narrow and open to the sky. The spring that rises here has made a series of pools of water that step down its slope. Each pool is progressively larger and deeper before the flow disappears through a V-shaped crevice at the base. Whatever stream it joins is underground, hidden beneath the dry soil and stone outside. Just being here, just seeing this spring takes away all of my nausea. I am filled with a feeling of well-being.

I do not know much of the language that my old people spoke. Back in the nineteenth and twentieth centuries, that language was taken from most of us by the schools my Navajo and Apache and Pueblo two-times great-great-grandparents were forced to attend. But my family did keep enough of our languages to pass on to us certain songs and prayers. And certain words such as those I speak right now.

"Thank you," I whisper in Chiracahua. "Thank you."

Then I dip my hands into the lowest of the springs, washing the blood and filth from them, watching as it is carried down into the earth through that crack in the bedrock. I cup up some of that water and fill my mouth with it. It tastes of minerals, a strong good taste that is like food. I feel its strength washing through me

"Thank you," I repeat. "Thank you."

I pull off my boots. I put my feet into the healing water. Perhaps I could just stay here forever, lean back against the water-smoothed wall and become stone myself. That would not be a bad thing.

But it is not something I can afford to do. Other lives—and other deaths—still depend upon me.

I take a very deep breath and then let it out slowly along with the pain which came with that deep inhalation. I reach down to feel my ribs on my right side with the palm of my hand.

Ah! Sharp stab like a knife with that pressure. One or more of them cracked or broken for sure.

I undo the belts and straps that secure my holsters and my body armor. I carefully lay everything on the wide shelf of rock next to me where I've already placed my boots. Armor, staff, guns, knives, canteen, pack, all my clothing. In this quiet, secret place I feel safe enough to do so, though I keep everything in reach just in case.

Then I slide into the water. It's cool, but not cold. The only part of me not under water is my face. The water is at least two feet deep and the stone pool is shaped like one of those luxury bathtubs I've seen pictures of in old magazines. Like the tubs that the Ones are said to have in their private quarters at Haven. Not like the few cups of water in a bucket each of us peons are allowed to use every now and then to cleanse our bodies as best we can with the stained cloths that hang in the communal washroom.

I hold my hands up out of the water and look at them. These hands I have used to take many lives.

And I ask the water to cleanse my hands.

And my hands feel clean and renewed.

I wipe my fingers over my eyes.

And I ask the water to clear from my eyes, if only for a moment, the sight of death.

And my eyes feel clear and renewed.

I wipe the deep slash on my cheek, the water mixing with the dried blood and washing it away. And the throbbing of the wound stops and my breath, which had been quick and labored, slows and calms.

I run my hands along my body, touching every place that

feels bruised or broken from the battles I just fought. And I ask the water to heal me, to restore my strength.

And my body feels strong and renewed.

Then I lift my hands to my forehead and I ask the water to empty from my mind my memories of loss.

And even as I do so, I know it is more than I can ask, more than this water can give.

And my memories remain with me.

But do I really want those memories to vanish? For those memories, hard as they are, are also part of who I am and who I must be.

So I thank the waters for allowing me to keep those memories.

And as much as my troubled mind can be, it feels renewed.

It is still night when I crawl out of the cave of the spring after cleaning off my clothing and my gear and dressing myself.

There's no point in trying to return to Haven in the darkness. It is not just that they would not let me in if I arrived after dark—the door of Haven is never opened to the night. It is also the simple fact that in this world as we now know it, setting out on a journey in the dark—even with moonlight to guide you—means that you will probably never reach your destination.

Those who hunt in the night are better left unmentioned.

But there is enough space for me to stretch out here among the little verdant oasis at the mouth of the cave, where the roots of the bushes and other plants reach down to draw life from that water before it disappears. I unfold the blanket from my pack, put the pack under my head as a pillow, and look up at the stars in the clear desert sky. I feel safe hidden in here.

I also have the safety off on the .357 held by my right hand across my chest.

CHAPTER THIRTEEN

Enough to Feel Full

I set out with the first rays of the sun. Objective Numero Uno is to return to the bike, at the place where I was trapped by the stone. It takes me as much time to reach the place as it does for the sun to rise two hands high above the ridgetop.

The bike is still there. And aside from a few scrapes, it is in just as good condition as it was when Guy first wheeled it out to me. I wonder which will be more surprising to him—that I actually brought it back intact or that I was just as undamaged myself.

Speaking of which, I suddenly remember those broken ribs on my right side. I'd forgotten completely about them after my bath in the cave where Lozen's spring flowed so sweetly. They hadn't hurt even when I strapped back on my body armor before I covered myself with my blanket and sank into a dreamless sleep.

I touch my side gently, then press hard. No pain. None at all.

I'd been expecting to have to just live for a month or so with my ribs bound and a knife point of pain every time I breathed in deep. That had been my usual experience the last four times I suffered cracked or broken ribs.

But not this time. Lozen's medicine spring healed me. It makes me wonder what else that place might heal. Or if it would work every time anyone went there. However it works, I also have the feeling—maybe from my Power whispering it to me—that going there anytime I have a booboo would not be right. What I need to do is accept the gift of that healing and not expect anything more.

I look back at the narrow space in the rocks under that chipped stone shelf, with the boulder that once trapped me casually tossed aside. I could still be in there, pinned, drying up like one of those Peruvian mummies I saw in an ancient issue of *National Geographic* magazine in the communal library at Haven—a one-room library of tattered, cast-off books and magazines the Ones no longer wanted. I was lucky in more ways than one yesterday.

There's a smile on my face as wide as any smile I ever permit myself as I glide down the hill on my iron horse. That is what my ancestors called the first bicycles they saw. Iron horses. Back when there were horses to compare things with. All we have now of those horses we loved so much is in our memories. I'm not sure if I feel sadder for those of us like Mom and me who remember horses and rode them and miss them or those like my little brother Victor, who never saw a real living horse and doesn't know what he missed.

Let it go, girl. Be glad you're alive. Enjoy this moment.

Lovely day. It is a lovely day. Especially because there is nothing circling in the sky except for those two kettles of turkey buzzards—one flock a mile behind me, where a certain hilltop holds a nest full of some good pickings and the other over the canyon, where I left another scavenger's smorgasbord.

It takes me almost no time at all to reach the arroyo where I hung my deer. I park the bike and walk down, my knife already out of its sheath to finish butchering off the better cuts of meat.

But my deer is not there as I had left it, high enough to be out of reach of the coyotes. And it is not, as I had feared, that some predator such as a mountain lion climbed the tree to drag it down.

It is far different from that. No mountain lion took my deer out of that tree. Unless mountain lions have learned how to use tools. There, hanging from the tree by the same rope I used, is exactly one quarter of my deer. The right rear haunch, skinned and strung up by its hoof, is waiting for me. It has also, I see as I come closer, been salted.

The sand around the tree has been wiped smooth. There are no tracks visible. Wiped away with a tree branch used like a broom as whoever or whatever left carrying the rest of the deer.

But you can follow the track made by wiping away other tracks. And I do that for a hundred yards or so until the sand gives way to rock. Clever. But not quite clever enough. For there is one partial print visible just where the sand and pebble mix before the ground becomes solid stone. Three times as big as one of my own prints. Almost, but not quite, the same as a track left by a barefooted human with proportionately longer-than-usual toes.

There is a bee sting in the middle of my forehead.

Little Food. You left enough for me to feel full. So today I will not eat you.

Where and what the hell are you? I think back.

Something like a chuckle echoes back into my mind. Then it is gone.

CHAPTER FOURTEEN

Lady Time

S tripped down to my underwear as usual. But this time I'm being taken to another of the Ones who own Haven and all of us the way ranchers used to own cattle spreads and all the beasts fenced inside. Back when there were ranches and cattle herds.

I know where we are going. I've never been to her part of Haven before, but as soon as I hear the ticking of the clocks I am certain that I am to see Lady Time. The air is already laden with the musky odor of the heavy perfume she bathes herself in.

We turn a corner and there in front of us is a heavy door with a painted clock face. The guard who stands beside it is already unlocking and opening it. I'm pushed forward.

I am ushered into one of the largest and most ornately decorated residences in the center of Haven. Once, it was Electronics Training Center. Back when men were locked in here for actual crimes and not for simply still being alive, convicted felons were taught how to repair outdated computers and viddy players that were—like them—of no use to society.

Of course I am not supposed to know that, just as I am also not supposed to have ever seen a map of the layout of Haven. Which, thanks to the Library, I have. I have a feeling the Ones do not know it's there. Only the Ones are supposed to know such things.

The Ones must know so much about the world, and history, and science, and . . . everything. The rest of us know only as much as is necessary to be useful to our overlords. The only other things we're taught are the manual skills needed to serve our leaders. Carpentry, cooking, farming, laundry, tailoring and shoe-making, how to repair and make the devices that still work since the departure of electricity. Plus those few allowed to use their very special abilities outside the walls. Scouts, couriers, hunters . . . and me.

Of course I am leaving out the guards. Their duty is to defend Haven against any attacking force. Or, if it comes to that, an insurrection from within. Those favored protectors of the status quo have the best food, the best beds, and a few other privileges that make me want to puke. Such as being able to choose whatever women they want.

That is another reason I have to find a way to get my family out of here. The thought of Victor, who is only eight, one day being recruited to be one of those loathsome mercenaries because of his size and strength makes me cringe. And Ana, at the age of twelve, is already such a beautiful girl that I have seen more than one of the guards look at her in a way that has made me want to rip their throats out.

Only the thought of what would happen next has kept me from that. It's not her fault that the men look at her that way—most of the guards are predators who look at all the women in Haven that way. But even so, Mom and I both coach Ana all the time on how she can dress and act and do her hair to make herself as inconspicuous as possible.

The door slams behind me and I am standing in the At Ease posture. My feet are shoulder width apart, my hands clasped behind my back.

Covering every wall are clocks—round ones, square ones, some ten feet tall that stand on the floor. They are all the type made a century or more ago—before batteries or electrical cords. The clocks are powered by springs wound up with keys. Next to each clock, in fact, is its own individual key hanging from a wall peg.

The cacophonous sound of their monotonous music fills the air. Some tick loud, some softly. But each has its individual notes. Just as every one has chimes or bells or cuckoos that pop out whenever the minute hand touches six or twelve. It would drive me crazy to dwell in this sonic pandemonium.

But the distance to crazy is a short journey for Lady Time. Like all of our overlords, she is more than half insane.

Lady Time is standing with her back to me, looking up at

one of her beloved timepieces, a grandfather clock that was once in a Phoenix museum and is over three hundred years old. I have heard it is one of her favorites and that it's one of the few she winds herself, rather than leaving it to the Clock Keeper who is on call here twenty-four hours a day. Like all of her clocks, it was brought here at her behest by her Time Team, a group of guards whose job it has been to scour the surrounding area for a hundred miles to add to her collection. I've heard it whispered that two of them died bringing just this one to Haven.

I wait and keep waiting, mentally counting—one and one pony, two and one pony—to keep myself from doing anything annoying like tapping my foot on the floor. The last person who did that found himself being held in place by three of her bodyguards while a fourth—Red, their slightly more sadistic leader—drove a nine-inch nail through the man's instep.

"Sooooo."

Lady Time's voice is as sibilant as the hiss of a serpent.

As she speaks, she turns to face me—if showing someone a mask like that of a clock face with exaggerated lips and black eyebrows painted between the numbers could be called "facing." She tilts her masked face down at me. Though I am six feet tall, she's half a head taller than me. She raises her graceful hands, the way priests used to do when giving a benediction, and glides a step closer.

I control my breath, keep myself from shrinking back as

she approaches. She wouldn't like that, either. Despite the fact that they like to scare the crap out of everyone, they also like to believe that we all love and adore them and are deeply honored to be in their presence.

Screw you, sweetie.

"Am I to understand that you have successfully dispatched all of those large nasty flying nuisances?"

"Yes."

"Ahhhh."

She seems about to say something more. But then she raises one hand, commanding silence. As if I was about to say anything more, which I was not.

Lady Time pivots like a dancer, faces the wooden Swiss clock on the wall to her left. The minute hand, which I now notice is set one minute ahead of all the other clocks, moves to the twelve with a loud click that is audible even above the din of ticking and tocking, clicking and clacking that surrounds us.

Whirrr. Thunk!

A gear turns. A door flings itself open below the clock face. A garishly painted yellow bird thrusts itself and opens its wooden beak with a clack.

CUUU-KOOO, CUUU-KOOO, CUUU-KOOO.

Whirr. Thunk.

The bird whips back inside. The door snaps shut.

Lady Time raises her arms and then pirouettes a full circle and a half so that she is again facing me when she stops.

100

"Perfect. Wasn't it?"

Which? The clock? Her twirl?

But I sense it is a rhetorical question that I am not expected to answer, especially since that extra minute has now passed. Every other clock in the room, dozens and dozens of them, is making its own little whirring, clicking, clacking, and *brrring* sounds that presage its forthcoming proclamation of time.

DING DING DING!

CLANG CLANG CLANG!

WHONG WHONG WHONG!

BONG BONG BONG!

Thank God, I think, that I wasn't brought here at noon or midnight. I feel deafened by the din, which is clearly music to the ears of Lady Time, who is still waltzing or gavotting or polkaing—or whatever the hell it is that she thinks she is doing—after the last bell sounds.

Almost. From the far corner of the room another clock suddenly whirrs and then, twenty seconds late, sounds the hour.

Bing! Bing! Bing!

It almost sounds embarrassed to be so out of sync with the others. I almost laugh.

Lucky that I don't.

Lady Time is not amused. A low growl emanates from that mask.

"WALTER!" she screams. I can't see her face, but I have no doubt that it is red with rage.

A small, thin man wearing a robe comes running from somewhere at the back of the big room, the errant clock his destination.

"No!" Lady Time says. Not loudly at all, but the coldness in her voice is even more threatening than her scream. "Here!"

The little man runs forward and stops five feet short of her as if he has come against an invisible barrier. His features are small for his round face, but they display on them the amount of terror that I suspect is appropriate for this moment. Sweat beads are popping out on his pale brow, and his empty hands are lifted up in front of himself as if he is holding a shield.

"Have I not told you?" Lady Time says.

"Yes, your grace," Walter replies in a voice that is deeper than you would expect from someone who can't be more than five feet tall. There's also pain in that voice, as if he is already experiencing the agony that he expects will soon be inflicted upon him.

"Three times," Lady Times says, her voice even more cold, more calm than before.

She looks at his hands. And as she does so the fear on his face becomes even more visible. Then she shakes her head.

"No, you need all those fingers, don't you, little time-keeper? To keep my lovelies wound and running . . . on *time*? All of them, except for my sweet little cuckoo, right on time?"

102

"Yes, your grace."

"Toes . . . ," she says to herself. "No. Can't have you limping about caring for my sweethearts, can I?"

"No, your grace." Walter's voice is beginning to sound less frightened. And his thoughts suddenly come to me as clearly as if he was speaking them.

Perhaps the punishment will not be that terrible. Perhaps the bitch queen will just whip me again. I can stand a whipping. I can. I can. I can. Oh, how I wish I could pull the hands off that grandfather clock and drive them into her evil eye and blind her. Into her ears and deafen her. Yes! Yes! Yes!

"Teeth," Lady Time says. Her voice is light and happy again. She twirls and signals to the three guards who have remained behind me at the door.

As they step forward, Walter seems to grow even smaller and his thoughts become an incoherent, horrified babble.

"Two—no, three," Lady Time says. "Back teeth. I hate the look of missing teeth in front. And do it downstairs. I do so hate the sound of screaming."

Two of the guards lift Walter up by his arms.

I stay where I am, looking to neither one side nor the other as they drag the whimpering timekeeper past me and shut the door behind them.

Lady Time turns back to me.

"Oh," she says. "And who might you be? And what just

103

punishment shall we mete out to you today, my dear?"

She's crazy, I think, *but not that crazy.* I stay as I am in my At Ease pose, even though my mind is not at ease right now.

Lady Time laughs, a laugh that goes on a little too long as she whirls and spins like a wheel in one of her clocks.

Finally, she stops and holds her palm out toward me in a way that makes me think of a picture I saw in a tattered book of fairy tales. The witch offering candy to Hansel and Gretel.

"Oh my, I am just joking, my dear. Of course I know who you are. You are here to be praised for your good work."

She pauses. Time for me to say something.

"Thank you," I reply in a level, expressionless voice.

"You are a bit dull, aren't you?" Lady Times says. Rhetorical. No reply needed. "But you are good at doing what you do, aren't you? Ridding us of large nasty things? Yes?"

Reply expected.

"Yes."

"Well then. Keep at it."

She waves her hand. Audience over. The one remaining guard steps forward to escort me from her room.

But as I leave, Lady Time's parting thoughts come unbidden to my mind. And they are less crazy than I might have expected—and more chilling.

That one bears watching. She may be more clever than the other three—fools that they are—give her credit for. She is useful. Yes. But dangerous as well. We do have her family as leverage, but will that always be enough? For a moment there she looked as if she was thinking about leaping at me and tearing out my throat! Put her down? Perhaps not yet. There may be more little jobs for her to do. Then . . .

Lady Time's thoughts move away from words in her mind to several very graphic images—quite pleasing to her—of what she plans to have done to me when she decides I have outlived my usefulness.

I am living on borrowed time.

CHAPTER FIFTEEN

Where the Heart Is

As I walk down the tier toward my home—cell, that is—I am taken aback by what I see. The door is open. The lock hangs freely from the bike chain. But only four people know the combination to my lock. Me and . . . I catch the familiar scent of herbal soap.

I look inside and take a relieved breath when I see who is there waiting as quietly as guests at a surprise party. Despite Lady Time's reservations about me, her haughty thank you is not my only reward after all. This place really does feel like home right now. The place where my heart lives as long as *they* are here.

"Mom! Ana! Victor!"

"Lozen!"

"Big Sis."

We wrap our arms around each other in what my dad used to call our Old-time Apache Hug.

"How long?" I ask.

"Until the lamps are lit," Mom says.

That's about four hours. A longer time than we've been allowed to spend together in weeks.

Mom steps back and examines me carefully. "Your face is all bruised," she says. I like it that she says it without pity or even surprise. Just making an observation. She reaches down to the pouch at her belt and brings out a jar of salve as I look into the small mirror taped to my wall.

She's right. My forehead is covered with a purple and yellow contusion. I have two black eyes and my chin is red and scraped. Amazingly, though, where the monster bird slashed my cheek, there's nothing. Not even a scar. Lozen's spring healed it completely. I guess I should have immersed my whole face in that medicine spring.

I look like a second-rate fighter after twelve rounds in the ring. All-out, bare knuckle combat, by the way, is one of the few sports that we are allowed here in Haven. Not that we enjoy it all that much. Since it is done for the pleasure of the Ones, it usually involves some poor outclassed ordinary getting the crap kicked out of him by one of the better trained and medicated guards. The best of them are Red, Lady Time's heavily tattooed head mercenary, and Big Boy, who heads Diablita's crew. Both Chainers, of course. Edwin is the third best ring fighter here, and as one of Diablita's men under Big Boy's tutelage he has been training in the hopes of beating Red.

"Sit." Mom points to the bed.

107

I sit while Mom applies the salve to my forehead, my chin, around my eyes. The salve is comfrey plus a few other herbs whose uses were taught to Mom by her grandmother. But it's not just the salve that is healing. It's also Mom's touch and the wordless chant she sings under her breath. I can feel my insides growing cool, my mind slowing down, the balance I didn't know I was missing returning to me. I know that salve and Mom's healing hands will do the job. In a day or two the bruises will be gone.

While Mom ministers to me, Victor and Ana sit quietly on the floor by my feet. To someone else outside of our family it might look like they are doing nothing. But they are actually doing something important: simply being with each other and with me.

"Anywhere else?" Mom asks.

I look at my arms, which had been covered with scrapes, cuts, and bruises yesterday. I pull up my pants to check my legs, which had been equally battered. But that was before I bathed in Lozen's medicine spring. Not a mark on me now from my neck on down. Again I press my hand along the side where my ribs were badly broken. Still no pain.

"No," I say.

"Amazing," Mom says.

More than that, I think. I don't tell her about Lozen's spring. But I keep it in mind. If—no *when*—the day comes that I can engineer our escape from Haven, that will be one of the places we can take shelter for a while. Better that no one other than me knows about that place or the other places I have mapped inside my head. Or the caches of weapons and food I've been gradually building outside these walls.

Victor climbs up to sit next to me on my cot. He's holding one of my books. I have a lot of books. I can't say that I have a lot of friends here in Haven. Aside from Guy and my family, there's not really anyone who's close to me. Or anyone I care that much about.

Well, not exactly. There's Hussein. I love his music . . . but I don't think he even knows I'm alive. Sure, he smiles at me—that shy beautiful smile of his—sometimes when he looks up from the strings. But he smiles like that at anyone who is listening to him play. So I can't call him a friend, or anything other than just someone to nod at, maybe say hi.

As far as other ordinary people go, I never exchange more than a word with any of them. But for some reason people keep giving me books. Word must have gotten round about my little cell library. I'll be walking down the bloc and a woman will come up to me with something wrapped in a scarf or an old towel.

"For you," she'll say. "I know you will take care of it."

And, as I always do, I'll mutter "Thank you." And then when I get back to my cell I'll unwrap it and find a book like the one Victor is holding.

"I'm reading this," he says.

That book is one of my favorites and also one of the most painful books for me to read. *Black Beauty*. It's about a girl and her horse.

"What were they like?" Victor asks, tapping the picture embossed on the cover. "Horses, I mean."

He's only eight and thus he's never seen a real horse. I have. But how can I explain it to him? What story can I tell? Not the real one. The one about how horses were gone from this continent for thousands of years, but then they were brought back to our people. Uncle Chatto told me that some of our elders used to say that they were the only gift ever given to us by Europe that was a welcome gift. So welcome that our horses were known by sacred names, were members of our families. We loved our horses. They loved our people. And then . . .

They called it equine pneumonia. It was worse than the normal pneumonia people get. It began at racetracks. The leaders of our nation liked horse racing and so it was one of the sports that got a lot of "scientific" attention to make it better. Dad said the sickness came about as a result of the stuff they did to make horses run faster. It was not a hormone or a drug, but an actual biological entity, a sort of symbiotic microbe. It was not injected into the blood stream, but inhaled in a mist. It didn't just dull the pain in stressed and injured legs—like cobra venom—it actually made the horses stronger. For a while—there was a trade-off. Burn out. You got faster and stronger horses—but only for a year or two.

What happened next, though, was that the symbiote

mutated. It got faster. A year or two turned into a week. The infected lungs filled with blood, yellow mucus poured out of the horses' nostrils. And they died. Plus it turned out to be able to spread itself through the air. Fast. Any horse within ten or twenty miles got infected. And because of our marvelously efficient rapid transport networks—which made it possible to run a horse in Florida one day, put them on a 500 mph sub-oceanic maglev train and then run them in London a day later—the mutated symbiote established itself on every continent other than what was left of two-thirds-melted Antarctica within a month after it was positively identified. Too late for any quarantine to work.

So, not long before the Cloud hit us, horses had their own apocalypse. And it moved into other hooved domestic animals as well. Cows, sheep, even the semi-wild private herds of buffalos that still existed. All wiped out. The only domesticated hooved animals it spared were goats—though for some reason it didn't affect wildlife like deer and antelope.

Which is why we are walking and running, not riding or being pulled in wagons by animals with hooves. And why the only horses Victor will ever know are in books and stories.

"Lozen?" he says. He's waiting for me to say something.

Can I tell him how Dad and Uncle Chatto and Mom and I all had horses of our own? Poor as we were, we had horses. Which made us feel rich. On the rare days when Dad and Uncle Chatto were not working—they each held down three crappy jobs back then to just barely earn enough to feed and clothe us and pay the mortgage on our little ranch—we rode together across the mesas, racing each other and racing the wind. Or sometimes just walking along, feeling as if our horses were part of our own bodies.

My horse. I wish I could sing a song about him like those sung by my Navajo and Apache ancestors.

About his hooves striking the red earth like lightning.
About his mane whipping back like the storm wind.
About his eyes made of stars.
About his teeth made of white shells.
About his tail like a trailing black cloud.

But I do not know how to sing. Even about my own beloved horse.

We called him Black, but that was not his secret name, his sacred name. Can I tell Victor about the morning I heard the weak thudding of his hooves against the stable wall and found him on his side in his stall, trying to rise? Blood coming from his mouth and his nostrils and even from his eyes? How I cradled his head in my arms and whispered his secret name into his ear? How I leaned close to his mouth and felt the warmth of his last breath?

No.

I take the book from my brother's hand and place my palm on its cover.

"Beautiful," I say. "They were beautiful."

CHAPTER SIXTEEN

Precious Things

I wake up, as I always do, before anyone else. I open my eyes the tiniest crack, just enough to see without it being noticeable to anyone who might be watching that I am awake. I have my cot pushed back against the far wall. That way, without moving my head I can see the door of my cell. Is the bike chain still wrapped to hold it secure, the heavy combination lock still clicked shut?

Yup.

But I do not move yet. I listen. No sounds of feet sliding across the concrete walkway or of anyone trying to breathe silently as they creep closer.

Am I being paranoid? Maybe.

Am I still alive? So far.

Never imagine that you are safe when there are enemies nearby. That was Uncle Chatto's advice. And here in Haven there are always enemies nearby.

But I don't feel a tingling in my hands here unless those enemies are intending to do me harm, and not just keeping me under control until I can be sent out again like one of those Tomahawk missiles from the time pre-C, when anyone annoying our nation was blown up with unmanned drones and guided missiles.

Tomahawk. An old Indian word. That's me. Their tomahawk. Their killer. But at least my missions of destruction have never involved killing innocent people ("collateral damage"). Those so-called smart bombs blew up everyone within a hundred yards of a bad guy.

I keep listening, counting silently. *One and one pony. Two and one pony.*

I reach one hundred. Still no sound or sight of danger, no message delivered from my Power to my central nervous system. I slide back my blanket and swing my legs onto the floor. No need to get dressed. I always sleep with my clothes on.

I sprinkle a few drops of precious water from my water container into my palms and rub my hands over my face. Then I take a small sip of water. In Haven everyone has learned how to live on the minimum amount of water possible for a human. Some have learned that lesson so well that they get dehydrated and die.

What are the most precious things in the world? Not gold or silver or diamonds or the possessions that people killed each other for in the old pre-C days. I mean those things that you need to stay alive.

The first is shelter. Without shelter you freeze in the winter or die of heat stroke in the summer. Without shelter from predatory beasts, you end up as an entrée. And shelter is what Haven offered those who chose to seek refuge here. That is why so many people came here of their own accord. Far fewer were brought here at gunpoint like my family and me.

The second precious thing is water. You can live for days with no food. But not without water. And there is also water at Haven. It flows up on its own from an artesian well. So there is no need for those irrigation pumps that used to bring water up from deep below the surface—so deep that hand pumps would not work. In the pre-C days that artesian well was a nuisance. Its flow was pumped away because the prison had a bigger water source from a community water treatment plant four miles away. That plant, of course, is a dry ruin now.

So that artesian well is far from a nuisance now. It provides enough water for every soul in here—if they behave. Misbehave and the daily water ration is decreased or cut off entirely. A single day without water is enough to bring most ordinaries back in line.

Of course our rulers are exempt from any rationing. The Ones use some of that water to fill a swimming pool they have installed in their secure enclave in the heart of Haven, while we only get enough water for the barest essentials. If it rains enough to fill the tanks on top of the shower shed, the communal showers can sometimes be used. But you only get four seconds of flow.

As far as the water from the well goes, each day we line up at the water house with our containers and ration cards. God help you if you lose your ration card.

That's another reason why people lock or barricade the doors of their cells. Water theft happens often. You might come back home to find your water jug drained.

Thinking of how important water is here makes me think of how we irrigate the gardens, which are a major source of the third precious thing needed to live. Food. Which makes me think of Hussein. It's about time for his morning ritual.

But I skipped one other source of survival. It's one we forget about until the cold or the dark close in on us. I climb up on my cot and look out through the bars. There, on top of the part of the wall I can see from here, is that old friend of human life.

Fire.

The fires on the fortress walls are still burning. I've gotten so used to their harsh smell—nothing is more pervasive than the stench of burning rubber tires—I can sleep through the night without thinking about what I'm smelling. A better option than dying with sweet-scented air. Without those hundred bonfires, creatures of the night might come close to the walls without being seen. Even worse, they might come over those walls.

As I peer up at the wall fifty yards away, I catch a glimpse of one of the wall watchers. It's a blocky man whose name I don't know. Like all the watchers, he's armed with a shotgun, slung by a strap over his shoulder. He squints his eyes, partly from the smoke and partly from four hours of staring out into the dark, looking for any movement. In his other hand is a torch. All the wall watchers carry one. See anything moving outside near the wall, throw the torch down in that direction and then shoot at whatever it discloses.

Then, if it's more than an unlucky coyote or a stray shadow, follow it up with one or two of the Molotov cocktails lined up in racks along the inner edge of the wall. It's amazing how effective a bottle half filled with gas with a rag stuck in it can be.

The wall watcher moves out of sight. I'm glad of that.

This part of the prison wall faces east. He won't block my view of the new light of the day. I always say hello to the sun as it comes up. I whisper a silent prayer to the Life Giver. I ask for health and help for my family. Then I listen for what always come next. Through some strange acoustic property, maybe the shape of the wall and the design of the cell blocs, I can hear Hussein's morning song from his cell a hundred yards away in the Men's Wing that also faces east.

He gets up at the same time I do every day. Garden work starts early. He goes to the window of his cell and sings—without his guitar, just his lilting voice—his own greeting to the new day. I don't understand exactly what he's singing. Not the words at least. They're in Arabic.

But that song has a lilt to it that reminds me of an Apache prayer being chanted. It sounds reverent. It makes my heart feel fuller hearing it. I am certain it is praising and pleasing the Creator.

I wait. But not long. Sweet as the notes of a cactus wren, Hussein's soft chant begins.

My concentration on his song is interrupted. Boots are coming down the corridor, scuffing the concrete, approaching the door of my cell. I hop down off my cot, straighten up and wait. They're coming for me. Could it be another summons, already, for a mission outside the walls? I don't know. There are reports of a monster not far from here that I've been expecting to be sent to dispatch for some time. Perhaps they're finally getting around to it.

But I can safely assume who it is this time. He's the only one who ever summons me this early in the morning. All of the Ones are evil and unpredictable. But none of them creep me out the way this overlord does. The one whose strange chamber I'll soon be entering.

The Dreamer.

CHAPTER SEVENTEEN

The Dreamer

The Dreamer's chamber—chamber, not room, is the only word for it—is as weird and otherworldly as he is. The room is hung along two of its walls with heavy red curtains, blood red. They are draped in such a way that they seem to be moving. That's because of the light reflecting from the third wall, the one to my right.

That wall is covered with mirrors of all shapes and sizes. Some of them seem to have come from a sideshow funhouse from one of those carnivals that used to exist B.C. They distort the shapes they reflect in bizarre ways. They catch and twist the light cast by the candles and oil lanterns hung in front of them. Look too long at those mirrors and you start to lose your balance. This chamber may be the smallest of the rooms occupied by our overlords, but the lights, the mirrors and those rippling vermilion curtains make it seem as if it has no boundaries in any direction.

It's as if I just stepped into the heart of a monster. Although that simile is probably not that good, seeing as how the monster himself is inside this shifting, dizzying crimson cubiculum. There he is, lounging on a divan that is as spotlessly white as everything else around him is scarlet, including the thick rugs and the ceiling itself.

The divan is large, but it barely holds the Dreamer's languid, sprawled form, wrapped in a red silk dressing gown decorated with Chinese dragons. He's the tallest of the Ones, perfectly proportioned like all of them, but over seven feet tall. His legs, feet encased in tight, ruby-colored slippers, hang off the end of the divan and one of his lanky arms is extended so that his hand, palm up, rests on the floor. His other arm is held up in a theatrical fashion, the back of his hand covering his eyes. He looks like a fop, a spoiled silly prince of the sort you used to see in very old films. That impression of harmless indolence is aided by the mask he wears that covers his face from his hairline down to his chin, leaving only one eye and his lips exposed. His mask, which resembles the bemused face of an ancient Chinese emperor, is covered with small garnets and rubies that twinkle in the bizarre, shifting light. It's so weird it's almost funny. But no one brought here ever laughs.

If what I have heard is true, the white slipcover of his divan has to be regularly changed. Otherwise, it would match the rest of his chamber. And it is not paint, but his sanguinary practices that stains them.

He acts as if he has not seen me. But as the guards step back, I can sense that he's well aware of me and about to act.

Stay calm, girl. Here it comes.

As sudden as a snake striking, the Dreamer uncoils, covering the thirty or so feet between us in a single, feral leap. He lands, looming over me with his hands held above my head like claws.

I don't move. I stay at ease, my eyes down.

He leans his head down close to my face.

"My little killer," he hisses. "One dreamt of you last night."

Not something you'd want to hear from his lips. Being the girl of his dreams may mean that once you are brought to his chamber of horrors (which is rumored to be even worse behind those curtains) you will never be seen again. Whenever new people are brought to Haven or manage to reach here to beg for admittance, the Ones are always there, standing on the wall walkway above the main gate to look them over. Ostensibly they are here to assess them to decide for what duties they may be best suited. Usually it is the Dreamer who speaks.

"That one, to the kitchens."

"That strong looking one—wood cutter."

"Machine shop."

"Gardens."

But every now and then, one of those sanctuary seekers—always a handsome young man or a lovely young woman—catches the fancy of Diablita Loca or the Jester. With a gesture of the hand, that unfortunate chosen one is led off . . . and is never mentioned again.

All we have are rumors. None of us peons are given access to the truth. But whispers do slip out from some of the more careless or squeamish of the guards, about what was done to that new fish who came swimming into our pond and disappeared without a ripple.

Now and then, though, it is the Dreamer who makes a personal choice.

I picture the Dreamer standing there on the wall. I imagine him raising one arched eyebrow as he takes in the unfortunate person looking fearfully up at the four gods standing in judgment. A chill goes down my back as I imagine him pointing down languidly and drawling to the other three, "One dreamt of that one."

Fast as the Dreamer is, I think that I may be faster. Even as nearly naked as I am, there are a dozen or more ways I could kill him before he could make a single move to defend himself. I allow myself the luxury of picturing him falling backward, blood oozing out of the corner of his perfect mouth after I have crushed his windpipe with a ridge-hand blow. But that is as far as I can go. Not if my family and I are going to survive.

One day, one day.

But not today.

The Dreamer spins on his heel, cartwheels, and drops back onto his couch.

"One dreamt," he whispers. "Do you understand dreaming, my little killer?"

I shake my head, as if giving him a negative answer. But I do understand dreams . . . and wonder if he does. Does he truly understand the power of dreams? He says that sees things in his dreams. But is what he sees just something he hungers for?

"One saw something one just *must* have," the Dreamer says in his soft voice. He waves a languid hand toward the two guards standing behind me. "Now, one might send one of them to get the object of my desire. Karl there and Samson and, oh, twenty or so others. You'd be delighted to do that for One, wouldn't you, my boys?"

I'm not sure which of the two my mind picks up. But as soon as he speaks their names a panicky thought from one of them knifes through my head.

Christ, no!

"But that is too risky," the Dreamer continues, his voice so low now that I doubt the two increasingly nervous men behind me can hear it. "One must maintain the balance of power to keep One's friends by One's side. Mustn't One?"

He is talking about our other three petty rulers. I'm one of the few who know just how much the four of them hate each other, and that is only because of my special abilities. If they could, the Ones would gladly cut each other's throats.

"No," the Dreamer says, his voice loud enough for the

123

relieved men behind me to hear. "One must disappoint you lads and not afford you the chance to undertake this mission for One."

He snaps his fingers.

A tall, bone-thin woman slides out from behind the curtains. Her face is pale as paper and just as expressionless. She's attired, of course, in the Dreamer's favorite hue from her high heels and sheath dress on up to the hyacinth hairpins that hold the thick, high-piled honey-blonde curls on top of her head. She's holding a book. As she approaches her master and presents it to him with upraised arms, bowing in a deep curtsey as she does so, I can see that it is a collection of color photographs from an art museum.

"Thank you, Lorelei," the Dreamer says.

Lorelei. The Dreamer's helper. I've not seen her before, but I have heard her name mentioned. It's said that those who do get to see her usually never get to see anything else.

For a moment, the Dreamer studies the large book that he holds easily in one large hand. Then he snaps his fingers again.

"Now go."

Lorelei nods and bows. Her perfect blue eyes take me in as she lifts her head. She licks her lips like a cat anticipating a delightful dinner. A smile—not at me, about me. A graceful turn. Four dance-like steps back and Lorelei slips smoothly through the curtain. Smoothly enough to prevent my getting a brief glimpse of what is back there. But my imagination fills in what I don't see. Another shiver runs down my back.

"Observe."

The Dreamer has just spun the book in his hand and holds it out for me to peruse an open page. He taps the photo in its center. "Can you remember this?"

"Yes," I say. It's the only word I have spoken thus far.

The Dreamer studies me. I focus on the photo in the book. It is of a small, ornate mirror, its rococo frame characteristic of a style of artistic expression prevalent during another time of self-centered monarchs. Excessively ornate, but interesting. I've always liked looking at art and learning about it, even though there was no way in hell our family would ever own any and I seldom got the chance to see any of it outside a viddy screen in the pre-C days.

The Dreamer slides his long, perfect finger to the text beneath the photo. "Can you read, my little one? This was owned by the Sun King. Louis the Fourteenth of France. Ever heard of him, my little killer? No? Ever heard of France?"

The self-satisfied sarcasm in his voice is so thick you could cut it with a knife. Just as I could cut his throat by breaking one of those mirrors and using a sharp shard of glass to part his breath from his lungs with one quick slice. It would be so simple to do. I could do it all in less time than it would take to count to four.

But four is the magic number. There are four of them. Kill one and it will just make the other three stronger. And my family and me deader. There's no other course now than to follow orders. While quietly doing whatever I can to plan for our someday escape.

So all I do is stare up at him with what I hope is a confused look and shake my head. I do not open my mouth to ask him how much he really knows about that mirror he lusts for, about the rocaille ornamentation of eighteenth-century France with its fanciful and frivolous use of curved spatial forms.

The Dreamer shakes his head, disgusted by my stupidity.

Is she truly this dense? One might as well be talking to a slug. But if anyone can accomplish this task, she can.

"Never mind. All that matters is that in my dream I saw it. I know where it is. My dream told me."

Dream, my ass. He may fool others into thinking he has prophetic ESP, but I noticed that it said very clearly on the page with the photo of the mirror exactly where it was located.

The Dreamer nods. "It waits there. Unbroken, perfect. It waits for One to claim it. Which you shall do for me, yes?"

I nod. Even though I am a little confused by his request.

Bringing back an art object for one of our overlord's collections is not exactly the sort of job I usually do. Which means there has to be more to it than simple retrieval.

CHAPTER EIGHTEEN

The Bloodless

The gates of Haven are now an hour's ride behind me. And I have a lot to think about. As I pedal along, the gentle whir of the rubber tires against the road, the slight clatter as I shift gears when the road rises, are a comforting sound. They're almost like a song. The wind is in my face, the scent of sage is in the air, and I'm out from behind the walls. And I can pedal this bike down the highway without fear of being squashed by a boulder dropped by a Monster Bird. I suppose I should be feeling good on some level. Aside from the usual knot somewhere in my stomach that I always get when I am sent out on one of these missions to kill—or be killed. But there's something else disquieting this time. Two somethings.

I stop at the top of the last bend in the road where I can look back and see the old prison. I lift up the motorcycle goggles

I've been wearing to keep the road dust out of my eyes. Maybe I don't need them all that much. But I really love them. My dad gave them to me. He'd liberated them from a museum exhibit in a little ghost town only a week before we were taken. His last gift to me.

I squint against the light, put a level palm across my forehead to shade my vision. The gates are still closed. I'm not being followed by anyone. Not yet, at least. But that feeling that I may be followed is something Numero Uno. Partially a result of my Power. Right now it is tugging at the back of my brain and telling me to keep looking back. And partially because I noticed the little group of men who were casually gathered together at the far side of the exercise yard past the armory. None of them were wearing armbands. And that was strange. All but one of them were carefully *not* watching me as I left. They were also making a point of *not* looking toward the armory. Which made me suspect that was where they were heading as soon as the gates closed behind me. To get geared up and follow me?

But not yet. The gates stay closed. I sigh, lower my goggles, shift my backpack—a little heavier than usual because of the weighty items at the bottom of it—and then apply my feet once more to the pedals.

And I begin to think about reason Numero Dos for my disquiet. Snakes. I am less than fond of snakes. That's a weakness of mine, I know.

Dad talked to me about snakes. I remember one day when we were out walking through the desert. It was after one of those rare soaking rains that bring everything into bloom. The ocotillos were vibrant with blossoms as red as flames and the green of the cactuses was so bright that they seemed to throb in the sunlight. Little buds started to open into delicate flowers on their spiny surfaces. Even the stones were brighter, glowing like the diamonds and emeralds and rubies I'd seen in a cartoon pirate's treasure chest. Only it seemed to me that the stones of our desert were much more precious than those in any old wooden box. I was only six years old and holding my father's hand as we walked and everything was perfect.

Then I saw something. It moved so fast. It was like a muscled length of rope throwing its coils out to the side as it moved along over the moist sand, leaving S-shaped patterns behind it. I recognized it as a sidewinder, a kind of rattlesnake.

It was not coming toward us, just crossing in front of us.

But I grabbed my father's hand tighter and shrank back in fear.

Dad dropped down to one knee and put his arm over my shoulder.

"Lozen," he said in that soft reassuring voice of his, "There is no need to be afraid. That one has his own job and is just doing it. If you do not bother him he will not harm you. The Giver of Life made him, too. He has as much right to live as we humans."

I understood. And I let go of my fear. I respect snakes. But that does not mean I have to love them. They go their way and I go mine.

Or at least that is how it has been until now.

I've heard the old saying that the enemy of my enemy is my friend. But not if the enemy of my enemy is also my enemy.

As I pushed the trail bike through the gate of Haven, I'd gotten a poisonous look from Edwin. He was the only one in that little group of men trying to look casual who had stared my way, his cheek twitching as he did so.

But the unbidden thought I read from his mind was not the usual one containing graphic images of his disgusting fantasies.

She thinks she's something. But just wait. Her time is coming, sooner than she thinks.

No. I can't worry about Edwin now, though. I need to concentrate, keep pushing on as far as I can before nightfall, planning what I need to do to survive until tomorrow.

This little carefree jaunt of mine is going to require me to spend at least one night in Bloodless territory. No way around it since the only way to reach my objective—what used to be the private estate of a wealthy and powerful art collector—is by passing through the outskirts of Sun City. Not into Sun City itself, which is fortunate for me. With care, I could survive a descent into that hellscape where no people—real people— live anymore. Just the Bloodless. But no one would attempt that if they could avoid it.

And it is a lovely day for a ride. I even pause for a few moments on a hilltop vista where I can look out over the hills, purple with sage, and listen to the lilting song of the cactus wren sticking its head out of a hole in a tall saguaro. I observe the rusting wrecked vehicles by the roadside and count the burned-out hulks of houses in the valley below.

What I need to find is a relatively intact dwelling near a handy hillside. Not an adobe, but a house made primarily of wood. There are going to be few trees where I spend the hours of darkness. I need the wood of that house for fire, not shelter. Unless you can lock yourself inside an abandoned bank vault, overnighting in any dwelling within ten miles of Sun City is tantamount to suicide.

Maybe I could find a bank vault. But no. Any such vault might already be occupied, seeing as how vaults are just as good at keeping out those nasty old sun rays as cellar holes and attics, where the Bloodless pass away their dormant hours. Another reason for me to stay the outdoorsy type.

I keep one eye on the sun as I pedal along, giving silent thanks to our old brother in the sky for its life-giving light. With my other eye I keep watch for just the right place. And there it is. Far enough out to be isolated and unburned, but close enough to make it a perfect stopping place three quarters of the way to my final (let's hope not) destination.

I park my bike and lift my goggles to look the place over. It's a large ranch-style house at the end of its own little driveway straight up from the road. Big windows that let in a lot of

131

light—and air, seeing as how the glass is all gone. A hill that rolls down behind it. And a dried-up reddish brown yard in front of where there had once been well-irrigated lawn. No trees or big stones for anything to lurk behind as it creeps toward me in the twilight.

I take out the eighteen-inch pry bar I've packed. Then, holding it in my left hand, my .357 in my right, I insert it between the front door and the frame. True, I could have crawled through the space where the plate glass window once looked out onto a verdant yard. But the chance of cutting myself and being in an awkward spot halfway in and halfway out when . . . well, you know. The lock pops free, but the door sticks when it is part way open. One front kick does it, not only opening the door but ripping it off its hinges to fall with an echoing crash on the floor of the hallway that—like the other rooms in the house—appears to have been stripped of everything valuable.

"Honey," I call out, "I'm home."

No answering hellos, growls, or slobbery snarls. An excellent start.

It's a ranch style, constructed on a slab since the bedrock is too close to the surface to make a basement. So aside from a possible crawl space overhead—which I am not about to explore—there is just one floor to check out before I start.

I contemplate how to do this. I reach back to the bag slung over my left shoulder and pat its lumpy contents. I could take

132

out one of the party favors that Guy provided me for the particular task I hope to accomplish at Dragoon Springs. Toss one into the house ahead of me and then . . .

Nah. Too noisy. Plus I may need every one of the seven he gave me at my ultimate destination tomorrow.

So I just grasp my .357 in both hands. I double check to make sure the safety is still off. (You'd be surprised, Guy once told me, how many people forget that one little detail until it is too late and something's teeth are lodged in your throat.).

Take a slow breath, start moving from one room to the next.

My back is against the wall with the gun held ahead of me till I reach each doorway. It's a long hall with one sharp turn in it. Then I take a quick step and a half turn to face into each successive room with the gun held ahead of me, ready to fire at the center mass of whatever is lurking in there as my eyes sweep from floor to ceiling, corner to corner.

Kitchen. Clear.

Living room. Nothing living.

Den with no denizen.

A trio of bedrooms. No Goldilocks, no three bears.

Three bathrooms without a single psycho in the showers.

Two-car garage with no cars within.

Nada.

Safe enough. But not a place I would want to spend the night.

Then I hear something. The unmistakable sound of heavy feet coming my way down the hall. Booted feet. With spurs. Coming from the direction of the last bedroom. Did I check the closet in that bedroom? I did not.

I put my back against the wall, lift the gun with both hands. I'm ready to shoot first and ask questions later. Then the footsteps pause and a voice comes from around the corner.

"Whoa, partner. Wouldn't shoot an unarmed gans, would you?"

I'm not sure I heard what I just heard. I'm even more unsure when the one who said that steps from around the corner. It's a frigging cowboy. With a big silver lawman's badge on his chest.

"Stop," I say.

The cowboy's wide handlebar mustache twitches as his mouth shapes itself into a wide smile.

"Whatever you say, little sister," he says. His voice is warm and reassuring, but the hair is standing up on the back of my neck. "I'm here to help. Just tell me what you want me to do."

I look at his face. It looks as friendly as his voice sounded. But something is wrong here. I slide away from the wall, back into the living room. The cowboy takes a step toward me and his spurs jingle as he does so.

I raise one hand and motion him to keep coming forward. "Slow," I say.

His smile gets even broader. "Sure thing, little sister. That makes sense. 'Bout as much sense as me looking like this, hey?"

"Sit," I say, gesturing at the couch he's just reached.

"Thought you'd never ask," he says. He lowers his long, lanky frame down onto the couch. And as he does so I notice two things. Numero Uno is that his face has changed. He looks younger now. His mustache is no longer gray, but black. Numero Dos is that the overstuffed couch cushions did not give way under his weight.

Gans, he'd said. I hadn't heard it wrong.

"Ayup," he says. "That's me." And as he says those three words his voice changes. His accent is no longer that of a cowboy out of one of those old western movies. It's as deep and resonant as thunder coming out of the mountains.

My namesake spoke to the spirits. They visited her from time to time, just as they visited all of our people who fasted and prayed for help from those ancient beings. The gans. The mountain spirits who have helped us now and then. In the old days, back in the early twenty-first century, there were still times when our people would put on the sacred paint, wear the tall cruciform headpieces, and dance as the Mountain Spirits.

But I haven't been fasting. Or seeking a spirit guide. Or have I?

The figure in front of me flickers, his shape blurs for a

moment. Like the flames of a fire moving when struck by a gust of wind. Or a dark whirlwind. And for just that moment he is so terrible, so beautiful, as beautiful as our ancient peaks, that it takes the breath out of my lungs. Then he is, once again, an old Arizona Ranger. With a smile on his face.

Why a cowboy? I think.

The gans chuckles. "Why not?" he says. "Seeing as how when white people used to see a guardian spirit, they'd say it was an Indian, more often than not. And you being Chiricahua, little sister,"—he spreads his arms—"you get to see a cowboy."

A spirit being with an Apache sense of humor. It figures.

What have I done to earn this? I think.

"Why have I come to you, little Lozen?" the gans replies. He's no longer smiling. His speech no longer sounds like that of an old cowpuncher. It's more formal, more serious. His shape is no longer human. "Do not look for any reason that your logical mind can grasp. Just know that we have seen you. And I have shown myself to you to encourage you, just this one time. You will not see me again, but you must remember that you are never alone on your journey. Be brave, little one."

He pauses. Is that it? But it's not. Just before he vanishes he looks over my shoulder, as if seeing something or someone there.

"I have also been sent to warn you that, in another way, you are not alone. There are enemies behind you."

And then he is gone. There's no sign he was ever here.

Perhaps I could explain it away by saying I've been under stress for so long that my brain is playing tricks on me. That is what my logical mind would conclude. But not the part of me that is Lozen. And his warning is apt—I've got work to do.

I holster my gun—but do not snap the strap in place. Then I set to work with my pry bar.

By the time I am done, I've demolished the interior walls and reaped an excellent harvest of nice, dry eight- to twelve-foot-long two by fours. I place them in three tall, carefully spaced piles along with heaps of trim—which will make excellent kindling to add to the brush I've gathered, all to be piled into three tipi-shaped stacks.

Stack Numero Uno: directly behind me and fifty feet from the front window of the house. It's the biggest of the three and the one I need to keep burning the hottest.

Stack Numero Dos: eight feet from the back fire and directly to my right.

Stack Numero Tres: an equal distance from the back and to my left.

Then I take my place in the center—more than halfway surrounded by my blazes, which I start with my flint and steel when the sun is still a hand's width from the horizon.

Build it and they will come. Uncle Chatto used to say that all the time and chuckle. I never quite got the joke, but it is for sure true about the Bloodless. Nothing attracts them more at night than a fire. Like moths to a flame, they come creeping in. The next thing the person huddled in front of that fire knows, there are two clawed hands around his or her neck and some very sharp teeth fastened in said soon-to-be-deceased person's neck.

If that person is stupid enough to sit staring into a fire. The proper place for a night fire is at your back when you are dealing with such former (we assume) human beings. I've heard theories about how they came to be. A virus, a genetic mutation, a gene-splicing experiment that was meant to cure a certain kind of immune-deficient disease that popped up a few years before the Cloud and caused severe anemia. Or maybe it had to do with some sort of old darker magic coming back after the electricity was dampened.

For whatever reason, the result was the rise of the Bloodless. And when they were set free by the chaos after the electronic apocalypse, it turned out they could propagate more of their kind. Getting killed is one thing, but it is way worse as far as I am concerned to get turned into a creepy-crawly who only comes out at night.

A lot of people—myself included—think that maybe the Bloodless have been around for longer than some think. Like the vampires of legend, maybe they (or others like them in the past) are the basis for such stories all around the world. Including among our Chiricahua people and the other original peoples of this continent. And when electricity and bright lights vanished from the world, they were free again to reclaim the dark.

So why build a fire if it attracts them? Because they will

come anyway, attracted to my own body heat. And with fire, especially fires like these I have strategically located, I can see them and have some control over the situation. According to Guy, they are drawn to fire, but also leery of it.

The creature shows up soon after the sun vanishes. Which makes me think that there may be some caves in the hillside off to the left of me. Of course he does not expect me to have seen him. Stealth characterizes the way they stalk up on you.

I clear my throat. "Ahem," I say.

My stalker freezes while still about forty feet away.

He (it's a male, a tall long-haired one wearing tattered jeans and a black jacket) stands up from where he was crouched down and creeping forward. He raises one hand and takes a step.

"Hello," he says, just a trace of a growl in his voice. "Good see you here. I join you? I sit with you? Yes? You tired. Why you not rest? Yes. Go sleep, rest now?"

Whatever it is that makes them what they are also makes them somewhat language challenged. They can speak English and even better Spanish. But only in short phrases and not always with good grammar. But they are clever and somehow they are able to hypnotize most people with their voices.

But not me. I hope. Despite the seductive, reasonable tone of his voice, I say nothing. I concentrate on staying awake and alert as I shove more wood into the fire in front so that it blazes up higher.

My false friend barely stifles a snarl before recomposing his face into a toothy grin. He brushes his hair back from his face, beckons with his hand. A hand whose fingernails are as long and sharp as the claws of a vulture.

"No. Fire too hot. Cool out here. Come out here, better out here. Fire too hot."

He's talking faster now, being more insistent because he's frustrated that I haven't fallen for his line of crap. Or have I? He's closer than he was before and I don't remember seeing him move. But I stay where I am.

His hands are trembling. His body is tense. But the fires and my obvious resistance have discomfited him. His mouth is slightly open now and I can see his sharp canine teeth. A little line of saliva is creeping down the right corner of his mouth.

I haven't unholstered my gun. I could shoot at him, sure. But shooting doesn't always work with the Bloodless. Unless you hit them just right, a bullet goes right through them. Then they just keep coming. And at the sight of a gun they move so fast that getting off an accurate shot—even for me—isn't a certainty.

Plus, I wonder if he's alone.

I've heard that they hunt in pairs, staking out their own little portions of the nighttime landscape as their own.

The female of the pair may be somewhere out there in the night behind him. Not behind me. My fire is too big for that direction to be to her liking. Without the protective wall of the fires I've built the two of them would already be on me like two mountain lions on a rabbit.

"Tired," the Bloodless male says. He has moved a step closer to me. That is not good.

Focus, girl.

"Tired," he says again. "You tired."

No, I'm not. I hold hard to that thought.

He is grinning even wider now, all resemblance to humanity gone. Showing all his teeth—more than the average human mouth could hold. Toothy, I think. I'll call him Toothy. And what should I call his as-yet-unseen mate who may be planning to sweep in on me like a storm wind as soon as Toothy makes his move? How about Mariah? Like that old, old song my mother sometimes sings. "They Call the Wind Mariah."

"Tired, tired."

He takes two steps closer. I'm awake. I see those steps.

"Sleep now. Sleep," Toothy repeats in a growly whisper. And my eyelids are feeling heavy, despite my attempts to concentrate, to stay awake.

Another step, nearly near enough to leap.

I close my eyes. And as soon as I do so, that familiar stab in the middle of my forehead comes along with his breathless, ravenous voice.

Yes!

Timing is everything. I open my eyes just in time for my feigned slumber to work. Toothy is in midleap as I lift my staff, its sharp blade already extended. It catches him square in the throat. The butt of the staff *screaks* as it grinds against the bedrock under his weight.

Toothy's eyes are wild and his clawed hands are trying to reach me. But the staff is too long and the angle of penetration into his throat has taken it up into his skull. Somehow it has missed the spine, but it is not doing any favors for the back of his brain. His thrashing is no less wild, but it's not as focused.

Damn, these things can be hard to kill.

This is all only taking me a few heartbeats. But if his mate is out there about to attack, it's a few heartbeats too many!

I twist the staff and thrust it to the side, using all of my strength. Toothy's struggling body is pushed toward the fire on my right. His heels catch on a burning two by four and he falls backward.

"EEEEYAAHHHH!"

His scream is as high and ear-splitting as a blade drawn across metal. No wonder, though. As soon as he hits that blaze, his waist-length hair becomes a nimbus of flame, and his parchment-pale skin blackens and crinkles like dry paper. The fear they have of fire is well-founded. Apparently the Bloodless burn as quickly as paper soaked in kerosene.

All that, from Toothy's leap to his metamorphosis into a Roman candle, has taken no more time than for me to count from one to four. Almost too much time.

Like a sharp-fanged whirlwind, Mariah comes flying out

of the night. No clever hypnotic monologue this time. Just claws and canines aimed for my eyes and my throat.

I sidestep and swing my left arm—holding my faithful Arkansas Toothpick—at the back of her neck. The Bowie knife's razor blade parts bone and flesh with one smooth sweep.

Her decapitated head bounces three times to land sizzling in the largest fire. Her lifeless body falls at my feet.

And now, though the larger problem preventing a good night's rest may have been eliminated, I am faced with another annoyance—the rank odor of two crispy critters frying in my bonfires.

CHAPTER NINETEEN

Dragoon Springs

've traveled another twenty miles toward my destination. The sun is high in the hazy sky and the desert lands I'm now leaving behind as the road climbs are rippling with the heat. It is so hot that five miles back I passed a hungry coyote trying to catch a jackrabbit. Both of them were walking and taking rest breaks.

That's my own feeble attempt at making a joke. I'm afraid that I am nowhere as good as Uncle Chatto or my Dad at humor. And I am going to have to get serious all too soon. According to the rusty, bullet-perforated road sign I just pedaled past as the road turned around a rock outcrop, I am nearing my destination.

DRAGOON SPRINGS   5 miles

144

The Dragoon Mountains are one of the places my people found safety for a while. Cochise had his stronghold here. Safety from the Mexicans and New Mexicans who took us as slaves. From the Americans who sided with our old enemies and then, at the end of our wars of resistance, put us all on a train and shipped us to Florida, then Alabama and then Oklahoma. Hard places of exile.

My namesake was one of those put on that train. And that is where she disappears from their histories. Lozen, the warrior woman. Was she buried in an unmarked grave in one of those faraway places?

However, hard and bitter as it was for us, we Chiracahuas did not just politely curl up and die as many hoped. Those of us who survived became that much tougher. And eventually, the children and grandchildren of those old resistance fighters found their way back to the Southwest. Most went to our cousins, the Jicarilla Apaches, but some like my dad and Uncle Chatto, returned quietly to Arizona. Not on a reservation, but on land they purchased with the money they had set aside when they were in the Marines and then doing private security work. And then came the Cloud, making all that history more or less irrelevant.

But I still remember. And so do our mountains. And, if I didn't just hallucinate my ironic mountain spirit's visitation, so do the gans.

I park the bike, leaning it against a state historical marker that is almost readable despite the bullet holes. I push my goggles up on my forehead and start up the narrow trail between boulders toward the high place I've spotted. A few feet along the trail, a piece of my torn sleeve catches on the dry branch of a shrub. I tug it free, a strip of frayed cloth hanging down where the short sleeve falls over my bicep. Not enough cloth to sew it back in place—easier to just rip it off.

I always carry a needle and strong thread with me. I've already sewn the two other tears that were ripped into my clothes last night by Mariah, who came closer to nailing me with her clawed right hand than I'd realized. One of the razor-cut rips was on the left inseam of my shorts just above the knee. Two inches higher and deeper and she would have gotten my femoral artery and I would have bled out.

I hold up the four-inch-long piece of red cloth. It looks like a prayer tie. I reach into one of the pouches hung from my belt and pull out a little tobacco. I wrap it in the cloth and then tie it to the branch that had caught hold of it as if to stop me, to remind me. I'd forgotten last night to give thanks properly for my survival. I do that now. Then I continue up the trail to the place that was once a lookout point for some of my own ancestors. It's a perfect spot to see in all directions, to see if enemies are on your trail, to see the enemies that may be just ahead.

When I reach the top I stand on top of a flat black boulder, its surface of rippled stone glistening in the sun. It's beautiful here. Familiar. My dad brought me here when I was little.

So I know this place by the name it's held since long before I ever breathed. We Look Far From Here. It is a name that is like a track, telling me what was here before, connecting me to a memory that might otherwise be lost.

I turn slowly to face each of the four sacred directions. The view from We Look Far From Here is far, indeed. Breathtaking. The land is spread out before me like a living map. And so is the sky, stretching farther than any human eyes can clearly see. As I face the direction where the winter lives, there's something gliding across that endless sky. Not just one, but three eagles. Real eagles, not monster birds. A wind comes whistling in, washes over me, then passes by and all is calm again.

Look down at your feet, my Power tells me.

I do. An eagle feather is right there, almost touching the toe of my left boot. It is a perfect feather just like those in the tails of the distant, sailing birds. Except for the black of its tip, this feather is pure white—so white that it seems to vibrate in the light. I don't ask myself where it came from and why I didn't see it when I first stepped onto this flat stone surface that is like a great black table. It doesn't matter if it was blown here by the wind or just appeared on its own out of thin air. It is here. That is what is important.

I go down to my knees to reverently pick it up. I lift the feather, feeling the quiver of wind held within it. Then I touch it to my forehead, my chest, my shoulders.

I ask for help, Great Creator.

Still holding the eagle feather between the thumb and index finger of my right hand, I raise my arms and turn them palm out. I slowly begin to turn again. The tingling sensation in my palms comes just when I expect it, facing the direction of my destination, a walled estate that houses what was once the largest private collection of art in the Southwest. The place where the Dreamer expected me to believe his extra sensory perception told him that mirror he is lusting for was hanging.

I know why he's aware of the crawly creature that guards the place. The one he told me he saw in one of his dreams. Guy laid it out for me as he was outfitting me for this latest task. A month ago the Dreamer sent out a group of a dozen of his best guards on a little collecting mission. Only two came back. The others, heavily armed men, met their demise on the grounds of Dragoon Springs.

Swallowed by a giant snake. Which will soon be viewing me as yet another desirable entrée.

But when I turn back to face the direction away from the place where danger awaits me, that sensation—as if I was holding my hands against a stone heated until it glows red—returns to my palms.

I immediately drop down to my belly, slide back where to I am no longer a silhouette against the sky. Then I lower one hand to pull out the small collapsed 40X telescope that I carry in one of the numerous handy pockets in my vest. I flip it and it clicks out to its full length.

I scan the road I've just traveled where it comes out of the desert several miles back. Movement. Just coming into view between the hills. And there they are at last, the ones following me. Two, three, four, five of them loping along at a brisk military pace. Following their leader, a big bear-like man wearing a red armband. He stops and looks down. I know what he's seeing. The tire treads of my bike in the sand that drifted over the dip in that part of the road. His head starts to turn my way. I quickly lower the scope and drop down out of sight. Did his peripheral vision pick up a brief gleam of sunlight reflecting from the lens of my scope? If so, maybe I'll get lucky. Maybe he'll think what he half-saw was nothing more than sun bouncing off stone. Or maybe not.

Crap! Everybody wants to get into the act. But not actually everybody. Just one Overlord in particular. Only Diablita Loca's men wear the red band. The huge man leading them is the head case everyone calls Big Boy. Boss of an outlaw biker gang back when motorcycles still worked. Now Diablita's head of security. I recognize him by not only his boxcar bulk but by the two jagged lines of raised flesh across his right cheek. Plus the signature machete hanging at his waist. He's never without it and uses it for you-know-what. I don't have to guess whose head he plans to cut off with it this time.

Big Boy was a Chainer even before the coming of the Cloud. It's surprising he's still alive. Chain isn't just addictive. It eventually kills its users, burns them out in a few years. At the very end it's like there are chains inside your body, wrapped around you, being pulled tighter and tighter until your own bones begin to snap.

Why are Big Boy and his crew after me? Perhaps there is no logical reason other than that the Ones are always at odds with each other. Sending a killer team after me would be one way to thwart the Dreamer's wishes. Done just to spite him? Getting what he wants for herself? Take that prized mirror to Diablita Loca, who can let the Dreamer know that she plans to hang it among her trophies? Or maybe she'll just have it smashed to pieces in public?

Then again, it just might be that their job is simply to get rid of me as soon as possible because I am being viewed as a potential risk by the one who dispatched them on their mission. They're obviously not backup for my mission.

So which will it be? Engineer my immediate demise or hang back to see if I manage to retrieve that stupid mirror and wipe out a baleful beast or two in the process? Then, if I am still alive and ambulatory, ambush me on my way back?

Not that it matters in the long run to me which objective they have been instructed to accomplish.

After all, either way, I'll end up as dead as alternating current.

CHAPTER TWENTY

More than One

I've never killed a human being.

Even though I have fantasized snapping Edwin's neck, tearing out Diablita Loca's jugular, I have yet to do anything like that. I would gladly have killed those men who took the lives of my dad and Uncle Chatto and then gunned down Lobo. The first few weeks I was in Haven I dreamed about the revenge I would take on them. But I never got that chance because something else got them first. Whatever it was took them by surprise while they were on patrol not long after they brought us to Haven. What was left of them was found by another crew a week later.

On the other hand, I have broken my share of other people's bones. Back when I first got to Haven, some of the bad boys decided to see just how tough this skinny Apache girl was. Three against one. Odds that were lessened when I broke the first man's knee cap with a kick and then smashed in the next attacker's nose with a palm strike.

That discouraged any testing of me till a week later. That was when I stuck a guard's bolo knife through his left hand, pinning him to the wall. But that was only after he held its point to my throat as a gentle persuader to convince me to allow him to, shall we say, have his way with me? That was sufficient to convince him that no really does mean *no*! I didn't need to make his attempt at undeserved intimacy his last date.

It was lucky for me—and them—that none of them were Chainers. Because even broken bones and impaled palms would not have stopped one of them. Nothing short of killing discourages a Chainer. Which I could have done, though I'm glad I wasn't brought to that decision point.

Now, though, I may have to make that kind of decision. Neutralizing or shaking that five-man hit squad, before I go up against the denizens of Dragoon Springs, might be the smartest thing for me to do now. My brief glimpse of them was enough to see that two of them were carrying sniper rifles with those old-fashioned but still effective mid-twentieth-century telescopic scopes that do not rely on any of the electronic stuff that took over in the next millennium. Telescopic scopes are easily effective from half a mile away in the hands of any halfway decent marksman.

As I begin my climb down from We Look Far from Here, keeping the mountainside between me and my stalkers, I consider my options.

They have to see me to get me. All they know now is that I'm somewhere ahead of them. I could try to stay unseen and pick them off one by one. It might take a few hours, but I could possibly decommission all five of them before sundown.

But do I have to do that? I might if all I had on my side was my stealth, my strength, my weapons, and the training given to me by my family, passed on from generations of the greatest guerilla fighters the world ever knew. The last Apache to fight against the United States was Geronimo, but our people then—like other American Indian nations before us—began to apply our skills to fight for the country that had been their enemy, all through the twentieth century and into the twenty-first. My dad and Uncle Chatto were only the most recent Chiricahuas to serve as special force soldiers. And they kept on passing me their knowledge and training until the day they died. Like them, I am a warrior.

However, I have one additional choice other than just using my fighting skills against the men tracking me. I can use my Power.

I begin to climb down from We Look Far from Here.

Little Foo-ood!

I almost slip on a loose stone that goes bouncing and rolling down ahead of me.

I should have known it. Just when things are looking bad, my silent admirer would show up to make them worse.

What?! I think back at him.

Somehow, though I've not seen more than a partial glimpse

of this sardonic kibitzer who has been describing me as a future menu item, I know that he or it is a male. Back once again to taunt me. But the unspoken words that enter my mind surprise me.

I could help you.

There's a sort of sincerity in those words. As I start climbing down again, I consider that. And he did help me before. But I have to ask.

Why?

Because.

And the old irony is back again in that telepathic message to me. I stop again. I look carefully downslope, upslope, to either side. Nothing living in sight aside from a horned lizard sunning itself.

Where are you?

Somewhere.

Why did I even ask?

I'm halfway to the bottom now. Then it comes to me. Something is different. What is it? No pain in my forehead when his words touched down in my mind. We've been having a conversation just now—frustrating though it may be—as easily as if we were speaking aloud. Actually, for me, easier than talking.

You are not really going to eat me, are you? You've just been messing with me.

You think?

Ho ho ho.

I thought it was funny.

I hop down from one last rock and I am back on the road. The crossroads that lead south into the mountains are just ahead of me to the east. I pick up a stick and crouch down by the side of the road in front of the sign, which is leaning at a forty-five degree angle and still reads US10.

My silent partner is quiet now. No mental messages. But I can feel that he is somewhere nearby. Perhaps no more than behind one of those boulders back up the slope. I can feel him watching me. And suddenly I think I know now who—or what—he is. Of course! And I feel stupid for not having figured this out sooner. He is not a gemod. He's far older than that, a being who lives in the stories of not just my people but those of Indians all over this continent. Not exactly a human being, either. Or a gans. Someone more ancient than that, from a time before us humans, him and his people. All of our Native people have stories about him or his relatives. They've called him by many different names. Big Elder Brother, Sasquatch, Bigfoot. To us he was just Tall Hairy Man. Perhaps if I turn around quickly I'll see his large-toothed face before he can duck back out of sight. But I won't.

I feel the presence of my hairy friend beginning to fade. He is moving away fast, back toward the direction where I saw that sniper team. I can almost see him in my mind.

Why has he chosen to help me? I no longer think that it is,

as he so sardonically put it, because he sees me as his Little Food. He's doing more than just protecting a potential protein source.

Maybe I'll survive long enough to find out the answer. But I need to get my mind back to this task if I expect to eliminate the additional threat to my existence posed by my well-armed pursuers.

I bring the words of Lozen's chant to my mind. I learned it not from my father, but from my mother. She passed it to me soon after we were brought to Haven. The blood of Lozen's family came down to me from Mom's side, not Dad's. Mom is just as strong, in her own way, as Dad was in his. If she weren't, she would not be able to take care of Ana and Victor the way she does, making them feel safe as long as she is by their side.

I can see Mom's calm, unlined face, her dark, knowing eyes. She was holding both my hands in hers. And though I was already half a head taller than her, I felt in that moment as if I was the one looking up at her as we stood there. We were in one of the few quiet places in Haven that day, by the wall behind the shed where Hussein stores his tools. Mom had just been assigned to the job she still has working in the garden. We really knew nothing about him. But Mom and I'd known, somehow, that we could trust him.

We'd both walked up to him where he was adjusting one of the drip hoses for his beloved tomato plants.

"Hussein," I said.

He stood gracefully, turned to look at me. His brown eyes were really kind. My voice stalled out.

"Can you help us find a quiet place for just a few minutes?" Mom asked him.

I didn't say why.

He didn't ask.

"Come," he said

Then, without another word, he had led us both there and then left us in private.

"Are you ready?" Mom asked. "I can only sing this once. Then it will have passed from me to you and I can never sing it again."

I nodded. And then in her soft, strong voice, she gave me Lozen's song.

I am ready now to sing it. As I do so I need to think not just of myself, but of my family. But not just of them. There are other innocent people back in Haven caught like flies in a spider's web. Far more of them than those who have chosen to follow the dark path shaped by the Ones.

Hussein is not one of those who've gone that shadowed way. Though he could have, at least physically.

Because of my job, I'm allowed to work out in the gym. They have heavy bags and weights. It's the favorite hangout for guards to keep in shape—or what they think is shape. All that bulky muscle slows you down, in my opinion. I hit the gym at least three times a week. In part it's a show of defiance.

I know a lot of the muscle heads in there resent me. But the Ones passed the word down that I was not to be messed with physically. I was too valuable as a monster slayer. So mostly I just get hostile stares or remarks like those Edwin always makes.

"Hey girl, want to work my heavy bag?"

Because they can't do anything else to escalate their harassment when I ignore their taunts, eventually those making the nasty comments get bored and I can work up a sweat in peace.

To my surprise, the fourth time I went to the gym Hussein was there. And he was busy. Though he saw me and nodded politely over his shoulder to me, it didn't interrupt his concentration on what he was doing. He was wearing a tight black t-shirt that showed the long rippling muscles of his arms and shoulders and torso. He was working not one but two heavy bags that were hung within ten feet of each other. And he was doing it not just with his hands, but also with his feet, his elbows, and his knees. Back and forth between them, his limbs moving so fast that they were blurred, the two man-sized bags folded in the middle from his kicks, rocking back and forth from his elbow and knee strikes. All of his hand strikes, though, were open handed. Palm strikes. Not wanting to break his knuckles, preserving his fingers for his guitar strings.

He went on like that for ten minutes straight, according to the clock on the wall, at a pace none of those doped-up, muscle-bound thugs could have maintained for a minute. By the time he was done, he was glistening with sweat. Then he stopped and began doing a breathing exercise.

I realized then that I hadn't moved. I'd just been standing there watching him. And thinking how much fun it would be to spar with him. But I didn't say anything.

He came over toward me—to pick up his towel from the bench next to where I was imitating a statue.

"Muay Thai," he said as he wiped his forehead. "It keeps me in better shape for my gardening. Now I have to get back to work." Then he smiled. "It was nice to see you."

And I didn't even nod in reply.

Despite my obstinate silence that day—and other times, Hussein has still been nothing but polite and kind whenever he sees me. Probably because my mom is such a nice person.

But Hussein is not alone in being one who has kept a good heart. Every day when I am in Haven I see good people—mothers and fathers trying to take care of their children, young people of my own age whose hearts are still good. I can sense that, even if I never even say hello to them. Maybe they'd be friends with me if I let them. My true task in life must be not just to protect my family, but to try to somehow save us all in this dangerous world. Somehow. Even if all that I have now is the faintest glimmer of an idea about how I might go about that monumental task.

There are tears in my eyes as I begin to chant the words, far more words than I usually speak out loud. But every word is needed.

In this world,

this world of many dangers

only our Creator has the power

it is from our Creator

that this power comes

so I ask for this help

I ask so that I can help the people

I ask for this gift

this gift to confuse my enemies.

I've been drawing in the earth with my stick as I chant, drawing a shape that begins with a circle and continues until the lines within the circle seem to glow like silver touched by moonlight.

I'm vulnerable as I do this. There is a chance that the killer team trailing me might come up over the rise in the road half a mile behind me and see me here in the open. I just hope my ally is helping me right now as he said he would.

But when I am halfway done with this task I hear something. I should have been expecting it, but I still jump at the cracking boom. A shot fired from a high-powered rifle—but more than a mile away. As its echo reverberates between the rock walls, a small smile comes to my face. I can imagine Big Boy cussing out whoever fired that shot. Just as I can imagine what led that person to do something as foolish as shooting a gun while engaged in what was supposed to be unnoticed pursuit of their prey—me.

Actually, I am not just imagining what happened. A picture of it has come into my mind, like the images poorer people used to be able to see on the inside lenses of the viddy glasses or the corneal implants of the elite back when television was still possible.

I'm seeing it through the eyes of my hairy ally. Hairy? Hairy Ally? Nah. What the heck, maybe I'll just call him Hally.

Hah. Good name. Better than some I have been called.

I can really see him clearly now.

He's crouched down, concealing his sizeable bulk behind a mound of stones and earth surmounted by several clumps of rabbitbrush. I don't see him. But I see what he is seeing, which includes two hairy hands. Three times as big as my own, those hands of his are juggling a melon-sized rock back and forth between them.

I hear him chuckling. Or maybe I should say I feel the growling chortle building within him at this moment.

Hmmmrr, hmmmrrr, hmmrrr. Watch this, Little Food.

One of his hands whips forward so fast in a sidearm underhand throw that it's a blur. The rock sails out swift as a ball shot from a cannon. It doesn't look like it is heading toward the confused mass of men perhaps two hundred feet down slope from him. Until it bounces off a wall of rock to their left and ricochets back to strike the ground in their midst, sending up a sharp spray of small shards.

One of the men with the sniper rifle lifts his weapon and points it in the direction of the wall of rock that the stone

161

rebounded from. But he doesn't fire a shot this time. The barrel of his gun is pushed down by Big Boy's lightning-quick right hand. The man with the gun, who is almost as big and muscular as Big Boy himself, takes a quick step back and reaches down toward the knife at his side. Big Boy starts to raise his machete.

Are they going to end up at each other's throats? Maybe just kill each other and save me the trouble of having to figure out how to get rid of them? It's a pleasant thought that brings a little smile to my face.

I smile even broader when I realize my old buddy Edwin is the one who tried to fire his weapon. There's a trickle of blood coming down Edwin's forehead from being struck by one of those pieces of obsidian kicked up by my unseen ally's stone. His teeth are visible in a snarl. He and Big Boy are standing there as stiff-legged as two bulldogs about to go for each other's throats. The faces of the two big men are distorted with the kind of illogical rage that is a side effect of Chain.

Then another rock, bigger than the first two, slams into a tall saguaro cactus next to them. All five men, Edwin and Big Boy included, scramble down into an arroyo for shelter, out of Hally's sight—which I've been sharing with him.

Then his perspective shifts. I'm no longer looking at the retreating team of would-be assassins. I see two large hands brushing off rock dust and then folding themselves together in a self-congratulatory handshake.

I go now, Little Food. Bye bye.

A moment of darkness. Then I am back to seeing through my own eyes.

Over and out. And over to me. Even though I'm sure Hally could have harried them all the way back to Haven, he has done all he will do to assist me.

But they've been delayed long enough. I have finished my drawing. And now it is time to see if it will work. As I descend the trail I break off a broom-shaped stalk of dry rabbit bush. Perfect. Then, retrieving the trail bike from next to the cracked roadside, I walk it up the road edge where the tire treads and my feet leave visible tracks in the dry earth. I continue straight on, right to the place where the roads diverge. The first branch, the one I have to follow, leads to the right, while old US10 just keeps going straight. Instead of taking the turn, I keep walking the bike straight along the road edge of US10, leaving more tracks, fifty paces past the intersection. Then I lift the bike and return to the intersection, staying on the unbroken pavement. I stop and look back. The only tracks visible are those in the soft ground of the road's edge. Perfect.

I'm at the turn off, where the side road has aged away, leaving only earth. There's a smaller, two-sided metal sign here on a single post. It reads DRAGOON SPRINGS on each side, with arrows pointing the way. I put down the bike and the stalk of rabbit bush, step over to the sign. I grasp it with both hands. Time to use that deceptive strength of mine. I set my feet firmly, bend my knees a little, take a deep breath and then twist. The metal post resists at first and then it turns.

I step back and view my handiwork. Now it looks as if US10 and not the side road is the route to Dragoon Springs. I scan the unpaved route I'm about to take and the sandy soil to either side of it. No way to avoid walking through more soft earth and making prints. I pick up the bike and the stalk of rabbit bush. With the bike on my right shoulder, I walk backward, making good use of my improvised broom with my other hand to wipe out my prints. I also stop every now and then to bend down and grab handfuls of dried sticks, leaves, and small stones to strew across the places that have been swept clean.

If I truly have inherited that power of the first Lozen to confuse my enemies, all of this back tracking and track covering might not be necessary. But the one being hunted is wise to use more than one method to deceive those on her trail.

After I've gone a way down the side road to Dragoon Springs, I put my bike down where it's out of sight behind a pile of lava rocks. I climb the slope that will give me a view of the place behind me where the roads diverged. I shrug off my pack and lay down flat behind a clump of sage. Its clean scent fills my nostrils as I watch through its screening branches.

At least half an hour passes before anything happens. But eventually I can feel them coming. Then I hear them well before I see them. They're trying to walk quietly, cautiously, but they don't know how to do it. And through the scent of the sage, I can smell them. Fear and adrenalin have made their body odors even ranker than usual.

Despite my good buddy Hally's delaying tactic, they've gotten back on track. Perhaps they've convinced themselves that those stones which slowed their pursuit were not hurled by a long anthropoid arm but merely round rocks that rolled down at random from the nearby hill.

"Most people have this way of fooling themselves," Uncle Chatto said once when we were out hunting. "Especially when they are in dangerous places. They imagine they're safe." He put one palm on my shoulder and the other over his heart. "We never do that."

Big Boy holds up a hand just as they reach the junction. He stands with his right foot next to my drawing in the dirt but is not looking at it. If I have done it right, he will not see either my markings or the road sign reading DRAGOON SPRINGS. Nor will the other four.

The huge former biker looks right, then left. Taps his fingers on the handle of his machete. Starts to take a step, stops, takes a step backward. Stops again.

The power to confuse my enemies.

The others seem even more bemused. One of them sits down and pulls a map out of his backpack. The two men with the sniper rifles move to stand back to back to each other, their heads moving back and forth like mechanical toys. Edwin takes a kerchief out of his back pocket and dabs at the bleeding wound on his forehead.

"Hut!"

All four of them turn toward Big Boy at the barking sound

of his voice. He holds his right hand out, points it at the tread marks of my trail bike. He raises his other hand, fingers pointing at the sky, chops it forward toward the northeast along US10, and starts off that way at a half-trot. The others fall in behind him.

If the medicine I've made works half as well as I hope, they will keep going for hours, on and on until the sun is about to set. By then, they'll have reached the deserted ruins of the next town down the road, Wilcox. Like Sun City, it's a haunt of the Bloodless. And with night falling, the team trying to track me will have no choice but to find the best shelter they can. Then their fires and their guns may protect them through the night.

Or not.

CHAPTER TWENTY-ONE

Crawly Things

I t is still well before midday when I reach Big Ranch. Big Ranch is the name that was given it by Doctor Samson, the mega-wealthy and powerful man who built it and the high walls that stretch around it. Some, especially those currying favor, called Big Ranch the "Seventh Wonder of the Southwest." I have no idea what the other six were. Others called it the scariest place they had ever been.

Why? Well, Doctor Samson (an actual doctor whose special field was something called replacement genetics) had an interesting hobby. Or maybe obsession is a better word. He liked to keep, breed, and—as he put it—"improve" large reptiles. Some of it was through the genetic modifications that produced the gemods of the sort I've had to hunt.

But Doctor Samson was one of those men to whom size really mattered. So just mixing and matching was not enough for him. Bigger was better. That is why he recreated the Super Snake.

Despite my lack of fondness for snakes, I have always been fascinated by them. As a little girl, I clicked every text or viddy I could read or goog. The biggest snake that used to exist in the wild was the anaconda down in South America. An adventurer named Percy Fawcett who made a survey of the Bolivia/Brazil border in 1906 wrote that he shot one that measured sixty-two feet from tip to tail.

So, of course, the anaconda was chosen to be part of the mix.

Back in the mid-twenty-first century, there was little chance of finding a big anaconda in the watery swamps in what was left of those jungles. Jungle rivers had been poisoned by gold mining, the great forests of giant trees had been clear cut. But there were still anacondas in the private menageries of the privileged. Easy sources for the necessary DNA.

There were also fossil remains of something that paleontologists called the Super Boa. Long extinct, but twice as big as the largest recorded anaconda, according to one vid-arty I googed from way back in 2011.

And so, with unlimited wealth and the developing gen-tech to do it, Doctor Samson decided to recreate and improve that ancient creature. It was rumored that he succeeded. He made a Super Snake. But he kept it secret. Until the Cloud, everything within the walls of Big Ranch was kept hidden from the public. Unbreachable barriers kept the uninvited out and Super Snake—and perhaps other behemoth beasts—within.

As I pedal along I pass a succession of guard posts that once blocked the curving road that winds between stony hills. The guard posts are not just empty now, their gates broken. They are flattened, as if by a giant foot stomping on them. Not an encouraging sight.

Then I round a corner and find myself looking down into a wide valley. Big Ranch lies below me. And as I stand here, in admitted awe, I am struck by two things.

Numero Uno is that wall. It crawls like a giant snake itself, way off as far to left and right, encompassing the entire valley here in the folds of the surrounding hills. How many acres in there? More than a thousand, I'd guess. Taller than the Great Wall of China, I bet.

I push up my goggles, train my scope on its top. Wide enough for a two-lane road up there. It's strung with electrical cables that must have lit it so brightly every night that it was visible from space—back when humans flew beyond Earth's gravity.

Even without its electric lights this set-up is more than just impressive. There's no way anyone could build anything remotely similar today. It brings to mind an ancient film made before CG made anything imaginable possible in viddies. Despite its primi-tech, I loved that movie as a little kid. I got goosebumps every time I viddied it. *King Kong.* And right now I feel as if I am on Skull Island. I can practically hear that antique film's foreboding music playing in the background as I stare at the hundred-foot tall rampart.

I study that wall. How did people get on top of it? It seems to run in an unbroken circle with the exception of the gate. No outside stairs visible. But there had to be access to the top. How? Interior stairs. That must have been it. Maybe even tunnels from the mansion that came out within the hollow interior of the wall. But most likely the main entry point would be at the front. Something to keep in mind.

Which brings me to Numero Dos—the entryway into Big Ranch. It's a wide portico, eighty feet across. It was formerly closed by the mammoth door that is jammed askew part way across that opening. Beyond the entry is an equally wide roadway protected on both sides by heavily reinforced electrical fences. There the good Doctor could drive or walk at his leisure and observe, to either side, his scaly lovelies. Plural because Super Snake was supposedly just one of his overgrown cold-blooded prizes. There were other crawly things.

I can see over the wall into what must once have been an ideal roomy habitat for something like a big crocodile, replete with running stream, marshy pond, and palm trees.

But, like the crushed fences that no longer protect the driveway, that running stream is no more. There's only a dry streambed lined with the broken stalks of dead coconut palm trees marking the upper reaches of where it once flowed. Once the pumps stopped, the water features of Big Ranch must have evaporated. All dead and dessicated.

There's a wide roadway that leads up from the gate. I shift

the scope and see half a mile further up that road an extravagant mansion. It is seven stories tall with countless windows, tall turrets, a crenellated roofline, and battlements like those of a castle. It's built up on a bluff in the center of Big Ranch's thousand-acre spread. That mansion is my main objective. And it looks as if luck is with me. The drawbridge over the dry moat that encircles it is down.

Far to my right is the gigantic enclosure that had been the big snake's habitat—including a man-made cave half a mile up the hill. The cavern's mouth gapes wide and dark. Is the snake in there? My Power is not telling me that it is. Just that danger is nearby. But where? Is Super Snake anywhere within the walls of Big Ranch or is it out hunting miles from here? There's no motion at all within the walls. And there were no recent gigantic crawl marks on the road I've followed to get here.

The shapes of the hills around the valley show me that there are other passes, trails that could be followed on foot—or by slithering. Other ways out of this valley in addition to the dead-end road I followed.

I can't stay here forever. I have to do something. At least get close enough to get a better look. I put away the scope, lower my goggles, hop on my bike, and coast down the hill. Soon I am standing by that wide entryway looking in. And I see that I was partially wrong about everything being dried up. The swamp still remains. The springs that gave this place its name are still seeping up enough water to cover a wide expanse of perhaps ten acres of deep green water. It almost comes to the edge of the wall itself, less than forty feet from the entryway where I stand. The water is stagnant. Its rank odor of decay is so strong I crinkle my nose. Gnats buzz at my eyes. I keep brushing them away, not taking my eyes off the pond.

Although there must still be a natural spring feeding this and keeping it from disappearing, it is mostly dead water. Only a small trickle flows from it into the large channel that passes under the roadway. It disappears within a few yards through a crack in the basalt basin.

Normally you'd see wading birds, turtles, all sorts of animal life around a pond such as this one, an oasis in the midst of the dry lands all around. But there are no signs of any life other than dragonflies, gnats, and the green algae slicking the water's surface. Bubbles, likely from swamp gas, rise here and there to the eerily placid face of the pond. The slow, steady popping of those bubbles is almost hypnotic.

I tear my eyes away from the pond and shade them against the sun to peer up the mile of roadway that terminates at the overblown building ahead. It is more like a castle built by a crazy king than a zillionaire's mansion. Therein, untouched or viewed by human eyes since the demise of electricity, lies the objective of my quest: the room housing the art collection that includes that stupid mirror.

This close, I can now see there used to be lots of interior walls at Big Ranch. Heavy chain link fences surrounded the castle and lined the roadway. But they are all crushed. Some might think they were flattened by a hurricane, given the force it would take to pull down such strong fencing.

But not me. I don't really need to speculate about what took down the fences or what happened to whatever animals used to inhabit that pond and all the other deadly denizens of the ten other once-securely-electrified enclosures I count from where I stand.

Something there is that does not love a wall. Especially when that wall stands between it and lunch. Big snakes do have big appetites. And once the normal supply of food furnished to it was no longer being supplied, that Super Snake was still hungry. So it began catching and eating everything (and everybody) living within Big Ranch. Alligators and crocodiles, immense Gila monsters, supersized Komodo dragons or whatever turned into main courses.

And then what? Did Super Snake die of hunger? It had been years since the Cloud came. So maybe all that was left of it is a mountain of massive reptile bones somewhere way back in Big Ranch. That was what the first team sent here by the Dreamer had assumed.

Snakes don't have to eat every day, or every month. I knew that as a little girl. I'd vidded that big snakes can go for a year without eating anything at all as long as there's water to drink. And they can just lay around for days or weeks hardly moving, dozing until there's food to be had.

And that was what the Dreamer's unfortunate men had become. Just another serving of appetizers.

I'd studied the hundred foot high wall from the hilltop. Close up now, I can see that its interior surface is mirror smooth. Even a giant snake would have found it hard to climb. But that's clearly not what it did when the food sources inside the walls ran out. When it had to venture outside Big Ranch and seek food elsewhere—like in the empty towns around this area. Which is where it probably is now.

I look at what remains of the gate that once closed off the entry to Big Ranch. It was not just pushed open. The heavy metal was bent as it was battered, then it was levered off its runners by a giant, rock-hard head. Just how strong does a creature have to be to be able to do something like that? I feel a chill go down my back.

The two survivors told how their bullets could not pierce its skin, so they'd aimed for its eyes. But that didn't work either. But the eyes of snakes are not soft and moist like those of birds and mammals. Snakes have no eyelids, just clear scales. When they shed their skin the scales over their eyes peel off as well. The heavy rounds just ricocheted off its eyes.

You can do this, girl.

Right.

Be careful, Lozen. Both my memory and my Power are telling me that.

CHAPTER TWENTY-TWO

Inside

I'm still standing just outside the gate leading into Big Ranch, thinking about one of Mom's stories. The one about the Swallowing Hill.

Long ago, Mom said, there was a huge being they called the Swallowing Hill. It was a monster so big that it looked like a small mountain. Whenever any person or any animal came close enough, it would open its mouth and suck them into its belly.

Coyote noticed that the people and the animals were all disappearing. When he found out they were all being sucked in by the Swallowing Hill, he got an idea. Coyote is always getting ideas.

But this was a good one.

Coyote got his sharpest flint knife. He wove a strong belt out of fibers and tied that knife tight to his waist. He also made four torches out of cedar bark and tied them to his belt as well.

He put a hot burning coal and some dry decayed wood to keep that coal alive into a clam shell. He put that clam shell into his bag. Then Coyote was ready and he went walking along to the place where he knew the Swallowing Hill lived.

Sure enough, it sucked him into its belly.

As soon as Coyote was in the monster's belly, he used that coal and that punk to make a fire and lit one of his torches. He looked around. It was all moist and pink and warm in there. The air smelled bad and it was hard to breathe. By the light of that torch he could see all the people and all the animals. They all looked weak and sick.

"Coyote," they said. "now the monster has got you, too."

"Are you sure about that?" Coyote replied.

Then he went walking. As he walked along he spoke.

"Where am I now?" he asked.

"You are in my belly," answered a deep voice that came from all around him.

"That is interesting," Coyote said. "I have never been here before."

"Who are you?" the deep voice asked.

"I'm just walking around," Coyote said, and as he kept walking he lit his second torch.

The passageway got narrower as Coyote walked. "Where am I now?" he asked.

"You are in my chest, Just-Walking-Around," came the answer. "What are you doing?"

"Looking," Coyote said as he kept walking.

Now he could hear a sound like a drum beating. He lit his third torch and walked toward that sound. He came into a red chamber. In the middle of it was a big pulsing thing that hung from the ceiling. It looked like a huge ball and was the color of blood. It was making that sound like drumming.

"What is this?" Coyote asked.

"Just-Walking-Around, that is my heart," the voice answered.

"That is good," Coyote said, taking his sharp flint knife from his belt.

"What are you doing, Just-Walking-Around?" said the deep voice. It sounded frightened.

"I am just killing you," Coyote said. He stabbed the heart of the Swallowing Hill with his knife and Swallowing Hill died.

Then Coyote went back to the other animals and people. He used his knife to cut a hole in the Swallowing Hill's side and let everyone out. Swallowing Hill's body turned into a real hill and it is still there to this day.

That is what Coyote did.

So, is that my brilliant plan? Get that giant snake to swallow me? Then pull out my Bowie knife and kill it from inside its belly?

Are you kidding me? No way am I going to do that. A constrictor squeezes its prey until all the air is pressed out of its victim's lungs. Its victim dies before it is swallowed. And even if I was swallowed whole without one of those nice warm hugs, the stomach acid inside a snake would turn me into mush. It's strong enough to digest an entire giant crocodile, armor-plated scales and all.

The only way I would get out of the belly of Mr. Super Snake would be as whatever is left of me inside a big pile of reptile scat!

I don't even know if Super Snake is home today. One way to find out. I hold up my hands and turn slowly, waiting for the touch of my Power.

There! The warmth that suddenly begins to burn the center of my open hands tells me that my enemy is not within the walls. But it is closer than I would like . . . and getting closer. I can feel it.

But I don't see anything. Especially not a two-hundred-foot-long reptile. And why is that? The reason comes to me right away—fortunately a little faster than the monster that is slowly crawling my way. It's approaching me from the outside. I can't see it yet because it is still hidden by the curve of the gigantic wall. What next? Get on the bike and pedal as fast as I can, either back up the hill or along the roadway up to Doc Samson's castle?

Not that good an idea. Though its approach is slow and stealthy right now, as soon as I try to make a break for it Super Snake will speed up for sure. And who knows how fast a giant snake can crawl?

Hide?

But where?

My Power is pulling me forward. I put the bike aside where I hope Super Snake will ignore it, then I take one step, and another, until I am standing within the arc of the entranceway through the wall. As is the case throughout its mammoth length, the wall is eighty feet thick at its base and tapers up a hundred feet until it is forty feet wide at its top. The surface of the entrance tunnel is ornately decorated with twining bas relief vines and flowers, a duplicate of the imitation rain forests that once thrived within Big Ranch. Nothing like it could be constructed today. To build it must have cost billions of creds. But money was no object and no problem in the pre-Cloud world.

I can feel the big snake getting closer. I try to calm my breathing, feel what my Power is telling me. I hold out my hand and feel it drawn forward as if it was a piece of iron being attracted by a magnet.

There. An ersatz vine that thrusts out from the inner surface and looks most like a doorknob or a handle. I grasp it, twist it, feel it start to turn.

Let it be simple. Let no electronic key be needed. Let it be unlocked.

The click of the latch comes just as an impossibly huge head, wider than a banquet table begins to appear around the outside of the entryway. Its eyes are deep and black as midnight, gleaming with malignant intelligence.

Its thought washes over me, rank and sickening as the

stagnant water in the swamp. Not words. Just an image of my body crushed by the snap of its jaws that look big enough to swallow one of our long-gone-back-to-rust maglev buses.

Got you!

Oh no, you don't!

I dive through the opening as Super Snake's head strikes down where I was. The stairs start so close to that door that I slam into them and almost bounce back out the opening. Almost, but not quite. My out-thrust hands hit the door frame and I push myself back to land sprawling on the first wide stair.

Who cares about form when your life is on the line? The snake is right there on the other side of the door. It thuds again and again against the door frame. The door is still open, it can't get through. Its head is at least twice as wide as the doorframe, which is made of the same impregnable material as the rest of the wall and not breaking.

Ka-boom. Ka-boom. The echoing sound of Super Snake's noggin bouncing off the unyielding surface reverberates through the hollow stairway like the beat of an immense drum.

Now might be the time to try my plan. If it will just open that big mouth.

I reach back for my pack. As always, it is tightly strapped to my back. Thus it stayed with me as I dove to safety.

But as I do so, one very large and much-too-knowing eye peers at me through the doorway. And before I can undo a single strap—*whoosh*—Super Snake's head is whipped back out of sight.

180

Am I going to lean out that doorway to see where it went?

Am I feeling suicidal right now?

I start up the stairs. It's a winding climb, but I manage to reach the top without running into any obstacles. There's just enough light from the open door at the bottom for me to see the handle on the hatchway overhead. I lift it and step out. I am atop the wall. I walk to peer down over the waist-high railings into Big Ranch.

Quite a view from up here. The roadway that runs the inner length of the encircling wall is in front of me. Not only is it as wide as a highway, fifty yards down to my left are two maglev Caddies. Both as dead as the industrial system that birthed them. I look over the outside wall. No sign there of my would-be meal companion. (His meal, that is.) Is he inside now? I walk to the other side of the wall and look down again into Big Ranch. Nothing moving but the bubbles on the stagnant pond. No giant reptile hungry for my flesh visible down there, either. I suppose I am safe for now. At least I hope so.

But there are two things that I know for sure.

Numero Uno, my serpentine adversary is somewhere down there.

Numero Dos, Super Snake has not forgotten about me.

CHAPTER TWENTY-THREE

A Simple Plan

As I walk along the wall, never taking my eyes off the ruined panorama of the thousand acre serpentarium below me, I'm wondering if my idea is going to work.

"Sometimes the simplest plan is the best." That is what Dad told me.

But is my plan so simple that it is just plain stupid? How could something that big move that fast? I hadn't expected that. Somehow, in my mind, I'd pictured the giant gemod anaconda as being slow, ponderous. But the creature I've just seen and narrowly escaped is far different from that. Rather than bloated and fat, its huge body is rippled with muscle and it moved as sudden and deadly as the snap of a steel trap. And then there is the intelligence that I read in its cat-like eye as it studied me through the doorway.

A shiver goes down my back again at the thought of that measuring gaze. That last look it gave me before it suddenly whipped its head out of sight. It was not an angry or frustrated look. I could feel that. Instead it was a look that seemed almost amused, a knowing, self-confident, arrogant stare.

And the thought came to me then, just as it returns to me now, that even though I have a plan to kill it, the giant snake has a plan of its own that ends with me down its gullet.

But what could the snake's plan be? Although the great snake is even bigger than I had expected—the result, I suppose, of consuming uncounted tons of other cold-blooded main courses, as well as the unfortunate populations of nearby towns—it still is not large enough to reach up to the top of this wall. Its weight is so immense that even with its great strength, lifting more than a third of its two-hundred-foot body shouldn't be possible. And the inner side of the ring wall around Big Ranch is still as concave and glassy smooth as it was when it was first made. The only ways up to the top of the wall are almost certainly no wider than the staircase I just took—relatively narrow entrances, tunnels, and stairways.

Does that means I'm safe up here? Maybe. But I am also still trapped. And I have only enough water in my canteens to last me for a few days at most. I could go back down that stairway and try to make a run for it. But that may be what Super Snake is expecting as it lies in wait.

Not only that, I would be leaving a trail for it to follow. Right back to Haven, whose walls are far from impregnable to something that big. I can only guess at why it didn't follow the survivors of the Dreamer's last expedition—perhaps it was sated enough with their friends that the trail went cold before it attempted to do so. Much as I hate to admit it, selfish as the Dreamer's primary motive may have been for sending me here after that mirror, the secondary duty he assigned to me—of getting rid of this creature—is the kind of job I was made for. It is right that I am here.

Sooner or later, that creature's appetite would have brought it to Haven. The picture that comes to my mind is far too vivid. Walls being crushed by its coils, buildings broken by its immense bulk, our weapons having little or no effect as it seeks out its screaming prey.

Time to hunt.

Uncle Chatto was the best hunter in our family. His advice comes to my mind.

"Prepare." One simple word that meant so much. Prepare your mind, prepare your weapons.

I sit down and take my pack off my back. The first thing I remove is a roll of wire. It is deceptively thin, supple as fishing line. But the way it was spun—by a molecular process far beyond any technology left to us humans in our new Stone Age—created a nearly unsnappable filament. This line could pull in a sea monster twice the size of a blue whale. And angling, in a way, is what I hope to do.

I lay the coil of wire to one side and take out a zippered pouch. I like the heavy weight of it. Then I pull out a rounded green object about the size of a fat avocado.

I hold the grenade up and tap a finger against its hard plastic surface. Taken, like its six brothers still in my pouch, from the basement of an abandoned army warehouse, it's the timed fuse variety, standard in wars since the early twentieth century. Grip it in your throwing hand tightly, holding the safety lever in place with your thumb. Pull the pin with your other hand. With the safety lever depressed, nothing happens until you let go—preferably as you throw it, unless you are feeling bored with breathing.

As soon as that safety lever is released, a spring strikes the firing pin and ignites a wick that takes a few seconds to burn its way down the detonator. Time enough for the grenade to have flown seventy or eighty feet through the air, beyond the effective killing radius or fifty feet or so. And then:

Ka-boom!

It's not just the blast that does the trick, but also what the explosive was surrounded by inside that little bomb—a layer of ball bearings that add to the shrapnel from the shattered shell.

Am I planning to throw this at my large reptilian playmate? Nope. The only result then would be to bounce shrapnel off the crawly critter's armored body. Even a rocket launcher—if we had one—might not pierce it. But all that tough, impregnable skin is on the outside. What is within said monster is a lot more vulnerable—as Coyote discovered when he destroyed the Swallowing Hill.

So all I need to do is to get Super Snake to swallow one or two of these. Easy . . . right?

185

CHAPTER TWENTY-FOUR

The Best Laid Plans

The best laid plans of mice and men oft go astray.

That, more or less, is what an old Scottish bard named Robert Burns wrote in one of his poems.

Maybe he was referring to the time when a tribe of mice decided the best way to make their lives safer would be by tying a bell to the neck of the cat that was always hunting them. That way they would know wherever it was and it could no longer creep up on them.

Capital idea, my dear rodent!

Perfect solution!

Hurrah, squeak, whoopee, huzzah!

Much mouse celebration and self-congratulation ensues.

Until one pointed question is asked.

How are we going to put the bell on that cat?

And that sums up my current task. How? How does one get a snake to swallow a hand grenade?

Plus I have this nagging feeling that there's something else, something I haven't taken into account. But what? It is just not coming to me.

Okay, as the saying goes, if you can't remember, just forget about it.

Back to work.

Numero Uno. I take out another grenade. I'm tempted to use them all. But it is best to keep most in reserve. Two should do it. I loop the end of one of my two lengths of wire through the removable safety pins. The wire flexes easily and I tie it off so that it will not slip out of the pins and spoil things. One yank and they'll be simultaneously released—and the armed grenades will be only a few seconds away from exploding.

Done. Good.

Like a gambler producing the final ace that makes a winning hand, I pull a coyote skin from my pack. Folded up, it hasn't taken up that much space, but when I spread it out, it almost looks like the animal whose pelt was taken and tanned by my mother's father long before I ever lived. It's not like a rug. It was sewn together to make it into a bag, so the only opening is through its mouth. The sun beating down on the top of the wall warms the coyote skin. That's a good thing. Snakes respond to heat from their prey.

I remove the large balloon that's the third element in my plan, work it carefully down the throat of my coyote bag and then, leaning so close that it probably looks like I am giving a coyote CPR, I blow the balloon up. As it inflates, the skin bag takes on more of the shape of a living animal. There is still enough space for me to, even more carefully, insert those two grenades down into Coyote's throat.

I put my hand on the skin.

"Help us, Old Brother," I say. And then I can't help but smile at the way we're recreating that story about him and the swallowing hill.

I can almost hear Coyote's laughter.

I take the second length of wire and tie it around Coyote's neck. Tight enough to hold the grenades in place while also making it possible to use that wire to lower my decoy toward the great snake.

Which is nowhere to be seen.

Where is it? I feel tense, and my hands are tingling. So it has to be somewhere relatively close.

Focus, Lozen.

I walk back to the middle of the roadway and start to lay out the wires, careful not to tug on the one in my left hand, which is connected to those safety pins. I take out a piece of cloth and begin to wrap it around the loops I've made in the end of the second wire to both identify it as the one connected to the pins and make it easier to grasp, since the wire is so thin it might slip through my fingers.

Then it comes to me. When I looked at the far side of the ring wall I saw something without knowing what it was that I was seeing. Could it be?

I put down the wires. I reach into my pocket, pull out, and

click open the scope as I rush over to the wall and begin to scan the wrecked grounds of Big Ranch.

Where was it? There! That distant spot on the wall where no sunlight reflected back.

Oh crap!

What I observe is just what I was afraid I'd see. Super Snake is even smarter than I thought it was. Piled against that distant stretch of the wall are slabs of wood and chunks of stone and concrete ripped from the demolished structures. A ramp giving access to the top.

My Power has been tapping me on the shoulder all this time, trying to get me to pay attention. But I've been too stupid to . . .

I hold up my hands and as I turn the burning sensation in my palms is so strong that I almost lose my breath. Or is it because of what I see that I feel this tightness like a rope being cinched around my chest? There, filling the roadway pretty much from one side to the other, is the one I was looking for. Who has politely decided to save me the trouble. It has crawled up on me so silently that it is less than a hundred feet away. Super Snake.

It raises its head up and up, so high it seems as if it is going to thrust itself into the clouds. It stares down at me with what I can only interpret as self-satisfied amusement in its eyes. It knows I've seen how fast it can move. I'm too far away from the stairway to reach it before the big snake can catch me.

But there at my feet are both wires. And Coyote's skin is

fifty feet closer to the snake than I am. I slowly bend down and grasp the wires. One in my right hand, one in my left. But which is which? When I put the wires down the cloth slipped off the string. The cloth fell closest to the wire on the left. It has to be that one. I wrap the cloth back around it as I slide one foot back, then another. My eyes are on the giant snake. Its head is swaying back and forth, but it's not striking. I'm still out of range.

I count under my breath as I walk backward. One and one pony. Two and one pony. When I hit fifty, the snake moves forward, just a little. If I turn and run, it will get me before I can take a dozen strides.

All the while I'm doing this I am keeping my mind as blank as possible. I have the feeling, a feeling being passed to me by my power, that just as I can pick up what that great snake is feeling, it can also sense my own thoughts. Not in human words, but in emotions. When it feels my fear is when it will strike. That's what it is waiting for.

Nothing, nothing, I am thinking of nothing.

I pull gently on the wire in my right hand. And it is the right one. Coyote slides an inch in my direction. I pull again and he moves a second time, looking almost as alive as when that skin embraced a breathing body.

The snake's gaze shifts down.

And now is the time.

No, no. Mine. Don't. No, no!

The giant reptile has felt that thought. I know it. It looks at me, pleased that it has found another way to play, cat-like—with my emotions before it devours me.

Then, its gaze still on me, it lowers its head to Coyote, opens its mouth to grasp the inflated skin—almost delicately—then raises its head to swallow it with such force that the wire I've released from my right hand snaps back toward it like a whip being cracked. It is pulled across my hand so fast that I am jerked two stumbling steps forward as it slices into the skin of my palm. Blood wells out.

I would have lost the left-hand wire, too, if it hadn't been so much longer. I catch my balance, begin to move backward again as I play out that longer wire, slick with my blood, through my right hand. One backward step, another, the snake staring down. And at last I've backed up enough to take in the slack. I tighten my grasp on the wire.

The snake still hasn't moved. But it is working its mouth, feeling those two wires in it. Is it going to regurgitate Coyote before . . . ?

No!

I jerk the wire back toward me hard. As soon as I do so, in response to that pull, Super Snake snaps its own head back. Still holding the wire, I'm yanked off my feet to go flying through the air toward the snake.

And then over the guard rail.

CHAPTER TWENTY-FIVE

Take Your Choice

As I plummet downward I am thinking two things.

Numero Uno is predictable.

Oh crap!

Numero Dos, though, is something less self-centered.

Did I yank hard enough to pull the pins?

Well, actually, more than that is going through my mind, which seems to be moving at something close to light speed. It is not my entire life rushing before my eyes, as people sometimes say happens when you think you are about to die.

Numero Tres. Part of what I am thinking is this corny joke that Dad told me, about a man who fell off the top of a hundred story building. As he passed the fiftieth floor, he was heard to yell out, "So far, so good!"

Numero Cuatro. While all this is happening, mentally I am still counting. *One and one pony. Two and one pony . . .*

Numero Cinco. More practically, I am taking note of the fact that I am still holding on to the end of that second wire. And that it is not going to do me much good if I maintain my grasp on it. I'm falling so fast that if I come up short of its length before hitting the ground, the jolt might rip my arm off if the thin wire doesn't cut my hand in half first. I yank it one more time and it takes up the slack with just the faintest hint of something finally giving at the end of that pull. I open my hand and the wire spins around before it rips free from my grasp.

Numero Seis. The last thing that goes through my mind is what I now see. I'm not about to hit the ground after all. The wide whip of that snake's big head has thrown me all the way back to . . .

KER-SPLASH!

I land hard on my back twenty feet out into the croc pond. The air is knocked out of my lungs. I'm so stunned that I sink for a second, not knowing which way is up or down. Everything around me is this hazy brownish green, visibility about six inches. Perfect definition of murky. My foot hits something hard that moves as I kick against it. A fish?

It's something sizable. As it moves away from me I'm pushed back by the displacement of the water.

Oh, double crap!

I kick again and I'm heading up toward the light. My head breaks the surface as I gasp for breath and spit out green slime.

I've swallowed so much water that I think the level of the pond must have dropped a foot. But I don't flail my arms or splash the surface. Not a good idea if what I hit down there in the depths is what I think it is. I side stroke as quickly and quietly as I can to the edge. I pull myself out like a crippled sea lion onto the muddy shore.

Can't stop now, Lozen.

I push myself up to my feet. Holding my stomach and still coughing out water, I stagger back away from the pond toward the wall.

All this has taken me no longer than getting to twelve and one pony and there has still been no explosion. Were the grenades too old to work?

THWUMP-THWUMP!

The two muffled explosions come right on top of one another. I look up and see the upper third of the giant snake's body raised high above the parapet. Its head is thrown back. Its mouth is open and it looks for the briefest moment as if it is a dragon breathing fire—as well as a gory spray of macerated esophagus, stomach lining, heart, and whatever other internal organs have been turned into borscht by the multiple blasts.

It's been killed, but its writhing body doesn't know that yet. Its convulsions throw it from one side to the other. Its tail, lolling head, and body keep hitting the roadway, making a sound like that of a rhythmically challenged musician pounding on the world's biggest bass drum.

BOOM-BA-BOOM-BA-BA-BA-BOOM BOOM.

The mammoth snake's coils are partway over the inner edge of the wall. As soon as more than half its weight slips over the railing it is going to fall. This way.

My way! And if I don't get out of the way I am going to be way dead.

I turn toward the pond and see just what I did not want to see. The snout and then the entire head of what my brain tells me is a not-at-all-dined-upon, immense, genetically modified saltwater crocodile are emerging in slow motion. Time enough for it to register on me that crocs, like snakes, can live a long time between meals. And this one must be very hungry by now.

One clawed front foot sinks deep into the mud, then the other. And now the top third of its body is visible. Far too visible. Too much visible. I shove myself frantically backward, but not as fast as I'd like. My hands and feet are slipping in the mud.

In the wild, the original saltwater crocs from which this one is partially descended could get to be as much as twenty-three feet long and weigh over a ton. Try five times that big for this one!

It has to be at least a hundred feet in length. Another stalking step toward me as it raises up higher on its tree-trunk legs. The double rows in its upper and lower jaws of two-foot-long teeth are now being displayed as its mouth gapes slightly open. Just open enough to swallow a hippo! Slimy green water slides off its ridged scales, thicker than the armor on a tank, as I manage to push back another twenty feet.

No wonder Super Snake adopted a live-and-let-live attitude toward it. Trying to eat this thick-plated titan would be like brunching on a boulder. Thinking of meal time, that croc's massive eye turned toward me is surely seeing me as sustenance.

Still moving backward, I glance quickly up and over my shoulder.

Oh great!

I've managed to push myself further from the immense oncoming croc, but now I am closer to the wall where Super Snake's noisy death throes seem about to carry it over the top in another few seconds. And the croc has positioned itself right between me and the entryway into Big Ranch.

And now, ladies and gents, you pays your money and you take your choice. Which will it be?

The frying pan or the fire?

The devil or the deep blue sea?

Crushed by a snake or consumed by a croc?

I think I want my money back.

CHAPTER TWENTY-SIX

Food?

Sometimes things happen in ways you can't predict. I'm in the middle of one of those moments right now. That's when you have to trust your reflexes and have faith in them as much as your conscious mind.

And that is why, as more tons of writhing reptile than I can guess come tumbling off the wall, I dig my feet into the mud, lean forward and dive. I don't leap to the side, but toward the mammoth saurian looming over me. I can move fast and I'm hoping this leap of faith will be fast enough.

Fast as I am moving, my mind is moving faster. It's repeating the reasons I have chosen to fly through the air in a low, long leap that I hope will end with me ducking my head into a roll rather than being chopped in half by one snap of those giant jaws.

Numero Uno: crocodilian heads are connected to stiff, thick

necks that flex much better back and forth than they can in the downward direction my dive is taking me.

Numero Dos: I've seen little intelligence in the eyes of that giant croc and sensed even less with my sixth sense. Unlike the deceased-even-if-its-body-hasn't-yet-gotten-the-message anaconda now answering to the law of gravity, this immense saurian menace is the reptilian equivalent of a dumb bunny.

Numero Tres: My suddenly dropping out of its line of sight will take its focus entirely off of me and place it on another, much bigger target.

WHA–BA–BOOOM!

The earth shakes from the impact of the snake's rendezvous with terra firma at the exact moment I land on my right shoulder, beneath and just past the big croc's left leg. I roll, my momentum taking me into a second roll before I come halfway up to my feet and dive into the deep green water.

Thwunk!

Or not so deep. The place where I hit the water is shallower than I expected. I do a faceplant two feet below the surface into the oozy odiferous mud. It takes all my self-control not to thrash about and thrust my head above the surface to clear my nose and mouth and eyes. Instead, I push further into the deeper water, hoping to get away from the sweep of the crocodile's tail. I raise my head enough to take a breath and look back to see just what I feared. I bend my body into a frantic dive just deep enough to avoid being swatted by the tip of the crocodile's armored tail.

When I come up again further out, I see that tail swipe was purely incidental. Just part of the croc's pushing itself out of the water toward the objective I had hoped it would choose once I was out of view. Not an unreasonable hope, I might add. Even a stone stupid mutant beast couldn't help but take notice of the earthquake-inducing impact that heralded the arrival of—

FOOD?

Now that thought has come through loud and clear. As do the next three.

FOOD? FOOD. FOOD!

And then this slightly more sophisticated one.

EATEATEATEAT!

The immense crocodile's cold-blooded metabolism has been in a state of semi-dormancy that enabled it to go for a long, long time without eating. But enough is enough, already.

The big crocodile covers the distance between it and Super Snake's twitching body with leaping strides that propel it twice as fast as any human could run. It turns its head slightly sideways as it engulfs the snake's head, then it begins to back up toward its pond, dragging the snake's body with it. Quite a feat, seeing as how the immense anaconda's body is twice as long as the croc is. But this is not the moment for me to pause in admiration.

Time for all the leisure swimmers to leave the pool! I scramble out and sprint upslope as fast as I can without bothering to look back. I'm heading for a spot I've seen where the crushed fence is leaning over the elevated roadway to the mansion. I clamber up it, drop on to the pavement. I roll onto my back, exhausted. Breathe, breathe again, and finally I feel able to push myself up to my feet and and look back down to the pond.

If I was wondering how any croc, even a mammoth one, could consume something twice its size and body weight then I needed to wonder no more. The waters of the pond look like they are being hit by a typhoon as the crocodile, its crushing jaws gripped tight on the snake's head, is spinning in the water to rip off just enough meat—yup, there it goes—to be able to swallow it. It vanishes under the water. Doubtless it will be back soon to drag the remainder of the carcass into the water where it can chomp off juicy bits at its leisure.

Enough food to keep it alive for another year.

I actually feel a little sad as I watch. There's a certain beauty to a big predator doing what it was meant to do, even one blown out of normal proportion by genetic manipulation. But this may be the last food it will find here.

Should I be thinking about killing it, too? Why? There's no reason. Unlike the snake, this croc is a true water animal. If it ventures out beyond its pond for too long in search of food it will not get far. Perhaps a few miles. And then a more powerful enemy than any beast or human will overcome it as it falls victim to the heat and dryness of this land.

Then again, it might just survive if animals such as deer

are drawn into Big Ranch by the water, come too close to the pond edge to drink, and then . . . *whomp!* Even so, it's not on my agenda today to hunt this croc. It's no longer an immediate threat.

Half of what I've come here to do has been accomplished. But now I have to finish my task by finding the Dreamer's mirror. It'll be the easy part after this. I look myself over. The slice across my palm was shallower than I'd feared. It's already stopped bleeding. I heal faster than most, so I should be fine. As for the rest of me, there will be bruises, but nothing seems broken. I'm limping a little but that will pass.

I follow the roadway back to the entrance, climb the stairway, and regain the top of the wall. My pack is right where I left it, untouched by the massive serpent's death throes. I put things back into their places inside it, sling it over my shoulder and walk over to the broken guardrail.

There is no sign of either snake or croc. The pond's surface is placid. I look up the roadway toward the crazily crenulated castle on the hill. And as I do so I feel my Power twitching at me again. More danger.

Maybe this last half of my assignment is not going to be just an easy stroll through the park after all.

As I walk up the elevated road to the open gate of the castle, the midday sun is shining down on me, drying me out after my little dip. I might be grateful about that were it not for the fact that it is baking the layer of green scum I gathered from the swim. Even my eyebrows are covered. The only clean thing is my pack, which did not take that mud bath with me. I look like a sickly, stunted version of the green giant printed on our bags of freeze-dried peas. My jeans and my khaki shirt make a crackling noise as I move.

And then there is the smell. A redolent, delightful combination of muck, rotted vegetation, and reptile poop. At this moment I am less than grateful for my over-developed sense of smell. Skunks would turn up their noses at me right now.

The thought comes to me of what it would be like to report in this very condition to the Dreamer. Despite the fact that I stink worse than a dead polecat left out in the sun for a fortnight, I can't help but chuckle at the expression that might come to his blasé countenance.

My amusement is brief. The stench is so bad that it's hard to control myself from bending over and puking up everything in my stomach. But I am not going to waste the precious water in my canteens by using it to wash off some of the putrid layer.

Despite my disgusting condition, and my overwhelmed olfactory, my ears are still working fine. I'm beginning to hear a faint gurgling sound. Water. Trickling somewhere nearby. It's coming from within a pipe that leads from somewhere up ahead down to the pond.

I continue to walk, crackling like a pot of corn kernels being popped.

This small stream of water may be what is keeping the croc's pond below from evaporating into nothingness. Maybe from the spring that gave this place its name.

And just before I reach the open door of the crazy Doctor's mansion I see it. Welling out of the exposed rock just to the left of the building is the most beautiful thing I have seen today. Pure, flowing water that fills a small natural basin before disappearing into that pipe. It's so clean I almost don't want to touch it and contaminate it with my filth.

Almost. But not quite.

I kneel down by the spring basin. I clean my fingers, wipe them dry. I take a pinch of pollen from my pouch and offer it.

"Thank you," I say in a voice as cracked as the layer of dried goo clinging to my body.

Then I stick my head into that basin of water.

I strip, wash myself, and thoroughly rinse my clothing. As I do so I take note of my new minor injuries. Nothing serious again. My left knee is skinned from scraping it against a rock during my dive into the pond. My left shoulder is a little sore and the tenderness on my right thigh is probably going to blossom into a big purple bruise. I am in a hurry, but doing this cleansing and personal injury inventory gives me time to think. I sit naked in the sunlight next to my drying shirt and jeans and underclothes, quietly considering things.

Step Numero Uno is the most obvious. Go inside and retrieve that mirror.

But I can sense more waiting for me inside the mansion

than just that mirror. Probably not anything living, anymore. Not after all this time. But there may still be something that could result in my dying.

What do I know about Doctor Samson from the evidence before me? The hellscape below me is a reminder, as if I needed one, that he was fixated on mammoth cold-blooded beasts.

But behind me, its ramparts leaning over me, is another clue about his psyche. His medieval mansion. Within it is the other love of his twisted life—his hall of mirrors, in that book the Dreamer showed me, was said to rival the hall in Louis the Fourteenth's eighteenth-century palace in Versailles.

And all of this leads me to deduce . . . what?

I put my clothes back on and stand for a moment in front of the mansion's open doorway. I can see clearly into the cavernous front hall. It is naturally lit by gigantic windows of unbreakable glass set high in the walls.

I don't sense any immediate threats. Any electronic security devices stopped working long ago. But I still walk slowly and carefully as I pass through the hall. There's a wide marble stairway at the back. It gives me my first broad hint that the Doctor's interest in medieval things extended beyond architecture.

There's a skeleton at the foot of those stone stairs. Not human. It's some kind of twenty-foot-long lizard which must have come in here either to escape the snake or to look for food. It's clear what killed it. Its bones are still pierced through by the big portcullis-like device that dropped from the ceiling to pin it to the stone as soon as it started up the stairs.

No need for me to go up there, so I don't. Curiosity killed even the cat, and I am totally lacking in feline genes. My objective, as I recall from the Dreamer's instructions, should be off to the left, down that narrower hall. Lined with cut stones that make it look as if it was built with hard-carved blocks centuries ago, it looks right to me.

If I had any doubts, the sign on the wall dispels them. It states, as politely as if this place were not a million miles from normal, THIS WAY TO HALL OF MIRRORS.

The passageway takes a hard turn to the left just ahead.

Perfect place, my conscious mind suggests.

You betcha, my Power agrees. I drop to my stomach and crawl forward. My assumption is that this trap will be set for someone walking. And that it does not involve anything heavy dropping from the ceiling since that might mar the hardwood floor.

I am at the corner now. I reach around it with my right arm and press hard. The board under my hand depresses half an inch with a barely audible click.

Swoosh! Swoosh!

I peek around the corner. Stuck in the wall on either side are the two crossbow bolts that were fired from recesses to either side of the passageway.

Nice. I stand up and examine the bolts. Deeply embedded,

but I can lever them out easily enough. I look carefully into the recess on my right. It holds a modern crossbow. It's made entirely of composite material with strings of braided metal. Same thing in the recess on the left. Beautiful weapons. Unlike those in medieval times that might be made ineffective by moisture or aging, it has no parts that cannot withstand the passage of decades. I lift one from its cradle. It weighs about the same as a .303 rifle. Doesn't have an automatic cocking feature—no CO_2 tube—nor does it have a retractable mechanism to wind back the string. I hold the crossbow down, put my foot in the stirrup, reach down, and draw back the string with both hands.

Maybe a hundred and fifty pounds of pressure. Not that hard to do—for me. Uncle Chatto owned a crossbow much like this one and taught me how to use it. When you cock it, you have to be sure not to pull harder on one side or the other. Use a nice even pull so that the release won't throw the bolt wide of its intended mark. Each of these crossbows is an efficient weapon for killing silently at fifty yards or less. Good additions to my illegal arsenal. Maybe in a certain dry, deep crevice two miles to the south of Haven near Place Where a Stone Stands Like an Old Man. Or the hollow under a flat rock beneath Old Saguaro Who Looks Tired in the arroyo just a few hundred yards beyond Haven's west wall.

Next to each crossbow are quivers, each with a dozen spare quarrels. I imagine them being used by the servants whose jobs it had been to reset them—after dragging off the carcass of whatever intruder (or merely luckless guest) tried to pass this way unchaperoned. There are levers by each crossbow. I pull one and hear a click from the loose floorboard. The lever must connect to the floor and were probably pulled into the safe position whenever Doc Samson was leading a tour of his museum.

I remove the second crossbow and lay it down by the first one along with the two quivers of spare arrows. I take a piece of cord from my pack and tie the crossbows and quivers of arrows together. I heft them. Not that heavy. Then I put them back down on the floor. I'll get them on my way back, assuming I make it through the next obstacle I am sure awaits me.

I don't have to go far. I sense as much as see the almost invisible wire strung two inches off the floor across the passageway. Meant, no doubt, to do more than just trip an unwary intruder. I take one of the crossbow bolts, slide it under the wire, lift hard. A large pendulum ax swings down at frightening speed four feet in front of me. I would have had a split personality for sure. Like the crossbows, it has no automatic reset. After its initial cut it swings back slower, moves back and forth a few times and then stops. I push it aside by the handle and slide carefully past the razor sharp edge.

Two trapdoors later. I'm standing in the ornate entrance to a room where my own image is reflected back at me in dizzying multiplicity. Aside from a bruise on my forehead, I have no further injuries. But I am a little disheartened. There are too many danged mirrors in there. How am I going to find the right one?

I study the entrance carefully. No sign of a steel-barred portcullis with daggered blades designed to impale me. No warning from my Power or all five of my heightened senses. But I still have to dope out where . . .

Duh! Talk about dopes!

Right there next to me, below a wall-mounted panel for a dead security system is a small ornate table. On it are several colorful little brochures. I pick one up. It's a printed guide to the Hall of Mirrors. Clearly meant for the favored few who were brought here as guests, it maps, with numbered photos, the location of every precious object in the collection.

A mere twenty seconds of reading and I know just where to go. I take my pack off my back and put it down outside the doorway. I flex my hands, take a deep breath. Then, I walk down the hall to the last of a dozen alcoves off the main hall, turn into it and look straight at the Dreamer's prize.

My own face gazes back at me, scarred cheeks, jet black hair, aquiline nose, and all. It looks troubled, as it should. Something tells me that trouble still lies ahead. As soon as I take that mirror, it's going to start. I take two steps back and look down the way I've walked. A hundred paces, a third that many running strides to reach the entryway and turn into that hall. I can run faster than any other person I've ever met, so it won't take me that long.

Snatch and grab. That's one of the oldest ways to take something. But is it the best way right now? The mirror hangs all by itself on this wall. It is ornamented with gold, studded with jewels and pearls. And it doesn't look more beautifully made to me than anything else. It might not be recognized by most eyes as one of the most special treasures in this vast collection. But it's the Dreamer's choice. It's also about twelve by eighteen inches. Just the right size to fit into the padded bag I was given to carry it in.

I study the wall and the mirror from all sides. No visible pressure plates or poison needles. I carefully touch the mirror's frame. No razor-sharp edges.

I take a breath. Time's passing. I need to get moving. Now or never. I grasp it firmly, lift.

Click! goes the innocuous hook as it snaps up, relieved of the mirror's weight.

Crap!

I press the mirror to my chest and take off like a deer being pursued by a mountain lion. I hit the corridor in two strides, turn and speed past mirror after mirror that displays my flying feet, my body bent forward over the artifact whose removal from that triggered hook may have just sealed my doom.

And ahead of me is the entry way and I can see that . . .

Double crap!

Can you guess what is now falling from the ceiling?

I was wrong about there being no steel-barred portcullis. Without slowing I drop to my side and slide beneath its spears

209

just before they drive into the flood and splinters fly up. I guess Doctor Samson didn't care that much about his hardwood after all.

You're not safe yet, girl!

I roll up to my knees, hook my pack with one arm and jet down the hall, around the bend and . . .

BOOM!

The sound of the explosive charges triggered by the lifting of that latch, which struck the spark to a long but quick-burning fuse, is deafening. The corridor behind me fills with smoke and flame from the explosives hidden under its floor. But I've gone far enough that the shock wave from the blast does nothing more than knock me to my knees.

I hold up the mirror, but not to look at myself. No, I want to make sure that this looking glass I've risked my life for has emerged unscathed. It's perfect. Not a scathe on it.

I pull the padded bag from my pack and slide the mirror into it.

Time to head back to my so-called home.

CHAPTER TWENTY-SEVEN

A Song

I am back in Haven. It's now two days since I left Big Ranch with the Dreamer's prize mirror. First came an uneventful bike ride back up through the pass and then an uninterrupted night protected by fires. Then an equally unmolested trek back to the walls of Haven. The only four-leggeds I saw were jackrabbits and ground squirrels and one coyote. The only winged creatures were no larger than hawks and the turkey buzzards I saw kettling far behind me over the Dragoon Springs valley when I paused to look over my shoulder.

My return trip was so un-anything that I was a nervous wreck by the time I got here. I'd been at high alert the whole time. I had been fully expecting at any second to be warned by my heightened senses that I was about to be attacked by some creature, waylaid by Big Boy's crew, or at least contacted by Hally. But nada—and that, in itself, was stressful.

So here I am—sound if not safe.

The evening guard at the gate when I arrived just before sunset was not Edwin. As of this moment, he is still out in the desert somewhere, holed up with the rest of Big Boy's crew that I sent wandering off my track. With any luck, none of them will ever make it back here alive.

My first stop inside, of course, was to report to Guy. As always, while I silently handed over my weaponry, he ticked each item off.

"One .357 handgun. Check."

"Sixty rounds of .357 ammunition. Check."

"One Bowie knife. Check."

"Two M67 fragmentation grenades. Check."

I smiled inside my mind as he listed those last items. Only two of the four unused ones. The other two were in my hidey-hole near Haven along with the crossbows.

As he did the debriefing I sensed a presence behind that one-way mirror. I could have guessed who it was, even before I heard her thoughts. It was not the One who sent me on my mission. Not the Dreamer or any of his surrogates. The un-spoken words that stabbed into my mind, sharp as needles, made it clear to me who was back there.

How did this little bitch survive?

Diablita Loca herself. Angry and frustrated at not having been able to dispose of me and thwart her cohort's desires with one lethal stroke.

Hurt her, hurt her, I am going to hurt her!

The images of my family being tortured that followed almost made me react physically. I wanted to turn around, smash through that mirror, and get at her. But I controlled myself, aside from the hairs on my arms standing up. If I tried anything now, all my careful waiting for the right moment would be for nought.

The Dreamer's lair was my next stop. He was pleased when I presented him with that mirror. So pleased that he told me I could spend the next day with my family.

"Do celebrate," he said to me, twirling in a circle as he held his new mirror in front of him with both hands. "Have a love-eh-ly day. Tomorr-ow, to-morr-ow!"

He actually sang those words. In a voice that was surprisingly melodious and not as sarcastic as I would have expected.

That tomorrow is today.

I tried to sleep last night. But it was hard to stop my mind from racing back and forth between one thing and another. Every time I did fall asleep I found myself dreaming that I was back in the middle of being attacked by the Bloodless, or watching the massive bulk of the mortally wounded giant serpent falling toward me. And in those dreams I didn't escape. Instead I felt talons pierce my throat or I was so paralyzed that I couldn't move and I was crushed. Just like the dreams of falling to my death that I had after defeating the giant birds, every vision that came to me in my slumber was of me losing my battle. And the worst part was that in every one of those dreams, somehow my mom and Victor and Ana were there, too. Watching me be destroyed. Me unable to save them. And I would wake up with tears in my eyes and the word "No!" on my lips.

I'm not sure why I always have those dreams. Shouldn't my subconscious be celebrating my victories? Is it because there is no one, not one person in the world, to whom I can express my hidden fears of failing? But I have to keep it all inside. I have to do it for Mom and Victor and Ana because they depend on my being strong. I have to seem unruffled and even oblivious to danger to the rest of the world because showing any sign of weakness or uncertainty might open me up to attack.

I run my brush, one of my few possessions, back through my hair to straighten out the tangles from all my tossing and turning. I need to look as good as I can for Mom. She worries about how I look, knows I'm just slightly better looking than a scarecrow. But she also tells me little lies to make me feel better.

"Lozen," she always says, "you have such nice hair. Why don't you let me braid it for you?" Or, "Sweetheart, your eyes are so beautiful." Or, and this is the most obviously false of all her little fibs, "You have a beautiful face. It just lights up the room when you smile."

I take a deep breath and practice that smiling which seems to please my mom so much. I am also thinking hard about how to tell my family about my latest exploit. Every now and then I slip up and say a little too much, like when I mentioned how I was a little worried when that porcupine cat swung its tail and almost nailed me with its needles. This look of deep concern, or maybe disquiet, came over my mother's face and she clutched at her stomach.

I hate when that happens. It makes me feel guilty because I know it means she's feeling sick with worry about me. She has enough to worry about taking care of Victor and Ana.

Keep it light, Lozen, don't let them think you were ever in that much danger.

I've been told that our meeting will take place outside. The Dreamer has arranged for us to get together in the reward area near the gardens where there are chairs and tables set up in the shade of Haven's few trees. These fruit trees have been lovingly tended to by Hussein and encouraged with careful drip irrigation to grow and even bear fruit. Those who have done something to please the Ones are allowed undisturbed time there—a rarity in Haven.

When I step out into the sunlight, Ana's already running toward me, her arms spread wide. She's tall for her age, even if she is bone thin. The top of her head already comes up to my shoulder. She barrels into me, wrapping her arms around me tight.

"Lozen," she says in her voice that is as sweet as a little bird singing. "Lozen, Lozen, Lozen."

"Ana, Ana, Ana," I reply, hugging her back.

Victor isn't running. That would be undignified. Even though he is the youngest of us three, he is very conscious that he is the only boy. The man of the family. And he wants to live up to his name, which is actually Victorio, even though Mom and I call him Victor and he's just Vic to Ana. His namesake was one of the great Chiricahua war leaders, the brother of Lozen.

But my little brother is walking much faster than he usually does and I can see that the look on his face says more than he intends it to. It's a look of both happiness and relief. It tells me that he was really afraid that this time I was going to die.

When he reaches me he can't control himself any longer. He grabs me, too, as I open one arm to fold him into this three-person family hug that makes me feel as if my heart is going to burst.

"I am glad you are back," he says, his voice tight. He's looking down to keep me from seeing the tears that I already noticed in his eyes.

"Me, too," I say.

I can see that there are some new scrapes on Victor's knuckles and a bruise on his forehead. He's been fighting again with some of the other boys his age. Fighting with each other is something that happens a lot among the kids in Haven. Some of them start fights because they want to be like older brothers or fathers who are in the little private armies of the Ones. Some just do it, as boys always seem to do, to establish the pecking order. My blocky little brother, though, always fights for his family's honor. And acts as if nothing can hurt him. Because of that, he's always the last one standing. Even when it's more than one trying to take him down.

I touch the bruise on his forehead.

"How many?" I ask.

"Three of them," he replies, looking up at me. "They said you were going to end up being eaten."

I just shake my head, push the hair back from his bruise and rest my palm on it.

"That feels good," Victor says.

"They were throwing rocks at him," Ana adds.

"Only one hit me," Victor says, as if that explains everything.

Mom stays sitting at the table, watching us. She's giving the three of us space to just be together. She knows how much that means to us. She's smiling, too, but only with her lips.

It comes to me once again that Mom is the strongest of the four of us. She never pretends that everything is all right, but she makes sure that we all make the best of what we have. She listens all the time to Ana and Victor—just as I suppose she would listen to me if I opened up to her. I know that what I do is an awful burden for her. But she never tells me not to do what I do.

"Be careful," is about all that she says about it. That, and "Remember what your father and your uncle taught you."

Ana and Victor and I walk over to the table, stumbling once or twice as we do because we are all still wrapped together in our reunion hug. When we are almost to Mom I catch sight of someone in the garden, maybe fifty feet behind the tables. I've hardly noticed him. It's not just because his clothing blends in so well with the foliage. It's also because of the way he just looks so right being there. It's Hussein, of course. His eyes make contact with mine and he nods. It's a polite nod, but also one that seems as if he is letting me know that he is pleased to be briefly sharing this rare moment of joy with me. It's amazing how much someone can say with just a glance. Then he raises one hand gracefully and turns back to tending his garden.

"Lots to eat," Mom says, ending her part of the group hug and putting her hand on the table.

And there is. Somehow she's made a little feast for us, much of it obviously drawn from the garden where she works each day. There's a corn and bean and squash soup, tortillas and salsa.

And as we eat I share with them my exploits, using as few words as possible, keeping it light.

"You know what the most dangerous thing was?" I ask.

"No, what?" Victor says.

I pause for effect, then point to my skinned knee. "Riding that bike. See what happened when I fell off it."

Victor and Ana laugh at that, but the look on Mom's face tells me that she knows it's more than that. But she accepts my reticence. Which reminds me again of just how strong she truly is.

And then, as if the sun has been in a race across the sky, it's suddenly almost evening. I've had a whole day to just rest and be with my mother and Ana and Victor. A day without something trying to catch, kill, and eat me. It was a day when, at times, my family and I were almost able to pretend for that we were not captives here, hostages to the mad whims of four powerful maniacs.

Now, though, that day is done. And what will tomorrow bring?

I look at the round object I'm holding in my hand. One of the four that Hussein gave us as he strolled by just before the time when we'd all have to go inside. Four perfectly ripe, golden apples from one of his trees. It was like sleight of hand the way he did it. He made them seem to appear from out of nowhere as he dropped them into each of our laps. No one further than a few feet away would have noticed, especially because each of us quickly put those forbidden fruits, meant only for the Ones and their closest associates, away into our pockets.

"Have a good evening," he said, his voice carefully polite, but with an undertone of amusement at the small larceny we were all engaging in. Then he had turned and continued on.

My mother had smiled. A broad smile, in fact.

"That boy likes you," she said to me.

My response was to knit my brows together and shake my head. But my mother, even though she was probably wrong, was undeterred.

"He is a very nice person," she said. Then she put her hand on top of mine. "You could talk to him."

Could I? Would he listen if I did?

From the B Bloc comes the sound of a guitar. Hussein's. He's the only one with a guitar. I listen. For some reason I am feeling sort of nervous. What is he going to sing? A few more notes are strummed and then I hear Hussein's voice. Though he sings his words in English, it is as if there is another language behind and beneath them, one that gives color and depth to his lyrics, as plaintive as the minor chords he's playing. And this song is one I've never heard him play before. I think it's one he'd composed.

I am the bird who flies at twilight
No other wings can match mine in flight
And if I should tap upon your window
Would you ask me to stay or just go?

Is that song actually directed at me? I think of what Mom said. I could talk to him. It would be nice to have someone to talk to, really talk about how I feel. Someone to be that kind of a friend.

But do I really wish that? It's not safe for anyone to be my friend. The Ones have their eyes on me all the time now that

I am their best monster eliminator—to say nothing of the fact that one of them has already tried to eliminate me. And who knows what tomorrow will bring for me?

Don't dwell on that now, girl. Just relax while you can. Think of other things.

Is it possible that Hussein actually does like me, actually has noticed me despite how big I am? I mean I am at least two inches taller than him. Plus my hair usually looks like a dirty dish mop and my face is scratched and dirty and my clothes always make me look like a field hand. I give new meaning to the word disheveled.

I take a bite of that golden apple. It's the sweetest fruit I've ever tasted. Some of its juice starts to run down my chin and I catch it with one finger and lick it off. Then, as Hussein's song continues, I eat the whole apple, even the core and the seeds, which I crack with my teeth and chew up one at a time.

I lay back on my bunk and close my eyes. Then I open them and sit up. The words that I think he's just sung are not just romantic. They're dangerous. And as he sings them again, I know I'm right.

We birds remember the freedom of another age
A time before cruel hands locked us inside a cage
Oh how we remember, remember the free sky
But those who own us now, will not let us fly

Hussein, I think. *Stop singing that song.*

Doesn't he know, as I do, that there are always people listening? People who might interpret what he's singing as subversion and tell the Ones.

As if he's heard me, he strums one final chord and then is silent. I breathe a sigh of relief. Then he starts playing again. This isn't one that he composed, as I think was the case with that first song. It's an old tune now, one I have always loved. My father used to play that song and say, half-joking, that because of its message it must have been written by a Chiricahua Apache. Dad had a guitar. Dad even taught me a few chords. I think I could still pick out a tune or two.

But I'd rather listen, as I am listening now while Hussein sings:

I am a poor wayfaring stranger
just traveling through this land of woe . . .

That's Haven, all right. And this world we're all living in now is one of woe for sure.

I'm going there, to meet my father
I'm going there no more to roam
I'm just a goin' over Jordan
I'm just a goin' over home.

I wish I could go home. Just click my heels like that brown-skinned girl name of Dorothy in an old old viddy called *The Wiz* that I watched when I was nine. Or at the very least, I wish Hussein's song could go on longer. But it can't.

He finishes it just as everyone in Haven hears the long bugle blast for Lights Out. Just like that, all the lanterns in our blocs are extinguished except for those of the guards in the main corridor. The enforced night silence begins. No singing or talking. It's part of life here in Haven. There are rules. Rules must be followed. Even—or maybe especially—those that make no sense.

I close my eyes, not certain if I'll be able to sleep. There are so many—too many—thoughts going through my mind. I may not say much aloud, but it seems as if my internal dialogue never stops.

Exhaustion, though, may be stronger than I thought. As soon as my eyes close I am asleep and dreaming. And for once it is not a dream of falling or being torn apart or crushed.

There are two Lozens in my dream. One is me, watching. The other is a girl even younger than my sister Ana, a six-year-old girl with a smile on her lips. She's barefoot and wearing a dress, a light cotton dress of the kind I used to love when I was little and I could hold my arms out and spin and it would billow round me and I'd feel as if I was a top. Everything around here is as bright and light as her smile. But she's not alone in her dream. As she stands still for a moment to reach up into a peach tree, just like the peach tree that my mother planted in front of our house, just as she is about to grasp a ripe piece of fruit, he comes up behind her. His big jaws are slightly open, his huge canine teeth visible. She doesn't know he's there as he creeps closer and then . . .

"Yiii!" Young Lozen jumps at the feel of his cold, wet nose thrust up under her dress and pressed against the back of her thigh.

She turns and points an accusatory finger at him as he sits back on his haunches, tongue lolling out, his eyes bright with amusement.

"Bad Lobo, bad Lobo." She drops to her knees and throws her arms around his neck. "You bad dog, I love you so much."

I close my eyes just then in my dream because a wind has whipped across my face. When I open them again, I am still not awake. I'm sitting on my bunk here inside my cell, but I must be asleep because Lobo is here with me, not using his last strength to try to crawl back to me.

Lobo. He is sitting in front of me, alive and whole. The wounds burned in his chest and side are gone. His German Shepherd and wolf forebears show in his massive body and the quick intelligence that gleams from his eyes. He raises his right front paw and places it on my knee.

I stare at him in disbelief.

"Lozen," he says. "Don't you know me?" He's speaking like a human person, something he never did when he was alive. But it seems natural to me.

"Of course I know you," I say. My voice is thick in my throat. "I haven't forgotten you. I'll always remember you."

"Lozen," he says. "Sometimes you are so stupid. You don't have to remember me. Don't you know that I am always with you?"

Then he leans forward to rest his big head in my lap. I place both my hands on his shoulders and lean over to embrace him and whisper my secrets in his ear as I used to do every day before he was killed.

That's when I really wake up. It's probably not just because of that dream. It's also because it's a windless night and without fans or air conditioners it can get so hot inside my cell that I get covered with sweat. I sit up and wipe the salty water off my face and out of my eyes, especially out of my eyes.

Lobo. He's always there in the back of my mind. It's just so hard to think of him, to think of yet another loss.

Dogs. Dogs are forbidden here in Haven. Not that it makes that much sense, but apparently at least one of the Ones has an unreasonable dislike for dogs.

It's the oldest partnership in the world, that one between canines and humans. When the first dogs decided that they would join with us, hunt with us, help care for us, stop living apart from people as the coyotes and wolves would continue to live, everything changed.

"Our dogs made us more human," my mother would say when she told me some of our old stories about our four-legged allies.

225

Not all of them were ancient stories. She told me about how the day all the people of our Chiricahua nation, men, women, and children, even those who had not fought, but had helped the Army, were loaded into trains and sent off as prisoners of war to Florida at the end of the nineteenth century. On that day, none of us were allowed to take our dogs with us. Those dogs ran after the train for miles and miles. Even after the train was out of sight, they ran. They ran until their feet were bloody and even then they kept running. But we were sent so far away, across wide plains and rivers too wide for them to swim, that they never caught up with us. Others who saw our train pass saw those dogs following, sometimes days later. They never gave up until their loyal hearts gave out.

That is what my mother told me.

But the spirits of those dogs who perished pursuing us didn't give up. They entered the bodies of puppies born in those distant lands where we were held as captives for three generations. In Florida, in Alabama, in Oklahoma, our dogs returned to us, born again.

And my family and I were never without dogs until we were forced to come here.

I wipe my face with a towel, stand up and stretch. It's quiet all around me, so early that no one else has yet risen. It's so still that I feel half in that dream of my lost dog and half in this place. And that is not a good way to feel.

Move your body, Lozen, I think.

226

Sometimes the only thing that will get rid of dreams, clinging to me like spiderwebs across my mind, is to put my body into motion. I do fifty push-ups, then a hundred crunches. Fifty more push-ups, a hundred more crunches. Fifty. A hundred. Fifty. A hundred. I keep at it till my stomach and arm muscles are burning and the physical ache is beginning to make the deeper pain of that dream fade.

TAH-TA-TAH THAT-TA-TAH THAT-TA-TAH!

The morning horn. But with a difference. Not a good one. Three blasts on that trumpet means only one thing. Everyone is to go immediately to Main Yard. That usually means to view a Punishment.

Someone is in big trouble.

It doesn't take long for everyone to be assembled in the Main Yard. Armed and arrayed in their four respective companies, the guards look down on us from the walls. Out of the corner of my eye, I recognize two of those wearing the red armbands. One of them, now glaring directly down at me, is Edwin. There's a large bandage over the top of his head that covers half his face. If this were not such a grim occasion, I'd almost smile. The other man I recognizes is Big Boy. That means that at least two of those sent by Diablita Loca to eliminate me managed to get back here alive.

On the raised platform near the northern wall, the chairs of the Ones have been placed. But they're not there yet.

Of course not. They always make us wait, nervously looking around to see who is here and try to figure out which of us is not here and thus the one who has been charged with some offense and about to be tried. This way we are reminded of the power they hold over us all. Plus they have the pleasure of manipulating our emotions that much longer. Four cats with hundreds of mice to bat around.

The one thing they don't do when we're all brought together like this is keep us in separate little groups. We're allowed to mill around—like sheep.

I don't know where my family is. But I see one familiar face. Guy's. He's so tall that he stands out in the crowd. Guy makes a quick sign with his hands and points with his lips and a small jerk of his chin to the right. Mom and Ana and Victor are over there. I slide through the crowd to reach them.

Mom pulls me close to her. One of the white strands in her hair has fallen over her face. My mother's hair was always as black as a raven's wing until we were brought here.

"Lozen," she whispers in my ear. "I was afraid it was going to be you."

"No," I whisper back. I reach out my hands to take the hands of Ana and Victor.

"Lozen," Victor says, his voice a fierce whisper. "if they did anything to you, I would kill them."

I look down into his face. For the first time I see Uncle Chatto in him, that look of one who would sacrifice his own life to keep his family safe.

I shake my head at him as I squeeze his hand.

"No," I say softly, hoping that I've said that word in a way that lets him know how proud I am of him for his courage.

Ana pulls on my other hand. "They're coming."

The door has opened at the top of the steps that lead from the platform up to the entrance to the main corridor of Haven, the corridor of the thirteen doors. The Ones emerge and extend their hands towards the crowd, raise their hands just a little.

We all know the signal. We all are supposed to applaud. The sound of nervous clapping echoes through the courtyard— even though I only pretend to do so, not bringing my palms together but just making a clapping motion. I'd rather have my hands around their supercilious necks.

The Ones take their places. The Jester is at stage left, Diablita Loca beside him, Lady Time next, and the Dreamer furthest to the right. Their masks cover whatever expressions may be on their faces, but I have little doubt that all four of them are wearing a similar slightly bored smirk.

They know themselves to be like the ancient gods of Olympus come down from their height to meddle in the affairs of us little mortal beings. But they also know they are not true immortals. Why else would each have four well-armed body-guards placed behind them? Aside from fearing for their own safety, is there any real humanity left in any of them? When I look at the Ones who rule us, I feel as if I am just looking at beings as alien from the rest of us as if they came from another planet.

I am sooooo tired of this charade. Why can't they just leave these poor people alone?

What? Those words that just needled their way into my head came from up on the platform. I can feel it.

But what can I do, one against three.

Those incongruous, unthinkable thoughts are coming from one of our rulers. The sadness and weariness in that unguarded thought are as startling to me as it would have been to have heard a praying mantis crooning a lullaby to a baby! And as I see him shaking his masked head, I know who it is.

I don't have time to consider what that might mean. Ana is tugging at my sleeve.

"Lozen, look who it is."

No.

But it is. The figure being shoved up the steps and pushed forward to stumble and then pause in front of the four who are judge and jury is Hussein.

I'm hardly hearing what is being said by Templeton, the baliff, who has stepped forward to stand, back half-turned to the crowd, as he presents the Accused to the Ones.

Templeton is holding a short cane in his hand, sign of his office as baliff. Like Guy, Templeton wears no colored armband to indicate his allegiance to any one of our rulers, but is dressed in a white tunic to indicate his supposed neutrality. Unlike most of us in Haven, he is well-fed enough to have a double chin. The thick black hair on his head should belong to a man half his age. It's either a wig or an indication that in pre-Cloud days he'd been wealthy enough to have begun the bodily transformations that might have made him appear ageless. He is theirs, not ours. His voice sounds as if he has a mouth half full of oil.

". . . voicing sentiments meant to lead others into dissatisfaction," Templeton is saying, waving his cane like conductors used to do with batons in the old days when there were orchestras.

It's all ceremony. Done to amuse the Ones and fool some of us into thinking there is some semblance of fairness in the enforcement of the rules that govern our little lives.

Templeton turns to Hussein and pokes the cane at his chest. "What say you, sir?" His voice is full of contempt.

Hussein straightens his shoulders. "I say that I am a gardener, sir. That is all. And sometimes I sing. My song was harmless. It was meant to please myself and . . . perhaps someone else."

Templeton chuckles and looks out to the crowd for approval. To our credit, the only ones who respond with laughter are the guards on the platform and on the wall. Most of the rest of us are just waiting with deadened senses for them to get on with it.

Except for me. I am filled with such anger that I am afraid I am about to explode. It takes every ounce of self-control for me to stand still.

Think of your family, Lozen. Think of them. Do you want them to be up there, too?

I don't want to see this. If I could leave, I would. But our attendance is just as strictly forced as this phony justice is enforced. Across the crowd Guy is trying to catch my eye. His hands make a small pushing motion.

Stay back. Stay calm.

I try to. But then Templeton moves on to the next part of the show. The act before the finale. The crowd becomes so silent I can hear my own breathing

Templeton raises both hands theatrically and then addresses the crowd in his oily voice. "As all know, we are fair here in Haven. Every Accused has the right to call one person to speak on his behalf. Does the Accused have someone to speak on his behalf?"

Just then, Hussein catches sight of me in the crowd.

"Lozen," he says in a soft voice.

CHAPTER TWENTY-EIGHT

Punishment

LOZEN!" Templeton immediately shouts. "Ascend the stage!"

Hussein's mouth is open. He's saying something but no one can hear him with all the commotion that began when my name was spoken.

"No," Hussein is saying. "No, no. I just saw her in the crowd. I did not mean to call her."

Too late.

I can't feel my legs as I walk forward and climb the steep stairs up to the platform. The Jester is still leaning back in a bored posture in his chair, but the other three have leaned forward. This morning has taken an interesting turn for them.

As I move to take my place in front of the Ones, a spot indicated by a dramatic wave of Templeton's pudgy left hand, I have to pass by Hussein. He's shaking his head, wanting to apologize.

I'm the one who should apologize. I already know that there

is nothing I can say that will make a difference. Even if I was used to talking, what words from me could possibly spare Hussein from some awful, inevitable fate?

Krensaw, the bald, long-armed man who is the Dispenser of Justice, has already climbed up onto the stage. He is wearing his heavy leather apron, standing near the front by the cutting table that has just been brought out by his two assistants. A heavy glistening knife is being placed on top of that table as another assistant carries out a charcoal burner in which a poker is being heated.

"Thank you," Hussein says to me in a quiet voice.

Templeton steps forward and shoves his cane between us. "The Accused," he says, "will now remain silent."

And so will I, most likely.

What can I say?

How can I say it?

And which direction should I face right now?

I look down from the platform. Everyone is looking at me. I know all of their faces, but right now all of those faces are a blur of different shades of brown, like the petals of a giant flower. I can't make out any individuals, not even my family. Standing in front of this crowd of people, my legs feel weaker than when I have found myself confronted by creatures eager to tear me apart and eat me.

Then it comes to me.

Of course. Never have your back turned toward a monster.

Four monsters to be exact. Forget about Templeton. Forget about the crowd.

I turn to face the Ones.

If you don't have anything to say, don't say anything at all. I've learned that from my mother, perhaps a little too well. Because now there has to be something I can say. Not that it will likely do any good. The Ones already have their minds made up and they are just playing now, playing with us all as they always do.

But do they have their minds made up? If only I could hear people's thoughts when I want to hear them. Not just now and then for no apparent reason. I've never sought other people's thoughts before, but maybe if I concentrate . . .

And then I feel that familiar stab in the middle of my forehead and hear in my head that same surprisingly sympathetic thought-voice I heard earlier.

I'd be glad enough to spare the boy, if my little monster slayer here could just give me something to work with and not just stand there with her mouth open.

I close my mouth. And as I do so I hear something else. It's a sound that everyone else is hearing right now.

Snick, snick, snick.

I don't have to look to know what that metallic rasping is coming from my left toward the front of the stage. Krensaw is sharpening the blade of his heavy knife.

There is hope. But I have to speak. Now. I take a quick breath.

235

"Sirs and madams," I say, a little louder than I intended.

But that's a start. Those are the words a mere mortal is supposed to speak when addressing our rulers in public.

I take another breath. "Thank you for allowing me to speak on behalf of the Accused."

The Jester raises a hand to his chin. The Dreamer actually leans forward toward me.

Interesting! he thinks.

That's good. The Dreamer's thought, and the Jester's languid gesture tell me that I've caught their attentions. Lady Time and Diablita Loca, though, appear unmoved.

My throat feels dry, as if saying another word will make me start coughing. I press my tongue against my teeth, forcing the saliva to flow. Swallow, breathe in through my nose.

If I had my .357 right now I could end this so quickly. Four quick shots before anyone else could move.

Oops. My eyes just narrowed when that murderous thought went through my mind. Diablita Loca, the One who is my worst enemy, has seen my facial expression change. She shifts in her seat and curls her hands into fists. I blink, as if that was what I was doing all along. I compose my face. She's so close that can feel her aura, her lust for destruction, and it sickens me. I don't want to hear her thoughts right now. They'd be so poisonous it might be hard for me to continue.

No expression, Lozen. Look blank.

I try to shut out everything from my mind aside from thinking about what to say and how to say it.

Then the Dreamer's unguarded thoughts touch me again.

Is she too stupid to say anything in defense of her singer?
Can't she just say it was nothing but a song?

A singer. Just a singer. That's it.

"I think," I say, "Hussein sang because he's a singer. He's like a bird that sings a song, like the bird in his song. That's all. A bird is just a bird, isn't it? And a song about a bird is just that, right?"

All four of them are looking straight at me now. Was what I said stupid enough to make sense? Or will they guess that my simple words were meant to be deep?

The Dreamer leans far forward in my direction. I can see his one remaining eye glinting through the hole in his mask. It looks . . . what? Pleased? Amused? He lifts his hand theatrically and then puts one finger in front of his mouth.

Thinking about what I said? Or is he telling me to quit while I am ahead?

But I'm done. I don't have it in me to say more than two final words.

"Thank you."

Templeton steps forward and taps me hard on the shoulder with his cane. Not a wise thing to do. I barely control my reflex actions—which would be to rip that stupid stick from his hand and stick it up his—

"Leave the stage," Templeton intones, not realizing just how close he just came to an unpleasant end.

I leave the stage, walking down the stairs in that same shaky state I climbed up, feeling the unreality of it all. Mom reaches a hand out and pulls me to her. I accept her hug, feeling drained. Ana and Victor have grabbed my hands.

I don't want to see what happens now. But I still turn to face the stage. I bite my lip as I realize that the place we've found ourselves in is right below Krensaw and his table. The strong smell of the burning charcoal and the hot metal of the poker make me crinkle up my nose and feel nauseous.

What have I just done? What did I say? Have I helped at all or just made things worse for Hussein? He's looking at me, but I can't meet his eyes.

"And nowwwww," Templeton says, his voice like a drum roll, "our benevolent Ones will offer their verdicts." He flourishes his cane and bows toward the seated four.

The Jester is first. Without turning his head toward the crowd, he slowly extends his right hand, curls it into a fist and then draws it back. Neither thumbs up nor thumbs down. Complete neutrality. Let the others decide.

Lady Time now. She languidly holds out her open left hand, palm down, curls back her four fingers and then ever so slowly twists her wrist so that her thumb points down. Guilty.

The Dreamer leans forward, his elbows on his knees. He links his hands together, presses them against his chin. Then he turns to look down in my direction, the hint of a smile visible on his lips, and floats out his right hand with a magician's flourish. Thumbs up. Not guilty.

There's an audible gasp from the audience. Abstaining from a vote is one thing, but one of the Ones deliberately going against a vote already given by one of the other four is something that just never happens.

Not that it will make that much difference. Without hesitation, Diablita Loca has raised her left hand high above her head and stabbed it downward, like an ancient bullfighter driving a sword into the neck of a bull. Thumbs way down. Guilty!

Two to one with one abstention. But what does it mean?

The Dreamer rises gracefully to his feet. He opens his arms, turns to his three confreres and extends his open left palm to them as he places his other hand over his heart.

"May I," he says, "decide the forfeit?"

The Jester nods, as does Lady Time. Diablita Loca is seething in her chair. She's so angry over what is happening that you could probably boil water by sticking her hand in the pot. But a show of actual discord right now is probably not something that she wants. Grudgingly, she nods.

The Dreamer smiles and strolls over to Templeton. He leans close and says something that only the baliff can hear. That's not just because he's whispering. It's also because of the murmur susurrating through the crowd like a breeze through a pine forest.

The baliff raises his eyebrows and looks nervously over at the other three. They all nod back at him, even Diablita Loca, whose jaw is clenched so tightly that I wonder if she is cracking a tooth. Whatever the Dreamer has decided has their agreement, if not approval.

Templeton steps forward as the Dreamer pirouettes back to his perch.

"We have a verdict," Templeton proclaims. "The Accused has been found to be . . ." He looks back at the Dreamer, who makes a sort of shooing gesture with one hand for the baliff to get on with it. "The Accused has been found to be, ah, *accidentally* guilty. Our benevolent Ones are sure that he will not make this mistake again. They also have noted that he is valued in his role as our chief agriculturalist." Templeton gestures in the direction of the gardens. "Therefore, a degree of mercy shall be shown."

Does that mean he's not going to have anything done to him?

But Templeton's pause was only for effect. He lifts his hand and then drops it, palm down. "However," he continues, "to be sure that our singer here does not forget, there must still be some punishment. His sentence is a day of solitary confinement . . ."

Templeton pauses, just long enough for my heart to leap in hope. But he's not done.

"And this," he adds.

Templeton gestures at the guards. They march Hussein over to the table where Krensaw waits, holding the heavy knife over his head to display the instrument of justice to the crowd.

"One joint of the little finger," the baliff says. The tone of his voice is such that you'd think he was announcing the winner of a prize. "Right hand."

Just one joint of one finger. One of those long fingers that caress the strings as gently, as lovingly, as a mother brushing back a lock of hair from her child's face.

No.

I have to watch. Everyone has to watch. I have to remain impassive even when his eyes finally do catch mine for a moment and he shakes his head as if to say he understands.

The two guards march Hussein forward. They position his right hand on the stained wooden block. He doesn't resist. Somehow he is calm in spite of what is about to happen. Calmer than I am. I want to scream!

He's looking down at his hand, the hand that is about to suffer an amputation. Is he thinking that it might have been worse? Is he thinking anything at all right now?

He's right over our heads where we've been pressed in against the stage by the crowd that has pushed forward to see. I want to run away. I can't. I pull my little brother and sister close to me.

The Dispenser steps forward, the heavy knife in his right hand. He positions it carefully, resting the tip of the big blade above the end of Hussein's little finger. The blade glistens as its shadow draws a line across finger splayed beneath it.

CHUNK!

And just like that the last joint of his little finger is removed as easily as a cook might cut one of the carrots that Hussein tends with such care in the garden.

But carrots don't bleed. The quick spurt of blood that sprays from his finger strikes my forehead.

Hussein does not scream in pain. Nor do I move or make a sound other than a quick drawing in of my breath, as his blood trickles down my cheek.

The Dispenser is holding up Hussein's hand now. He reaches back, grasps the wooden handle of the iron that has been heating in the nearby fire, lifts the white-hot poker.

SSST.

The bleeding end of the second joint of Hussein's little finger is cauterized by the searing hot iron, the flow of vital fluid stemmed, the chance of infection lessened. But the damage still done.

As everyone else is still staring at that smoking cauterizing iron, Hussein catches my eye. Despite the fact that he is bent over in pain, his mouth is shaping words. I'm hearing those words in my mind at the same time he is silently saying them. I'm hearing them without the little stab of pain that has usually come in the past when I've listened to the thoughts of another.

Lozen, I am sorry, he is saying . . . and thinking as he mouths those words.

No, I think back at him. *No, no. Do not be sorry. I am the one who is sorry.*

The look on his face changes to one of confusion. Has he heard my thoughts?

Lozen, is that you?

He has.

CHAPTER TWENTY-NINE

Am I Human?

And now what?

I'm walking around in a daze. Half of me wants to cry and the other half wants to go berserk and start breaking things. But neither of those is possible. I never cry. Never.

I lean back against the wall by the residency bloc. No one can see me here. I clench and unclench my fists. My body is screaming at me that it wants to take action. But there's no action I can take. The only target right now that would give me any satisfaction is Diablita Loca. She's my enemy more than anyone else in Haven, a place full of enemies. But attacking her would be suicide—and would result not just in my own death but that of Mom and Ana and Victor.

More than ever before I know that we have to escape. But my plan of getting them over the wall, collecting my store of weapons, and avoiding capture is only half-formed. I could get away myself easily, but finding the opportunity to save us all is another thing.

I hope Hussein is all right. I wish I could talk with him. Feeling the touch of his breathless voice answering mine was like nothing I've ever felt before. But it was brief, too brief for more than just that second of mutual recognition. Then he was taken away to his cell.

I need to calm myself down. I tried to do that by sitting with Mom and Ana and Victor, just chilling with them. No dice. All I did was keep gritting my teeth so much that Mom got all concerned and asked me if there was anything, anything she could do. Of course there wasn't.

Maybe if I keep busy.

I head to the armory. I have a legitimate reason to go there. Whenever I'm not on an assignment, one of my jobs is to help Guy with weapon maintenance. You can't just leave guns lying around untended—otherwise they rust. They need regular cleaning. I haven't gone in a while, with my latest missions coming so close to each other.

The guards at the door nod and step aside. Lucky for them. If they hadn't moved fast enough I was planning to accidentally catch my foot on something, stumble forward and break one of their noses with a seemingly awkward out-flung elbow. Maybe they read something in my body language because they gave me a much wider berth than usual.

"Lass," Guy said as I entered. Then he pointed to the table behind him where the cleaning rods and cloth and cleaning fluids were laid out on the bench. "The .44s today."

I nod and step over to the table. Guy usually talks some while I'm with him. But today he seems to sense that I don't want anything to break my concentration. I disassemble, clean, and put back together the first gun. Then I point it at the wall, where I imagine Diablita Loca standing, thumb back the hammer, and dry-fire it.

I repeat it with the second gun, the third, the fourth. I'm moving as mechanically as an automaton. No wasted motions, everything done as correctly and emotionlessly as a machine. Except I cannot stop my mind from racing and inside I am as far from emotionless as Earth is from the moon.

Who am I? I'm thinking. *What am I? What real good am I to anyone or anything? All I do is kill things.* Well, things with teeth and ravenous appetites and a lust for human flesh, true. So I guess that's not all bad. But there has got to be more in my life than just blowing holes in hungry horrors.

What is my purpose in life? What would Dad and Uncle Chatto have done? What would my ancestors have done?

I finish the job of gun cleaning twice as fast as usual. I wipe my hands and walk out of the armory. This time the guards practically leap out of my way. Lucky for them.

I'm not sure where I am heading. I'm just walking, the midday sun at my back, my shadow moving ahead of me.

Maybe I should go to the gardens. Mom will be there working by now. She and the other garden workers will have much more to do over the next day without Hussein there. A lump forms in my throat as I think of him. I stop halfway past the empty stage. Can I find him again with my mind?

I stop and look at the empty platform, where I feel someone coming up behind me.

"You!"

That commanding voice doesn't make me jump. From the place I'm standing in the main courtyard—right where I was when Krensaw's knife came down—there is still a darkening bloodstain on the wood of the platform below where the chopping table had been placed. Like the streak of dried blood I did not allow Mom to clean off my cheek.

I turn to see, somewhat to my surprise, that the one who spoke—like the two men accompanying him—is wearing a black armband. The Dreamer's mark. Strange. It should be red this time. It's Diablita's turn to make use of my services, which I suspect will involve setting up a more concerted effort to eliminate me.

"Come with us."

The Dreamer is not in his usual pose, lounging back in that huge easy chair. Instead, he is standing, his back to me, his hands clasped behind him. One of the black curtains just to the left of his lounging place has been pulled aside. And what's back there is surprising. It's not torture devices, as has always been rumored, or even antiques. It's bookshelves.

"Leave us," he says in that silky voice of his.

"Sir?" The guard who commanded me to come with them, nervously shifts the AK-47 he is carrying.

"Now!"

The three guards turn as one, go out the door and close it behind them.

Silence. I stand there not moving. So does the Dreamer. More silence, so much that I am almost tempted to break it by saying something. Almost.

Then the Dreamer chuckles. "Lozen," he says, "Lozen, Lozen. Do you know who you were named for?"

I don't answer.

He turns and walks to his bookshelves, begins pointedly running one long finger across the volumes on the top shelf. I can read some their titles from here. *Myths and Tales of the Chiricahua Apache Indians*, *Victorio*, *Reap the Whirlwind*, *Warrior Woman*. Books about us? Why would the Dreamer . . . ?

He pirouettes to look at me. "I have always been interested in your people, child. And their psychic abilities. Such as those of your namesake."

Are you surprised? he thinks.

"Yes," I say, so surprised by that unvoiced question that I speak without thinking. I want to take that "yes" back. But

I've said it. Maybe he didn't notice that I answered a question I should not have been able to hear.

"Ah," the Dreamer says, his voice still soft.

And how about this? Do you hate us? Want to escape us? Even kill us?

Those words are so deliberately *thought at me* that my legs grow weak and I almost stagger.

"Yes."

Another amused chuckle. "Of course, of course you do. Just as you know more than you show. Is that not so, Lozen?"

His voice is different than usual. It lacks the usual theatrical affectation that I've always heard. It is almost like a normal, human voice.

"You heard my thoughts on the stand, didn't you? Just as you heard them now. Don't say anything if I am right about that. But do answer this. Can you hear my thoughts all of the time?"

He pauses and waits, keeps waiting. I have a feeling he is ready to stand there for hours if necessary.

"No."

The Dreamer spins around, slaps his hands together and laughs, actually laughs.

"Well, thank God for that," he says. He takes a step back and settles into his chair.

"Lorelei?" he calls.

The tall, pale, bone-thin woman slides out through the

curtains behind him. But even though her garb is the same, her hair piled in the same way on her head, her stiletto heels just as tall, she seems different. What is it?

It's the look on her face. Concern.

"I believe it is time to show . . . you know. Do you agree?"

Lorelei shakes her head. "I don't know. Are you sure?" she asks. "Can we trust her?"

This is getting curiouser and curiouser. They're not speaking like a master and servant, more like two friends. Am I in the Dreamer's Lair or have I fallen down a rabbit hole?

"I think so," the Dreamer says. "Pull the curtain."

Lorelei steps back to the side and pulls on a rope. The long black curtain behind the Dreamer, the curtain that is said to hide the Chamber of Horrors, the place of torture rumored to be back there, that curtain is drawn aside.

And what it discloses is a small room lined with even more bookshelves, its walls hung with mirrors—including, I note, the one I just retrieved for him from Big Ranch. There are also tables with cards and devices on them that I do not understand. But nothing that looks even minimally harmful.

No racks, no iron maidens, no thumbscrews.

The Dreamer laughs again, a laugh like that of a delighted child. "Surprise, surprise," he says. "Not at all what you expected."

I shake my head.

"Power," the Dreamer says, "is kept by keeping secrets. That is why my friend, my one true friend here, is the only one until now to have seen my little lair of a library and psychic laboratory." Lorelei has come to stand beside him. He takes both of her much smaller hands in one of his large brown ones. "It is better for people, certain Ones in particular, to think that my tastes are the same as theirs. How long would a bookworm last in a jungle full of predators?"

The Dreamer motions for me to come closer. I take a step forward. "Before all this," the Dreamer says, "my true interests were in areas other than conventional technology. I was fascinated with psychic energy. The lost levels of the human mind. But my interests were archaic in the world before our silvery visitor. What need was there for telepathy when you could just have mini-vid and audio implants and communicate mind to mind by way of radio waves? So I consented to be somewhat upgraded. Not as much as my family members—who burned up like Roman candles from whatever feedback the Cloud caused."

He raises his free hand high in a closed fist, and then opens it.

"Poof! Gone. Ironic, is it not, that my fortunate family's fortune came from the tapping of energy resources? That great wealth meant that, like my compatriots here in Haven, I was surrounded by all the trappings of our station, including my own large, heavily armed private security force. Thus I found a foothold here, while hiding my true self. And continuing to delve into," he indicates his bookshelves, "the literature of extra sensory perception."

He cocks his masked head to the side to stare at me. "But you have those special abilities in abundance, don't you, my dear? Just as I do—but only in the tiniest degree. Just enough to faintly sense it in others. But you have the full spectrum, don't you? Clairvoyance, far-seeing, mind-reading? That is part of how you have kept on surviving even after being sent out to face one monster after another. Don't say anything if I am right."

I stay silent. Where is all this going? What's next?

"And what good were all those modifications? Even those genetic ones that mean I can, given the benefit of water and food and a certain amount of physical protection, live almost forever? What good? Let me show you."

"No!" Lorelei says.

But the Dreamer is holding both her hands too tightly. She cannot stop him as he lifts up his other hand and whips off his mask with a flourish.

"Am I human?" he asks.

CHAPTER THIRTY

Run

I do not shrink back or scream. After all I've seen in the past few days alone, the sight of the Dreamer's uncovered face is not that shocking. In fact, after what he's been saying, rather than being horrified by it, I'm actually saddened.

But I can also see why he would want to keep it hidden.

Half of his face is gone.

Where he once had a right eye, there is now a deep, gaping hole, webbed over by scar tissue. In the days before our extra-terrestrial visitor, if he'd been filled with nanobots like his other family members, even the loss of an eye would have been quickly remedied by his body's own healing and the quick implantation of another vid-eye to take the place of the one that spontaneously combusted.

His right ear is also missing. Though the hole there is not as deep, it's still thickly scarred. And there are pale scars drawn down the side of his bronze-hued face where the molten rare metals and plastics trickled down after they melted.

His jaw is strangely dented in on one side, a sign that he had one of those maxillary augmentations that would allow him to touch his tongue to the teeth on that side and link into and manipulate the com networks. Lucky for him that he was still using a 1.0 com link and not the deeper 2.0 direct-to-brain filament implants that enabled such manipulation of his environment as telling doors to open and close by just thinking a command. The 2.0s ended up with their cerebral cortexes sizzled like eggs dropped onto a hot frying pan.

I can see, from what is left of his face, how handsome he once was. Idealized features like those of a romantic hero in a viddy. All of the Ones were once like that. Impossibly gorgeous, unimaginably powerful. I can almost understand why losing that power, that physical beauty, might make one crazy and cruel. I almost sympathize with them.

Almost, but not quite.

"Well?" the Dreamer whispers. He wants to know the answer to his question. *Am I human?*

"Yes," I reply. And then I surprise myself by not just stopping at that one word answer to his question. "Completely human."

The Dreamer lowers his face into his hands and his shoulders shake. Is he crying? No, he's laughing.

He lifts his face to look at me with that one twinkling,

perfect blue eye. "Completely human by being rendered in-complete?" he asks, shaking his head. "Ah, Lozen, Lozen."

He lifts the mask back to his face and it slips into place like a second skin, binding itself to his flesh. He raises his head, but even though the mask is once more covering the ruin of his countenance, to me it is as if the mask was still missing. The real human being who revealed himself is still visible to me. His three cohorts may still be deadly and dangerous, but this One is different.

The Dreamer nods, as if he's reading my thoughts now. "Yes, protective coloration. Mimicry. Look like them, appear to act like them, pretend to think like them, even be feared as they are. All that just to stay alive."

But if that is all there is to it, then why has he revealed himself to me? What is going on? Does he want me to see him as a good person? Does he want to help me?

He raises his hand toward Lorelei to stop her from speaking. "No," he says. "My actions are not intended to help the in-nocent. I am too self-centered for that. True, now and then, thwarting the plans of my voracious compeers has resulted in some benefit to another. But that was unintended."

Another silent voice comes to me just then. I seem to be getting better at identifying who such messages come from, for I know right away it is Lorelei.

He won't admit that he's unselfish and cares about others. But he does. I know him.

The Dreamer looks over at her. Perhaps he used his own faint ESP to catch the drift of what she just thought because he shakes his head wearily.

"No," he says, "I am quite selfish. My motives are to protect my position or to weaken the others. To survive. That is my sole paltry ambition. And in doing so I am prepared to use anyone."

As I plan to use you right now.

He points a finger at me. "My prime aim," he says, "is but to play the game and continue breathing. Paltry as this little life of mine may be, it is all that I have. I am such a coward that I have to work twice as hard to appear the opposite." He opens both arms wide. "So, Lozen, now that you have seen the great Oz to be a pathetic little creature behind a curtain, do you despise me?"

I don't say anything. It's too complicated for a yes or a no.

The Dreamer laughs. "My, it *is* hard to get a word in edgewise around you, isn't it?"

I nod to that one, a small ghost of a smile on my lips.

The Dreamer laughs again, a laugh that I have to admit is rather friendly and a bit infectious.

"Well," he chuckles, "you do have a sense of humor." He settles back in his chair again, leans forward with his elbows on his knees. "But now I need to let you know why I have brought you here. Although I would love to run you through a whole battery of tests in my little laboratory here, alas, there is no time for that. Are you aware that it has been decided by at least two of my fellow Ones that you have been a bit too successful of late? That you pose a potential danger to them? That they are actually afraid of you?"

"Yes, I do know that."

The Dreamer looks back over his shoulder at Lorelei. "You see, she *can* say more than three words at a time." He turns back to me. "So you know that they are planning to eliminate you?"

I nod to that one. They've already started.

"Good. So I have called you here for two simple reasons, one of which is paramount. The first reason is to let you know that I am not your enemy. I say this not because I want to be your friend, but because I suspect that being your enemy is not what I would call a strategic choice if one hopes to see another sunrise. So, if and when you do gain the upper hand and wreak vengeance or justice or whatever," he waves a hand dismissively, "you will remember our little talk and spare me and my dear Lorelei. No?"

I nod.

"Aha! Now on to the second reason I summoned you to this tete-a-tete. It is to tell you what you must do, now, if you wish to both survive and aid me in my plan to weaken my peers."

A pregnant pause. I stand here, he sits there, both of us waiting. Finally I raise one eyebrow and cock my head slightly.

The Dreamer nods. "Run," he says.

CHAPTER THIRTY-ONE

Outside

I stand there staring at the Dreamer.

Run.

How helpful is that advice, eh?

Doesn't he know that if I do try to escape it is not going to be alone? It's going to include Mom and Ana and Victor. Leaving them behind would only leave them in danger.

The Dreamer nods at me. Is his ESP getting stronger by being in my presence?

"Yes," he says, "on both counts." Then he chuckles again. "And your escape must include your singer friend as well, is that not so?"

He rises gracefully from his chair. "Come."

He leads me over to a dark grayish brown table, taps its surface lightly with his knuckles. "Chippendale," he says, as if that should mean something. Then he unrolls a schematic that shows the entire layout of Haven.

"Here," he says, pointing to the area of the interior wall that is a blind area for the wall guards. "Your point of egress. But you already chose that spot, didn't you?"

I don't bother to nod.

"However," the Dreamer continues, "did you know about this? Or this?"

"No." I have to admit he's right. I did not know about those two secret passages that lead in and out of the family bloc and the solitary confinement area.

"Of course," the Dreamer adds as he re-rolls the schematic, "there are the problems of the monsters that shall likely be lurking out there in the darkness." He studies my expressionless face and chuckles yet again. "Or should I say the problem *for* those monsters when they encounter you in the darkness?"

As the Dreamer's guards escort me out of his chamber, I think about the steps I need to take to effect our escape.

Although Haven was originally designed as a prison to keep people locked inside (and is currently serving that purpose rather well), the lookouts on its ramparts, behind its gun turrets, and in its towers all keep their eyes glued to the space outside. Especially at night. That's one of the weaknesses I am about to exploit tonight.

Another is that one place where, even when Haven was a full-fledged prison and not a fortress protecting those inside from the hungry creatures without, a determined prisoner could reach the wall and scale it without being seen by any watcher on the walls or in the towers.

Once outside, though, one might be visible within the range of the light cast from the night fires atop the walls. And while one person with the right training—me—could probably be furtive enough to avoid being noticed, the chances of four further fugitives going undetected would be slim. Unless one could cause a diversion. Which I plan to do.

Step Numero Uno is to alert my family. And here is where more of the Dreamer's help comes in. I'm taken by his black-arm-banded men not to my cell but to the dining hall. It's time for the last meal of the day.

My audience with the Dreamer did not last that long—even though I feel as if more time than I can measure passed while I was in there. Mom, Ana, and Victor are in the hall, already sitting at the table we go to when we can eat together. I take my bowl to the servers, hold it out for the two ladles of mashed and gelatinous goulash that is this evening's gourmet delight. The brown flecks are pieces of venison jerky. There's never much meat in the food that ordinaries are given. My family and I would eat a lot better if we were away from here and living off the land as we used to do in our valley. I pick up a spoon and join my family.

As always, Victor has finished all of his food and Ana is playing with hers, shaping the mush in her bowl into little hills and valleys.

"Look, Lozen," she says to me, "I'm making a place for us to live. See the hills here. And this is a cave. And here's a river. Just like Valley Where First Light Paints the Cliff."

I bite my lip. It's almost as if she is reading my mind and describing the very escape route I plan for us to take. Not that we could stay long in our valley. That's one of the places any search party might come looking for us. But not right away. If my plan works they'll be too busy licking their wounds.

"Good," I say to my sister, making a seemingly random motion of my right hand that I know my mother will see.

Mom leans over her bowl so that her head is closer to mine. We've communicated this way before, just as Guy and I have done. Hand movements, gestures, code words. Our secret language for a time such as this. Getting out of Haven has been something Mom and I have been thinking about ever since we were captured a year ago and herded into here.

"Tonight?" Mom says in a very soft voice, not moving her lips as she speaks. Though I've never told her any details, she has known since we came here that I've been planning our escape.

I nod as I drop my spoon on the table and lift my hand to swat at a nonexistent fly. As I do so, my spoon slides to the floor. I pick the spoon up, tap it three times on the table top as if to clean off whatever may have stuck to it from the floor. As I wipe the spoon off on my shirt, my mother crosses her hands, laying three fingers across the back of her left wrist. I take a bite of my mush and nod once more.

Tonight after the three bells that signal for the changing of the guards on lookout on the walls.

My mother waits a while before asking her question. She leans forward. "Victor drew a really interesting picture today," she says. But it's not her words that she wants me to pay attention to. It's her left hand held close to her stomach making the sign for *where*.

Where will we meet?

That is what she's asking. I wish I could just talk to her by thinking the way I have with Hussein and the Dreamer and my "perhaps" friend Hally. Hally. I'd be willing to bet he is going to make make contact with me as soon as we get out of Haven.

If we get out of Haven.

I look at Mom, at Ana, at Victor. Then I hold out my index finger. One more. I trace the letter H on the table top.

Mom smiles then. She understands that my plan is going to include freeing Hussein, too, and she is happy with that plan.

I place my left hand palm down on the table. My index finger on my left hand stands for the east wall. My middle finger stands for the south wall. Ring finger, the west wall. Little finger, the north.

I wrap my right hand around the ring finger and crack the knuckle.

"I wish you wouldn't do that," Mom says, placing her hands on mine and grasping that same finger. West wall. "Cracking your knuckles may lead to rheumatism, you know."

I nod.

Ana and Victor look across the table at me.

"Mom is right," Ana says.

"She really is," Victor agrees.

Young as they may be, they also understand. We're getting out of here! Their faces are calm, even though I am pretty sure their hearts may be beating just as fast as mine right now. Although their time with Dad and Uncle Chatto was so much less than mine and they were still very little then, they remember what they were taught. Like that day when we walked with Uncle Chatto in the desert.

"Little ones can survive by staying still," Uncle Chatto said, pointing out the motionless quail chicks that were crouched down in the leaves under an ocotillo, looking like nothing more than part of the earth.

"Can you stay still and watch?" he asked my little sister and brother. And though each of them had no more than two handfuls of years between them, they solemnly nodded.

I know that Dad and Uncle Chatto would have been just as proud of them as I am now.

Two bells sound from the entrance to the mess hall.

They were struck by the monitor. His job is to keep everyone moving in or out of here according to the schedules set by the Ones. Two strikes. Time for us to clean up, whether we are done eating or not, and get ready to exit the room.

Even in this world after the end of electricity, we are still being run by time. Not our time, their time. There's this story that Mom told us. It's not one of our stories, but one that she heard from a friend of hers in vocational school who was a Salish basket maker from the northwest coast where their hero is Mink.

Mom told it to the three of us soon after we arrived at Haven.

"Mink," Mom said that day, "is the one who stole the Sun so that the People could have light and warmth. Before that, they were cold and living in darkness because the Sun was being kept on the other side of the world by selfish monsters. The lives of the people became better after Mink stole the Sun for them. He was always trying to help the People. Then the Europeans came and brought a new thing called Time. Mink saw right away that it was really important to them. So he stole Time. But as soon as he gave it to the People things did not get better. It turned out that Time began to run their lives. They no longer had any time to do the things they wanted to do. Time told them when to eat and sleep and get up and work. They longed for the old days, but those days were gone now that they were owned by Time."

"That is a sad story," Ana had said.

"Maybe Child of the Water could go and kill Time?" Victor suggested.

Mom nodded. "Perhaps," she said, looking at me. "But until then Time is here and we have to follow Time's rules."

And now that it is dark, I am at Step Numero Dos. I am sitting in the shadowed spot I chose near the west wall. I am listening and watching, waiting for the right moment to make my move. And also waiting for time to pass.

Of course I can only guess at the time. No one is allowed to have a clock of their own in Haven. The only time pieces, aside from those in the private chambers of the Ones—especially Lady Time—are kept by the monitors and guards. Those spring-wound clocks, like the one in the mess hall, are used to regulate us, keep us in line, herd us as if we were nothing but sheep or cattle. Docile cows.

A silly little song that Mom used to sing to us comes to my mind. It's an old, old nursery rhyme.

Hey diddle, diddle, the cat and the fiddle,
the dish ran away with the spoon.
The little dog laughed to see such sport
and the cow jumped over the moon.

Dad told me, though, that songs such as that one were often in code. The "dish" was a queen's serving lady and the "spoon" a young man whose job it was to taste the king's food to make sure it wasn't poisoned. So rather than just being for little kids, they were a way for common folks to comment on things they weren't supposed to talk about. Just like some of the spirituals that the black slaves sang were subtle messages. "Steal Away to Jesus" was about escaping from their masters.

And right now this cow is about to try to steal away and jump—or at least climb—over the wall in front of her.

I look up into the sky. From the position of the crescent moon, it is still perhaps an hour before the three bell signal for changing the wall sentries, one of whom is easily visible from my vantage point that is invisible to him.

As I watch him patrol the top of the wall, I'm counting.

One and one pony.

Two and one pony.

I'm making sure that sentry atop this part of the wall is following a regular routine, behaving as predictably just as most people do when they have a boring task to endure.

Ten and one pony.

Eleven and one pony.

His eyes are focused on the outside, the only direction from which everyone expects any threat to come. He never looks back inside.

Twenty and one pony.

Twenty-one and one pony.

Just like the last ten times, he is following the same pattern.

Twenty-nine and one pony.

Thirty and one pony.

And now he has reached the spot where he meets another guard walking from the opposite direction.

Forty and one pony.

Forty-one and one pony.

They stand, heads together, exchanging a word or two. Then each turns back the way he came.

Fifty-nine and one pony.

Sixty and one pony.

Just like clockwork, the whole thing takes a minute. And that should be more than enough space for me to do it. But can I? I take one deep breath, then another. Will my plan work? So much depends on my doing everything just right.

"Listen to the night, Lozen. It speaks to us."

That is what Uncle Chatto used to say.

And just as the memory of his words comes to me, from somewhere out in the desert outside, a coyote howls. Another answers and another until the night is filled with their high ululating voices. When the new people came to this land, they made war on the coyotes and tried to wipe them out. But no matter how many they killed, more survived. Even the powerful new genetically modified monsters that were loosed on this land have not been able to get rid of the coyotes. They are too quick, too smart, too much a part of this land.

As suddenly as they began, the coyotes fall silent. But the sound of their singing has given me back the courage I was beginning to lose. Beyond the wall in front of me is our old land, breathing, living, waiting for me.

True, there are monsters out there. I would be surprised if

I don't run into one or two of the Bloodless before this night is done. But as Uncle Chatto used to say, the Twenty-third Psalm is a little different when a Chiricahua says it.

Yea, though I walk through the Valley of Death
I will fear no evil
for I am the meanest son of a bitch
in this whole damn valley.

I slide my hand down my side and grasp the handle of my old friend, my Bowie knife. The Dreamer did just as he said he would—he arranged it so that my knife and a climbing rope with a grappling iron on its end would be left in a hollow under a paving stone behind the armory. The knife and rope are all I need for now.

Now!

I slip through the shadows, reach the base of the wall and start to climb. Unlike the smooth outer surface which drops straight down, the inner face of the wall at Haven is rough and slanted. Anyone with a little rock climbing expertise could easily scale it, especially here where two angles of the wall come together to make a corner. It takes me less than a ten-count before I slide an elbow over the top and lift my head just enough to look down the top of the wall to my left. Just as I hoped, what I see is the guard's back, less than halfway to his rendezvous point with sentry numero dos.

I crawl, silent as a sidewinder, on my belly across the walkway. When I reach the parapet, I take a quick look below to chart the course I'll follow when I reach the bottom. I carefully hook the grapnel so that it can be dislodged quietly and quickly with one fast snap from the bottom. Keeping pressure on the hook end with one hand, I drop the rest of the rope off the wall. It makes a hissing sound as it falls and then a *thwomp* when the end strikes the hard earth at the wall's base.

Even though it sounds as loud as a bass drum to my sensitive ears, the sentry—who I've kept in my peripheral vision this whole time—seems unaware and just keeps walking. But even so, as I slide over the top, I remember the advice that Uncle Chatto and Dad once gave me about how to move when there is danger. It was during one of the few times when they told me a little about their own experiences fighting in Mali when they were in the Special Forces.

"Flow like water, Lozen. Quick, jerky movements will catch the eyes of an enemy," Uncle Chatto said.

Dad had nodded at that. "Never hurry, especially when you have to move fast," he added.

Like when my feet touch the ground. I snap the rope and the grapnel comes flying down. I catch it as it bounces off the ground with a *thud* that I hope no ears—on either side of the wall—other than mine have heard. The area around the base of the wall is kept clear of any rocks or vegetation, but there are always shadows. Staying low, coiling the rope as I go, I flow into the shadows as I move swiftly. And though I expect at any second to hear shouts followed by a volley of gunshots aimed in my direction, I reach the clump of creosote bushes I'd chosen as my objective.

Safe, more or less. Staying low, I begin to trot in the half circle that will take me to the hidey hole where I stashed the helpful objects that will help me effect Step Numero Tres of my plan.

I can see things clearly for at least a hundred feet in every direction because of the strength of my own night vision and the thin light cast by the crescent moon. That is a good thing.

But what I see rising up to my left and beginning to lope in my direction, its eyes seeming to glow red from an inner light, is not a good thing.

CHAPTER THIRTY-TWO

Clever Repartee

The Bloodless pauses its approach because I've just turned to look at it. He's the biggest one I have seen yet.

"Buenos días, senorita," it says, taking a step closer.

It's night, you dumb bloodsucker, I think. But I don't say anything. I let one coil of the rope fall into the hand that is still grasping the grappling hook.

"Amigo. Me your friend. No?" Another sidling step in my direction, its hands curled at its side.

No, I think, setting my feet and judging the distance.

"I, me, I," it says, its hunger for my blood and flesh clearly getting the better of what little cunning it possesses. It's beginning to crouch, readying itself to leap at me.

However, I am not about to let that happen. I raise my arm, swing it once, let the grapnel fly so that the rope wraps itself around both of the creature's legs like a lassoed bull. I

271

yank on the rope and its feet are jerked out from under itself and it lands heavily on its back. I'm on it before it can move, bringing the Bowie knife down like a meat cleaver.

The razor sharp blade cleaves through flesh and bone. The head, a toothy horror, goes rolling across the sand.

I leap back from the body as it briefly arches its back and thrashes its limbs about before becoming still.

I snap the blade down to flick the blood off, and turn in a slow circle, crouched, my lips pulled back over my teeth. I'm ready for whatever comes at me next. Nothing is going to get between me and my family tonight. Nothing!

Come on, I'm thinking. *Come on.*

I hear something off to my left where the saguaros rise up like sentinels. It's creeping up on me. I turn in that direction. I can see a dark outline out there, maybe fifty feet away. Crouching and getting ready to leap. Suddenly a much larger shadowed shape looms up behind it!

"Warrggh!"

Then there is a crunching sound like something being broken under a heavy foot.

Followed by a needle-sharp touch to my forehead.

Little Food. You are so fierce. You scare me.

That very big shadow comes toward me. As it gets close, the light of the moon is bright enough for me to see what it is. The hulking is a very human-looking being—if humans were eight feet tall and covered with short fur from huge head to big bare feet. And if, like a gorilla, the top of that head stuck up in a sagittal crest where the parietal bones of the skull come together.

He—it is very clearly a he—is holding something in his right hand. It is the limp body of a second Bloodless. I look down at the knife I'm still holding in my hand. I shake my head, spin the Bowie backward, and slide it into the sheath on my belt.

Nasty thing, he thinks at me, holding the dead creature up and then tossing it so that it lands on top of the one I killed. *Not tasty to eat like you, Little Food.*

Then he smiles at me, displaying an impressive set of teeth that glisten in the moonlight.

Fangs a lot, I think back at him, wondering if he understands puns.

Ho, ho.

He does. And my maybe-friend Hally, who is looming over me like a hirsute mountain right now, appears to be just who I thought he was.

All our people tell stories about his big-footed people. In some of those traditions they are cannibal giants that were here long before our own human kind. In other tales they are friends and helpers. But in most stories they are just out there, living their own lives, staying away from us so elusively that despite their great size they are seldom seen.

My name is not Little Food. And why am I having this

conversation in my head with you? And why are you helping me?

Am I?

Hally's grin gets even broader, almost splitting his ugly face in half.

Well, if you are not helping me then you are doing a damn fine imitation of being helpful.

Hally turns his head to look in the direction of Haven, visible only as a glow in the night sky from the arroyo where the two of us are involved in this surreal dialogue.

Don't you have something to do other than engage in clever repartee with a Bigfoot?

Now I want to ask him where he got his vocabulary from. But he's right. Time's a-wasting.

I hold up both of my hands in one of those Time Out signs that professional athletes used to flash back in the days when there were organized sports on viddys.

"Later," I say out loud.

Hally nods.

I turn and leave the arroyo at a trot. I'm not running as fast as I can because, despite my excellent night vision, taking off at full tilt in the night is a good way to trip or run into something unpleasant like a hunting rattlesnake or a cholla cactus.

If my mental clock is working right, I'll be able to execute my plan on schedule. I just hope that my mother and my little brother and sister have been able to use that secret passage, as the Dreamer promised, to slip out of the family bloc and position themselves in the same shadowed spot where I was hiding only a few minutes ago. I'm worrying that my simple plan may not have been simple enough. So many things could go wrong. They might not be allowed out of the bloc. Someone might see them slipping out and follow them. There might be an unusually watchful guard on duty tonight.

But whatever does happen, I know that I can trust Mom and Ana and Victor to do their parts. Mom may be forty years old, but she is as strong and agile as someone half her age and part of my strength is inherited from her.

I'll never forget the first time I saw her pick my Dad up and hold him over her head.

Both of them were laughing and Dad was saying, "You see now who the person is who really supports our family, my daughter?" as Mom lowered him back to his feet and we all hugged.

Why is it that happy memories are so painful to me?

Stop Numero Uno is my hidey-hole under Old Saguaro Who Looks Tired. Yup, all three of the grenades I kept are still here. I put them into my pack. Then I pick up the two crossbows and the quivers of extra bolts and jog back.

Stop Numero Dos is the wall where my family will be escaping. The light of the moon casts just the right pattern of shadows for me to make my way unobserved to the base of the wall. It should be even easier now. The sentinels up there are near the end of their shift. They're tired and thinking about their beds in one of the four guard houses, quarters far more comfortable than those allocated to us ordinaries.

Right away I see the nearest guard. His white arm band, marking him as one of Lady Time's minions, is clearly visible in the light from the torch flickering next to him. He's just turning, starting to walk one more casual circuit before leaving the wall.

Now! I throw the hook and it catches on the first try. Good thing it does. I need to move very fast. I climb to the top quickly, but I do not unhook the grapnel. I leave it there in plain sight and drop down to my belly, slide back into an angle of the wall below and behind the nearest burning torch. Then I wait.

Sure enough, just as I've counted on, here comes my guard heading back to his post.

"What?" he says. He's noticed the grappling hook. He's approaching it, confused, trying to understand what it is that he's seeing. As he reaches out to touch it, I take him from behind. Right arm around his neck so far that I am touching my left shoulder, left hand sliding in behind his neck. I kick my foot into the back of his knee so that he drops down and we are both out of sight of anyone that might be looking at this section of the wall.

His carotid arteries clamped in my rear choke hold, the blood supply to his brain cut off, he goes limp in a few seconds, but I hold tight just a little longer to make sure. Not long enough to kill him. When I let go, he's still breathing but out cold. I take out the roll of tape that was another of the Dreamer's gifts to me, use it to bind the unconscious man's ankles and wrists together, then fasten a strip of tape over his mouth just in case he wakes up and tries to cry out an alarm.

Dong! Dong! Dong!

It's the three bells for the changing of the wall guards. It's also the signal for Mom and Ana and Victor to run for the wall and start climbing. I've already sensed them below me. And if my plan is working, Hussein will be with them. I stand up and see them starting across the short distance that separates them from the rough spot in the wall where they can scale it just as I did.

I pull the pin from the first grenade. I've never thrown one before, but I was told by Guy, who used a number of them during his time serving in the Maghreb, that the proper protocol when you toss a grenade is to call out "fire in the hole!" or "frag out!" So, as I heave it in a high, long arc, I whisper, "Frag out."

One and one pony, two and one pony . . . it's still sailing through the air and is heading right on target toward the furthest of the three guard dormitories, the one used by the Jester's troopers, whose green-arm-banded boys are the ones who should just be heading out to relieve the current guards.

Three and one pony, four and one pony. And it lands on the flat metal roof, bounces once and . . .

KA-BOOM!

It explodes before hitting the ground in a burst of flame. The shock wave caves in the wall and knocks out the windows on that side of the long, low building.

Shouting, incoherent screaming, general panic.

I do believe I have gotten their attention. But why stop now?

As I hurl hand grenade numero dos, Victor crawls up over the wall to my left. Perfect. But what I see beyond my family is less than perfect.

Crap. Hussein was late. He's running across the open space between the nearest building and the wall. Right out in plain sight where he might get shot.

KA-BOOM!

My second grenade was aimed at the Red Dorm of Diablita's boys. It's proven to be even more effective than the first. It didn't bounce off the roof when it hit. It ricocheted right into one of the cooling vents in the roof that used to be part of the defunct air conditioning system and dropped into the building itself.

More screams, some of which seem to be in actual agony. The enemies I have killed may now include real human beings in their number. But I can't take time to sympathize or feel guilt. Every one of those men who serve the Ones has blood on his hands. I can't even begin to count all the terrible things I've seen or heard about during the year we've been here.

Victor has grabbed Ana's arms to pull her up as Mom pushes from below. Now Mom has reached the top, too. I reach for her hands to help, but she shakes her head and in one quick athletic motion reaches the top on her own. I don't see Hussein. But I can now hear the scrabbling sound of someone, hampered by a maimed hand, making his awkward way up the rough inner face of the wall.

I point with my chin to the rope behind me. Mom nods and the three of them disappear from my sight as I lean the other way and look down. Dark hair, broad shoulders. I can't make out his face, but I can see the bandage wrapped around his hand.

I pull the pin from grenade numero tres, and launch it toward the White Dorm of Lady Time's myrmidons.

Before it explodes in another satisfyingly destructive blast, I've dropped to my knees, grasped Hussein's uninjured hand and yanked him up next to me.

Plus his guitar, which is slung over his shoulder in its soft cloth case and is another reason why his climb up the wall was a difficult one. His guitar! Talk about bringing a knife to a gun fight! Although maybe he actually has an AK-47 in there? But as he accidentally drops the case the hollow ringing sound from wood hitting the stone hard enough to make the strings vibrate, it's clear that his love of his music is at least as strong as his desire to be free.

I'm not sure if I want to hug him or hit him because of that. I am as glad to see him as I am sad to see him, but this is not the moment to sort out my feelings.

"Lozen, I'm sorry I'm late, but . . ."

I push him roughly toward the rope before he can say anything more. He doesn't hesitate. With his guitar case back over his shoulder, he rolls over the top of the wall and slides down the rope so quickly that I wonder if he is burning his hands until I realize that he has grasped the rope with his injured hand on the bottom so that the bandage is protecting his palm. Hussein may be more resourceful than I thought.

I hit the bottom a split second after he does, jerk the rope free with one hand as I gesture Hussein and my family back with the other arm so the grappling hook won't hit them.

Then, without another word—no time for hugs or questions—I arrange our little party. Me on point, Ana and Victor behind me, then Hussein, with Mom on drag.

Follow me, I signal.

Ana pauses for a moment to pick up a stick. Even though we're in a hurry, that makes me smile. I think I know why my little Chiricahua sister chose that stick. Perfect size and weight for throwing.

Then we start off at a pace fast enough to get us well away from Haven before the chaos I've created has been sorted out, but not too fast for Ana and Victor with their shorter legs to keep up.

CHAPTER THIRTY-THREE

Reasons to Run

I t's almost dawn, that sacred time of day when the promise of new life returns to us.

We've traveled through all of the rest of the night. We ran, just as the Dreamer told me to. We had good reasons to run. Once the Jester, Diablita, and Lady Time dope out what has happened by discovering my family and me missing, they are going to order pursuit. Maybe even through the dangers of the night.

We haven't stopped since gearing up at the place where I'd stashed the two crossbows and a few other useful pieces of equipment, including the two canteens full of water from Lozen's spring that I listed as missing—a true enough statement—when I checked in with Guy on my return to Haven. Unlike weapons and ammunition, I'd figured the loss of a few canteens would not raise any alarms and I'd been right.

Hussein took one of the crossbows and added the load of a pack to the guitar slung over his shoulder. We didn't speak. He has just silently followed my lead, nodded when I indicated he should follow behind me. Although I am sure that his wounded hand where he lost that finger must be paining him some, he's shown no sign of feeling it. Whenever I've looked back he's been there, never more than a hundred feet behind with Ana and Victor. He's keeping up, mile after mile, showing no sign of fatigue.

I knew already that he was strong, despite the fact that he's not bulky like Edwin or Big Boy, but long of limb and lanky. He's almost as tall as I am. I've wondered at times why he never thought of trying out for a position as a guard. I remember that day I watched him work the bags in the gym. Most men in Haven who have his physical abilities seem to want nothing more than a chance to join one of the corps. Dangerous, but a more exciting life than a lot of other jobs. Except Hussein was always content with his garden and his music.

Is he going to regret coming with us? He had to leave his garden behind. But it was his decision to come, wasn't it? When the Dreamer gave him the message about when and how to escape, he took the opportunity. Or was it just an opportunity? Was it an order from the Dreamer? Was he told to do it or else?

Was that why he was almost too late, because he was being forced to flee? Was he hesitant, uncertain? Or, for that matter, is he here as a spy for the Dreamer? Can I really trust him?

All those thoughts make my head hurt.

It's almost dawn and we've reached a good place to rest for a short time. There's an old fallen cottonwood tree here that provides some concealment from the direction any pursuers would come. The slope faces east so that we can see the sunrise from here. My next cache of supplies, one that includes dried meat and is near a hidden spring so we can refill the canteens, is just two hills from here.

I stop and slip my pack from my shoulder, wait for the others to reach me.

Hussein comes first around the bend in the trail with Ana trotting along next to him. Ana is carrying by its back legs the fat rabbit she brought down an hour ago. When it crossed our trail, she killed it with a quick sidearm throw of the stick she'd been carrying.

Hussein is carrying something extra, too. Despite everything else on his back and the crossbow in his right hand, he's also lugging Victor, who has his eight-year-old legs wrapped around Hussein's waist, his arms around his neck, his head resting on Hussein's shoulder. It gives me a funny feeling I can't explain when I see that. Maybe it's because I remember Dad carrying me that same way.

Victor wakes up as soon as Hussein gently lowers him to the ground. I notice how Hussein grimaces just a little as he does so because Victor accidentally grabs his injured hand for a moment. But he doesn't say anything. He just pats Victor's shoulder.

Ana takes Victor's hand and leads him over to a spot she's sighted where there's a flat stone next to the cottonwood trunk. She puts the rabbit down by the stone. Then they both sit down and begin to arrange sticks on top of that stone, talking quietly about the house they're building.

"This will be my room," Ana says. "And this will be Mom's."

"And this one," Victor says, "is where Lozen and Hussein can live."

I feel my cheeks getting red and I look away, hoping Hussein didn't hear that.

Another thought comes to me then. My little sister and brother don't look scared or anxious. They trust me to keep us safe. And that makes me anxious. Am I up to this, can I do it? Hussein, who is leaning against the trunk off to my right—probably out of earshot of my little brother—looks over at me as if he's about to say something. But just then Mom comes over the ridge to join us and he closes his mouth again.

"All clear behind us," Mom says.

I don't doubt her judgment at all. Mom was always as good a tracker as her brother, Uncle Chatto. And her eyes and ears are as keen as my own.

She turns her gaze in the direction of the eastern sky where the clouds are starting to turn red and gold. Then she looks over at me. I nod in answer to her unspoken question.

Yes, there's time now for her to offer a prayer to the dawn.

Victor and Ana stop talking and stand up, as Mom faces

the east, takes pollen from the pouch that she always keeps on her belt, then she raises her arms and begins to speak. Her voice is soft, but somehow it seems as if her words echo from every rock to touch everything around us.

Creator, we give thanks for another day.
All is good that we are able to breathe.
All is good that we are here together.
All is good that we may walk about.

For a moment as she speaks her prayer, it seems as if we are back together at Valley Where First Light Paints the Cliff. Time stands still.

And as Mom continues her prayer I realize that Hussein has stepped forward to stand beside us, that he is holding Victor's hand, while Victor holds Ana's and Ana holds mine.

Then the sun begins to show itself. The shadows lengthen and run across the land and the mesas turn from grey to blue and then to gold with the coming of the Oldest Giver's light. The dawn wind comes to us and touches our faces. The warmth of that sunlight passes into our hearts. I feel connected to everything. It is as if those webs of light are binding the five of us together.

Mom finishes her prayer. The four of us let go of each other's hands and Mom embraces each of us in turn. Hussein, then Victor, then Ana, then me. Her eyes are glistening. I know she's been thinking of Dad and her brother, my Uncle Chatto, as she made her prayer. Her face seems for a moment to glow and I remember what she told us about the Changing Woman Ceremony she did when she passed from being a girl into being a woman. In that beautiful ceremony the whole story of Creation was reenacted as she became for a time Changing Woman herself, her presence a blessing to everyone present. As the first beams of the sun touched her, Changing Woman began a series of dances that represented the stages of a woman's life, from birth to old age.

I feel sad deep in my heart as I think of that ceremony. It was denied to me and every other Apache girl because of the new Freedom from Superstition laws that were passed well before the coming of the Cloud. Those laws forbade all "antiquated rituals and practices" that did not contribute to the common good. I was nine then. Of course, those laws no longer held any power after the Cloud came.

So, in Valley Where First Light Paints the Cliff my parents had planned that they would bring that ceremony back to life again. I would be painted golden with pollen and become Painted Woman. I would dance blessings for everyone around me. That was what was supposed to have happened a year ago. But the scouts from Haven arrived exactly four days before then.

The dawn prayer done, Mom walks back down the trail to keep watch. Victor is now piling those sticks that were once a house into the right shape to make a small fire, one that will give off very little smoke. He piles tree bark and dried grasses together for tinder, then uses the flint and steel fire kit I'd hidden in my first cache to strike a spark and start it burning. Meanwhile, Ana is using one of the small knives from my cache to skin the rabbit. Victor is whittling another stick to make a spit on which the rabbit will be placed to cook it over his fire.

Mom just watches them, trusting that they know what to do. They may be young children, but they are young Apache children. Like Mom and me, they began early to learn the ways to survive here in this place that looks deserted to many people but has been the home of the People for many, many generations.

As I look at my family, I am wondering what it is that I have to do now to ensure our survival. It's all in my hands insofar as where we go now and what we do next. My plan is that one of our stops along our path will be Valley Where First Light Paints the Cliff. But is that safe? Does Diablita Loca know where it is? How to find it? The scouts from Haven are all dead who captured my family and killed my dad and my uncle. But they probably passed on the information.

Mom and Ana and Victor are trusting me to lead them when I am not even sure I trust myself. I've gotten us this far, but what exactly should I do next? And what do I do about . . .

"Lozen, can I talk with you?" a soft melodious voice says next to my ear.

I almost jump. But I don't. No one ever sneaks up on me, but somehow Hussein has managed to come over and sit down behind me on this flat boulder I've chosen as a seat without my having noticed him. I take my hand off the handle of my Bowie knife and nod.

Hussein takes a breath and then says nothing. He just slides around so that he is next to me and sits there watching the sunrise. Our shoulders are almost touching. I feel my whole body getting warmer—from the sun shining on me, I'm sure. I inhale the scent that the morning earth of the desert gives off as it absorbs the sun's gifts of light and life. People think the desert is dead, but it's not. It vibrates with life and I can smell that life around me, the heady odors of the sage, the subtler scents of velvet mesquite, ocotillo and saguaro, brittle bush and prickly pear, creosote and tough grasses. But I can also smell Hussein sitting next to me. His sweat, his body odor, the scent of tomato plants.

I look down at his bandaged right hand.

He holds it up. "It's okay," he says. "It was a clean cut. It will heal." He wiggles his other three fingers and his thumb as if strumming a guitar. "I'll play again."

"Good," I say. It's the first word I've spoken since he joined us.

He holds out his other hand and with a gesture that is so graceful it takes my breath away, he indicates the land around us. "It is so beautiful," he whispers. "I love it." He places his

288

hand over his heart. "My people, we were of the desert just as you are."

I wish I could read what is in his mind right now. But my gift doesn't seem to come whenever I want. But I want to know if he is for real. Is he as sincere as he seems to be or is this just an act?

Hussein leans forward and then turns his face so that he is looking right into my eyes. His eyes are large and brown, his lashes almost as thick and long as those of a beautiful, carefully made-up woman. But his face is not that of a woman at all.

"Listen," he says.

I look down and nod, not because I don't want to hear what he is saying. I just can't keep staring into his eyes like this. Plus the polite way to listen among my people is not to make eye contact but to look down.

"I am glad you made it possible for me to escape. Thank you. There is nothing back there for me, nothing. No friends, no family."

I don't nod at that, I just sit still, even though it's hard to do right now.

"When I was young, when I had my family, they taught me things. We were not of the rich, we were Bedoo, poor people who lived at the edge of their wealth. But we stayed strong as the desert was strong, worked hard. So my family were people trained to defend, to provide security. Our old masters brought us here to this land. They brought not just my father, but also myself, my mother, my brothers. To use us as leverage to make sure my father always did exactly as told, even when those were things his heart told him not to do. Plus my brothers and I, we had some promise. So they also trained us, too. Understand?"

I think I do.

"There is another reason why I was glad to escape last night. I know why you stayed there. It was because they had your family. That is why you took them with you."

I nod again.

He holds out his injured right hand and bends back his index finger.

"Now they have no hold on you by threatening your family. But I also know the way they think, the way all masters think. They will try to use your friends, threaten to kill them to try to get you to come back. But who will they threaten? The Master of Weapons? But he is far too important for them to injure. Would they injure him?"

I shake my head. Guy is safe as long as he does nothing himself in the way of outright rebellion.

Hussein bends back his third finger.

"So who is left?" He points at his shortened little finger covered by a bandage that is no longer white, but darkened by dirt and sweat. "It is me. Your only other friend in that dark place. A gardener. A very good one, to be sure, but only a gardener. And because I did not want to be a hostage, lose more fingers and perhaps my life, I was glad to run."

I want to say something. Like why would they think I'd care anything about him. And this time it is as if he is reading my mind.

"Why would they think you are my friend? It is simple. When I stood on that platform and called your name by accident, you came. And then there is what you said. Everyone knows how little you speak. But for me, you spoke. Not just one word or two. I counted. More than fifty words!"

Hussein smiles. Even looking away with my head down like this I can see that smile out of the corner of my eye. It's a really sweet smile, a little like the smiles I get sometimes from my little brother Victor. A trusting smile . . . and a little more than that. I wish Victor or Ana or Mom would come over right now and interrupt us. I am feeling confused and ready for this conversation to end. But they are just staying over there cooking that rabbit, pointedly giving us space. It makes me want to yell or say *crap*!

But I don't.

"So, Lozen, that is the other reason I came along. It is because I know that you like me." He pauses. "And because I like you." He takes an audible breath. "I really like you."

I need to say something. Not just shake my head. Am I happy or confused? Should I tell him I feel the same way? But what happens surprises me, because, in a real soft voice, I say a different word entirely.

"Oh," I say.

"I am also here to give you this," Hussein says.

He hands me a message tube. I take the rolled message out and read it.

If you have received this, I assume you are alive. That is good, for if someone else is reading this then there is an excellent chance that I may soon be defunct.

However, fingers crossed, if things went as planned, then whatever diversion you assured me you could stage has succeeded, having confused and occupied the attentions of mes bon amis. *Perhaps it has even set them at each other's throats, their ignorant armies clashing at night upon Haven's darkling plain, each One assuming the other was attacking her or him whilst my own hearty lads held back. (I do hope you spared my lads.)*

But now that the light of another day is upon you, mes bon amis *have likely discovered you, your family, and your song bird missing, and thus identified the author of their woes. A combined force, quite heavily armed I must note, has undoubtedly been set upon your spoor charged with but one task: bring back the Monster Slayer's head or return not at all. Thus, I must reiterate—nay, reinforce—my previous advice. To wit:*

Run, Lozen, run!

Hugs and Kisses,

D

I hand the message to Mom, who has come over to join us. She reads it and looks at me.

I nod. We need to eat and run.

CHAPTER THIRTY-FOUR

One Step at a Time

We've been climbing for the past two hours or thereabouts, judging how many hands high the sun now is in the sky. We are at least twenty miles from Haven.

I've heard it said that humans are the only creatures aware of their own bodily mortality. Knowing that you would die to protect and preserve all that you love—including Earth—makes you more than just bones and flesh and blood. It makes you stronger of spirit. It makes you better. Better for others and better for yourself. Better for the Earth.

And that is why I have to fight the Ones. For if they have their way, they and others like them will claw their way back to control the whole world. I can't let them do that again.

"I can't let them." Whoa, Lozen. You're beginning to sound like one of those overly noble characters in the old viddies who fight against all odds.

293

Enough grandiosity.

Forget about saving the world.

Just take it all one step at a time. That's the only way to get to the top of a mountain unless you have wings.

I look back down the slope. The dark rocks of every shape and size, some of them sparkling with mica, piled and stacked into all sorts of formations, have been making this climb like working our way through a maze. There, thirty feet below me, is Ana. She stops, waves up at me, and then turns to motion down to Victor, who must be just below her. I can't see him or Hussein or Mom. They are hidden by the twists of this trail, a path long followed by my ancestors. It is a path that can only be followed single file in many places. And for every choke point in this trail, there is a spot hidden above it and hard to see from below where a man or a woman with a bow could pick off any enemy foolish enough to follow.

The top is just ahead. That is where we'll stop and decide. We've already visited the place where I cached food, filled up our canteens, and added the two additional canteens I stored there three months ago. There are two ways we can go from here, both places where there is water. Here, in the ancient Rincon Range, there are many places that offered my ancestors refuge or places to stand off enemies. So my escape route is not just one place after another, but includes crossroads where I can choose which alternative to take.

As Ana comes into sight below, I scan the wide vista ahead. I don't see the pursuers that I know must be following. I hold up my hands and turn slowly. There, a light tingling in my palms. Back to the southwest, but still far away. That is where our enemies are.

Victor has now joined us with Hussein, who has become his special buddy. Victor smiles up at him and takes his hand as he stands here.

Mom's not joining us yet. As agreed, she stationed herself just above the next to last narrow spot in the trail. If anyone was very close to us, she'd see them. And if it was just one person, she'll use the crossbow she's holding.

But I trust my Power to have spoken truth. I gesture to Ana, who's still a hundred feet away.

Go back. Bring Mom up, I sign. Then I sit down on a large flat stone that is covered with petroglyphs. A sun, a coiled shape, a series of handprints, a man holding what looks like two tiny mountain goats in each of his hands.

Hussein walks across the top of this little mesa and sits on another rock to look out toward the east. Giving me space. Why is everyone always giving me space? And why do I feel irked about that right now? It's not like I'd want him to come sit close to me and put his arm around me and lean his head next to mine. Would I?

I shake my head, trying to untangle my thoughts.

Little Food, how are you?

I should have known it.

I am NOT Little Food.

Oh, Hally thinks back at me in a way that is like the sound

295

of someone chuckling because they are vastly amused with themselves. *Sorry. I try again.*

Don't bother!

No, no, is no problem. Here I go. Not Little Food, how are you?

Why do I even try? And why is my Power not working for me right now, warning me that an eight-fool-tall man-ape has somehow crept up on me? I slap my hands on the flat stone so hard that it makes a hollow sound like a drum. I look around in every direction.

Is he there? No tingle from my palms.

Is he over there? Still no warning warmth in my hands. I am getting super pissed!

Mom has now come up to the mesa top and is standing by Victor and Ana. They are looking at me, concerned. So is Hussein.

Crap!

I stand up and spread out my hands.

"Where are you?" I yell out loud.

Here.

The large flat rock on which I was sitting lifts like the lid of a chest, pressed up by two huge hairy hands—in whose grasp your average mountain goat would look tiny. Just like in the petroglyph I'd been sitting on.

I hear a sharp intake of breath from behind me, recognize it as coming from Mom.

I hold my hands out to my side. It's all right. I think.

One of the two large hands, connected to a long, long arm that disappears out of sight into the tunnel below that flat rock, lifts up a little higher, does a little wave at us, then gestures for us to follow as it slowly descends and disappears.

"Lozen," my mother's hand is on my right shoulder, "*Who is that?*"

Who, indeed? Are you coming?

I take a deep, deep breath and slowly let it out. The gang's all here.

"Lozen!" Mom says again. Her voice is getting impatient. "Who?"

"A friend," I say.

I hope, I think.

I take two steps forward to look down into the tunnel under the stone. It's a big tunnel. Carved into the living stone is a set of rough-hewn steps leading down and down into the dark.

Gesturing for everyone to follow me, I start down the stairs.

I hear the soft footsteps of Ana, then Victor, then Hussein, and finally Mom as they begin to descend behind me. Ten steps, twenty, thirty steps down into the dark.

Then, the small amount of light from above suddenly disappears. Somehow, that flat stone has closed down above us. Is it our weight on the stairs that did it? A hidden lever down below where Hally is somewhere ahead of us?

Waiting perhaps with a cooking pot?

Perhaps I am a vegetarian?
I doubt that.

Soft mental chuckling answers me.

Ana grasps the back of my vest. I reach back and take hold of her small hand, which is trembling a little. I squeeze it reassuringly. *It's going to be all righ, sweetie.* Victor, Hussein, and Mom are close behind. I can feel each of their presences.

And then, as my eyes grow accustomed to the dark, I see that it is not completely black down here. The walls are glowing, a faint luminescence that seems to grow brighter as I become aware of it.

"I can see," Victor says.

I give Ana's hand a little tug. *Let's keep going.*

The glow is brighter ahead of us. We round a corner and what I see there, waiting for us, shocks me as much as it does Mom and Ana and Victor.

This, I think, *is insane.*

CHAPTER THIRTY-FIVE

You Asked

'd been expecting a monster's lair with piles of bones from its victims stacked to the ceiling. Or a great echoing cave with giant stalactites hanging from the ceiling, bats fluttering about. Or a treacherous narrow bridge spanning a deep chasm filled with glowing lava and hissing clouds of steam.

Nope, none of the above. What we all see is a cozy room, its walls hung with Navajo rugs, a sort of fireplace built into the furthest wall in what is either a natural vent or one carved out of the rock to create a draft that lifts the smoke. Against one wall there are even more bookshelves than I saw in the Dreamer's lair. But what draws my eyes most is in the middle of the room. It's a large wooden table with chairs pulled up around it. On that table there are plates and cups, knives and forks, which is neatly set for five. This all might seem almost normal were it not for two obvious differences.

Difference Numero Uno—the plate, knife, fork, and cup at the head of the table are all three times the sizes of the other dining ware.

Difference Numero Dos—need I even say it? Yup. It is our genial host. Bent over by the fireplace stirring the large cast-iron cauldron suspended from a tripod over the flames is Hally. The aroma coming from that stewpot and filling the air is wonderful. It reminds me how long it's been since any of us have had a real meal.

Hally straightens up and turns to face us. He has put on an oversized white chef's hat, perched high atop his sagittal crest. It makes him look totally non-threatening, despite his size. He is also wearing a frigging apron that bears the embroidered words, I kid you not, KISS THE CHEF. Well, at least it makes him look more polite, or at least discreet, since it conceals his otherwise overly obvious nakedness. I am having a hard time not bursting out into uncontrolled and slightly insane laughter.

Hally holds out his huge, hirsute right hand, palm up, swings it to indicate the table.

"WELCOME, GUESTS," he rumbles.

It's the first time I've heard him speak, even though we've met in person twice before. His voice is rough, deep as thunder. It sounds like boulders rolling down a stony slope.

I can sense what Mom and Ana and Victor and Hussein are doing behind me—staring and thinking about retreating. And he hasn't even grinned at them yet. I turn toward them and gesture calmly with my own hands.

"Sit," I urge them, hoping my voice doesn't sound as strained or close to hysterics as my brain is feeling right now.

We sit down. Our hairy host lumbers over and deftly pours water into our cups from a stone jug that is as big as Victor, although Hally handles it as delicately as if it were a crystal pitcher.

"Thank you," Ana says, smiling up at him as sweetly as a little bird looking up from its nest.

He's nice. That is what she's thinking.

Victor's mouth is half open as he sits there. This is a lot for him to take in, but he seems to be accepting it. After all, he's only eight. Everything in the world can be surprising at first to an eight-year-old. Plus he can also smell whatever that stew is and his mouth is watering a little. Nothing ever makes my little brother lose his appetite. "Eat while you can" is his motto. He's a lot like Dad was in that way.

Mom is sitting quietly, studying everything. That doesn't surprise me. But Hussein's reaction to all this does. He has his hands together and is tapping his lips with his two index fingers. The way he is looking at Hally is not with uncertainty or fear, but something else.

"I know about you," Hussein says.

Hally turns his head. "OHHH?"

Hussein nods. "Not you, perhaps. One like you. Another desert, far away where my people called you Old People by the name of djinn. There, one like you helped my family before I was born. My father told me the story many times.

"HMMMMM," Hally hums. "GOOOD. NOW EAT."

By that he does not mean he is now going to eat us. He has lifted that pot up from the fire and is spooning out onto our plates a venison stew that contains vegetables like those from Hussein's garden back at Haven. Potatoes and beans and carrots. It smells as delicious as it looks.

I look up at Hally as he serves me.

Where did you get these?

My garden.

You have a vegetable garden?

Hally points at the huge opposable digit on his left hand. *Green thumb.*

So you actually are a vegetarian?

He drops a large piece of venison onto my plate.

That is what this deer thought when he came to eat my beans.

This time I can't hold it back. I have to laugh. It comes out as a loud barking cough that even startles me. Hussein and Mom and Ana and Victor all turn to look at me. I raise both my hands in a calming gesture to them.

"It's okay," I say. "Let's eat."

But even though I do not say anything else out loud as we eat, my meal is far from a quiet one mentally.

So, Not Little Food, how do you like my place?

I look around. And the thought that comes to me is that there is a feeling of great age all around me. That tunnel, this

302

room, everything else that I suspect is here within this mountain and hidden so well from the sight of normal humans, this has all been here for a long, long time. Plus that last thought which came from Hally was not in broken English. There's more to him than I thought.

Hally, just how old is this place? How long has it been here?

Since before your people were here.

Why help me?

Hally shrugs. *Every now and then we get interested in someone. We're not forbidden to help you little people, we just don't feel like it most times.*

Why do you hide? Why do you live this way?

It's quieter like this.

There's more than that to it, isn't there?

I feel a pause in Hally's thought. Is he wondering how much he should tell me? Then his silent voice asks me a question that surprises me.

Do you know why the Silver Cloud came?

The question shocks me. And it's not just because it is being asked by the least likely person. It's also his mentioning the Silver Cloud.

When the Cloud first appeared it was all that anyone talked about. Everyone wondered what it was, why it was here, when it was going away. Maybe it would just go away or disappear. But it didn't. And over the years that passed, the survivors all stopped talking about it. Certainly no one at Haven ever mentions it. What good would it do to talk about it? Just surviving takes up most of our time and energy.

No, I think back at him.

This time there's no hesitation as he begins to tell me a story.

My people have lived here a long, long time. We are from another age, old beyond old, before all of you were shaped from this earth by the Maker's hands. We, too, became powerful. We could fly. We could shape the courses of the rivers with the work of our thoughts, dig into the roots of the mountains, raise great structures up to the sky. Soon, we believed, we would dream a way to rise up beyond the Life Giver. Then the Maker sent us a message.

It came, a big light streaking across the sky. And there was a great explosion. Darkness filled the skies for cycle after cycle of the Giver of Light. Most of us died. But a few handfuls of my people survived deep in the earth. There was enough water and food to last through the dark time when most of the other plants and animals died.

When the sky finally cleared and we saw again the face of the Giver of Light, we were changed. We no longer wanted to shape the earth. We just wanted to live, to breathe, to see. We planted the seeds we had saved. We decided to just live and watch and listen.

Hally pauses in his story, rubs his big hands together, looks around his comfortable stone chamber. My brother and sister are busy eating, Mom and Hussein have their heads together quietly talking about something. No one is paying any attention, as if they could, to what Hally is telling me. But then I remember that brief instance when Hussein knew what I was thinking. Was it just a random moment? Or is there more to it?

Hussein, I think. *Can you hear me?*

No response. Did I hope for one? Or not? Whichever the case, I guess this is not the time to brood about it. I turn back to Hally.

So there are more of you? Are they around here, too? I think to him.

Hally nods.

Yes, there are more of us. But not here. Every now and then some of us gather together. But we enjoy being alone. So mostly we communicate with each other with our thoughts. Sometimes we have a big meeting of all of our minds. We had a big mind meeting of that sort just before what you call the Silver Cloud came. We were worried that something would happen because you little people were behaving as we did long ago. Your leaders believed they were wiser and stronger than Creation. They were crushing all other life on Earth beneath their weight.

Something would happen soon. We all agreed on that.

We were not sure what it would be. We knew you little

people had rockets to protect yourselves from any asteroids and comets that might strike Earth as that one did in our day.

But what came was not a comet or a meteor. It was something no rocket could destroy. It was the Cloud.

There's a lump in my throat the size of a fist. It all makes sense. I feel saddened and inspired. I think of all the old traditions that my mother still tells us about the past. How each world before this one was destroyed because of the misdeeds of humans or of Coyote, who is a sort of embodiment of all the craziest, most powerful and irrational aspects of humanity. What we need to do is find the balance again to make it right.

But Hally is not finished.

But some of my people think it may be another way.

Huh? I think.

Their theory is that there are other beings beyond Earth who do not care about balance. They just do not want any of us to become too powerful on this planet. So, whenever any of us beings on Earth seem to be growing powerful, they do something to hold us down. Send a comet careening our way. Or in this case, that Cloud.

And now I am feeling angry. *Is that all we are? Just flies to get our wings clipped whenever we threaten to break out of this solar system?* But Hally is still not finished.

But none of us know if that is true or not. And some think there may be another reason.

Oh, great! Just what I need. Another load of . . . uncertainty!

It is this. When there's a certain amount of electronic activity here on Earth it sets into motion an attractive field. And that field, like a magnet pulling iron in its direction, draws things toward Earth. One time a meteor, the next something like that Silver Cloud.

I look hard at Hally. Is that a smile on his face? Hard to tell with all those teeth when his mouth is open that way. My head hurts from trying to take in all this stuff.

Why tell me all this? Why make me so confused?

Well, he thinks back at me, *you asked.*

CHAPTER THIRTY-SIX

Your World Now

It's a nice room. But I can't stay here forever. Much as a part of me wishes I could. I'd like to check out those books on my huge hairy buddy's shelves, sit with my feet up in front of this fireplace and relax, really relax, for the first time in years.

That is what Mom and Ana and Victor are doing. Mom is sitting in a rocking chair that I suspect was brought here especially for her, seeing as how it is way too small for a bigfoot. A half smile on her face, her hands in her lap, she looks like one of those old Pueblo storyteller clay dolls, just waiting for half a dozen little kids to climb up and beg for an old tale.

Ana and Victor are on the floor in front of her. They are stretched out on their stomachs on a thick carpet spread out in front of the hearth, a checkerboard between them. They are totally engrossed in the game. They've always loved checkers. To Victor, checkers is what games are all about. He's too young to really remember holo-viddies.

It makes me think of the place that I hope to eventually take us all. Valley Where First Light Paints the Cliff. We had a checkerboard there. It was one of the things that my dad packed when we left the city and he and Uncle Chatto led us through the chaos of the looters, the Know Not mobs, the warring armies, the monsters of every shape and size that were starting to appear, to the safe, hidden place that became, for eight seasons, our little Eden in the hills. It was our home.

Until they were betrayed. And the men wearing red arm bands came and burned our homes and took those who survived as prisoners.

Hussein has blended right in to this idyllic little domestic scene. He's cross-legged on the floor, his guitar in his lap, strumming it with his thumb and index finger and keeping the bandage wrapped around his mutilated finger from hitting the strings. He is humming something softly as he plays.

It's all so peaceful. Too peaceful. It makes another part of me, the part that will never forget seeing my dad and Uncle Chatto going down in that hail of AK-47 bullets—the part that knows there are men somewhere out there trying to hunt us down—want to jump up and scream out something.

I shake my head in disbelief at the unreality of it all, at the way this tranquility, which our old people always said was the way life should be, seems so jarring to me right now, so confusing.

How can they all be so calm right now?

A huge hand rests on my shoulder—well, to be accurate, almost the entire right side of my body.

All of them look happy, do they not?

I turn and look at our host. And as I do so, it comes to me.

You did something. Did you hypnotize them?

Who, me? Hally puts a hand over his heart and widens his eyes.

If telepathic messages can sound disingenuous, then what he has just "said" to me is the dictionary definition.

Just tell me.

Hally removes his paw from my shoulder, presses both his palms together and puts his hands against his chest like a priest about to deliver a benediction.

I put them in happy place. They will stay there until I . . . wake them up. Then I will take them to a place where you can find them. They will not remember me. They will not remember being here. I will make them forget. That is something my people always could do to most of your kind. Like Lamont Cranston, the Shadow, we have power to cloud men's minds. Also women and children. How you think we manage to keep them from finding us all these centuries? Nyahhh-hah-hah.

Who is the Shadow? And what is with that weird laugh?

Golden Age of Radio? Never mind. I forget how young you are.

And how old is he? Hundreds of years, probably. I look hard at Hally and he shrugs. So he's used some kind of hypnosis to make everyone else chill? That's good. Because I do not want them following me—as I suspect they would all insist upon—when I go out to do whatever it is that needs doing now.

Which is what?

I look up into his eyes, deep brown. Like looking into two pools of deep water, little lights glowing somewhere deep beneath the surface.

It's not working on me. So cut it out.

Hally grins. *No harm, no foul.*

I go over to the place where I stacked my things. They are all there, as well as something else resting on top of it. A holster with a .357 Magnum in it and what looks like a hundred rounds of ammunition.

Where did that come from? I suppose the answer to that is easy. He took it away from someone who no longer needed it. And when did Hally have the time to bring it out from wherever he had it hidden away? We've been talking mind to mind almost the whole time we've been here. Or have we? Maybe I am not immune to mesmerism after all.

I look back over my shoulder at Hally. He lifts his eyes to the ceiling and twiddles his thumbs, innocence embodied. Then I pick up the gun. It's not mine, but it's in just as good shape as the one I had to leave behind in Haven. I check the chamber. Empty. Dry fire it. All in order. I load it, slide it in its holster, belt it around my waist. Ah! I no longer feel naked. Ready to go.

But which way? I look around Hally's stone chamber. It

seems at the moment to have just as many doors as there are windows. Namely none.

Which way is out?

Hally strolls over to the farthest wall, presses one large finger against its rough surface, and a section of it swings back to disclose a passageway.

Voila, mademoseille!

He and the Dreamer ought to get together. I lift up my very heavy pack, which clanks as I heft it, sling it over my shoulder.

I look back once at Mom and Ana and Victor and Hussein. I believe what Hally told me. They'll be okay here for now. If Hussein didn't have that bad hand to contend with, it might be nice to have him coming along with me. He's already proven himself to be more than a little competent. But no. Just like always, this is something I have to do on my own. And it will be so much easier to do with them safe and my not having to worry about them.

I enter the passageway, take a few steps. Then I stop. Hally is not following. I pause and look back over my shoulder

You coming?

He shakes his head. A look of regret passes over his craggy features.

Your world now. You defend it.

But what about the last few times you stepped in to help me? I think to myself. But not to him, not after that eloquent look on his face.

Though the walls around me are smooth, there must be some dust sifting down because I feel it irritating my eyes and have to reach my hand up to wipe them dry. As I do so, the wall starts to swing back into place, slowly blocking off my view of those I love.

I just stand there, not protesting, not saying or thinking anything. Just breathing, readying myself to do the job for which some kind of crazy destiny seems to have chosen me.

I just hope I have the strength to do it.

To be Killer of Enemies.

CHAPTER THIRTY-SEVEN

All Around Me

I t seems as if I've only walked a hundred paces, though for some reason I have found it hard to count my steps as I've walked along this passageway that has alternately been narrow, then wide, glowed golden, then silver. And the floor has seemed at times to be hard, then soft, rough, then smooth as ice. At times, even though the floor has looked level, I've felt as if I was descending, then climbing, stepping into holes that I cannot see. It's been disquieting. Everything is strange all around me. Time and space seem all jumbled up.

And now the passageway has ended at a blank wall.

Great.

Have I taken a wrong turn? I look behind me. All of the glow is gone. No gold, no silver, just deep, deep dark. Not going back that way.

How did Hally do it? I extend my right arm and press my

forefinger against the stone, which seems to give like a sponge and then . . .

Ah! A door opens in front of me and the light of day floods in with such intensity that I am briefly blinded.

Then my sight returns. I'm near the top of a hill, a little bowl between jumbled rocks is ahead of me. The sun is just rising in the east. More time passed in Hally's cave than I realized. The rest of yesterday and all of last night. But how could that have been? I didn't sleep. Or did I? I'm feeling awake and refreshed, not the least bit tired.

I take two steps forward, feel a rush of air behind me. I turn and see that the door has closed. In fact there is no sign that any opening was ever there. Just black volcanic rock, its surface speckled with lichen, and off to one side a series of familiar looking petroglyphs. Bird-winged beings. And among them, I notice for the first time another shape—that of a very large, human-like being with long arms.

I know where I am. Place Where Birds Flew. Just one ridge away from Haven. If I climb up that little rise behind me I'll be able to look down over its walls. How I got here is beyond anything I can explain. The range of small mountains where Hally invited us down into his den is at least twenty miles from here. But I only took about, what, a hundred steps before reaching that door? Somehow Hally has placed me right where I need to be if I plan to confront my enemies.

Hally, my man, you have some explaining to do when I see

you again. If I live that long.

I crawl slowly up until I can peer over the ridge top between two boulders. Good view of Haven and of the smoke rising. A lot of smoke rising! I slip my telescope out of my pack and focus it on the interior of the huge walled compound. Yup, buildings burned. Way more destruction than was inflicted by my few grenades. There's been a hot time in the old town since we left a day and half ago. The walls are still intact, the main gate is closed, but I do not see any people visible. Just smoking rubble left in three of the four guard compounds. The guard towers and the walls are manned, but no one else is visible. Every ordinary person is probably being kept inside the residency blocs, locked down.

That worries me. There are way more innocent people in there than there are those who want, at the very least, to kill me. What has happened to them? Has my escape with my family resulted in tragedy for people who never did harm to me?

I can't let potential guilt weight me down right now. Guilt is the worst thing a person can carry with them. It can lead them into foolhardy actions, putting themselves into danger because a part of them feels as if they deserve to be punished. Guilt can make you doubt yourself at the very moment when you need to proceed with certainty.

Whatever has happened has happened, Lozen. Don't think about that. Just put your mind on what comes next.

Which is what?

Locate my enemies.

I'm not going to stand on this ridgetop to do that, though. I sit back with my shoulders against the larger of the two big standing stones. The smooth stone below me is rippled like water, holding the memory of an ocean that was here before the desert. I can smell a storm coming soon. The faint scent of ozone is in the air. A few feet in front of me, a horned toad crawls on top of a stone that is banded with white crystal. It nods at me, then crawls down the other side and disappears into a crevice.

I hold up my hands, trusting now that my power can come to me like this. And it does. The warmth floods both my palms as if I am holding two stones that have been heated in a fire. To the east, to the south, to the west, to the north. Those are the directions in which my enemies may be found.

How lovely. I am surrounded.

Be logical, Lozen. There's no way they could know you are here. You just happen to have stepped out into their midst.

Comforting thought.

How many men were there in each of the Ones' little private armies? Twenty-four or so. Ninety-six in all. But I'm sure that some of them were put out of action by my grenade attack. At least a dozen. Leaving eighty-four. And there's no way that the Ones would dispense with their own personal bodyguards, at least four of which are always kept nearby. So take away another sixteen. Sixty-eight. Then subtract the twenty it takes to fully man the towers and on the walls. Forty-eight. Lovely, only forty-eight heavily armed men to deal with.

One of whom is so close that I can hear his feet.

He's coming up the only trail that leads to this lookout. There are steep cliffs on three sides of this ridge and a sheer drop of a hundred feet just beyond the two boulders behind which I'm concealed.

Whoever that one person is, I am fairly sure that he is clueless about the fact that I am up here.

Ambush time.

CHAPTER THIRTY-EIGHT

Civil War

Dad used to tell me stories about the Foolish People. They were Indians like us, but so innocent and just plain stupid that they did everything wrong. For example, when the first horses showed up, the Foolish People heard from other Indians that horses were useful, that having horses would make their lives better. So, the first chance they had, they traded everything they had to buy some horses from a passing Navajo. The horses were old and sway-backed, but they didn't mind. Now that they had horses they were sure their lives would be better. But what were they supposed to do with them? None of the Foolish People knew. They just looked at their new horses, waiting for them to make their lives better. They did that for a long time. Then, some days later, another Navajo came by.

"What do we do with horses?" they asked.

"You get on top of them and ride them," he answered.

"Oh, good."

So as soon as the Navajo was gone they tried getting on their horses. One of them sat on his horse backward and grabbed the horse's tail, trying to make it move. That did not work. Another tried sitting on his animal's neck. That horse shook him off. Finally, someone got on a horse's back the right way. But when the horse began to move, that man fell off.

"What can we do to stay on horses?" they asked each other.

Then a group of Chiricahuas rode past them. They were riding hard and fast. All of them were staying on the backs of their horses.

"I know," one of the Foolish People said. "They must have smeared pine pitch on their buttocks to stick themselves on the backs of their horses."

So that is what the Foolish People did. They all smeared their bottoms with pine pitch and then climbed on their horses. Sure enough, they stuck there. They did not fall off. They could not get off. They did not know how to steer their horses, so they were just stuck there for a long time while their horses wandered around.

Those men got thirsty and hungry. They began to cry for help. Finally their wives found them. The wives were not as foolish as the men. They drove the horses down to the river, and when the horses swam in the water it loosened the pine pitch and the men were finally able to escape.

○○○

'm thinking of the Foolish People now, I suppose, because in so many ways the men who are hunting me are like those Foolish Indians. Not because they are innocent. Every one of those guards who serve Diablita Loca and the Jester and Lady Time are men who have done bad things to other people and who behave as if they have no consciences at all. They are like the Foolish People because they do not know things that every little Apache child who was raised like my brother and my sister and me knows before they are four years old. Like how to find their way and survive in the desert with nothing more than a knife. Like how to walk quietly when there may be enemies around.

Unlike the person whose heavy feet are thudding up the trail now. From my place of concealment, his boots are jarringly loud as they scrape on the hardpan, loosen small stones that are sent rattling by his careless steps. His rifle butt strikes against a rock as he slips. He curses under his breath.

Ah, only three words. But enough to know that I know that voice.

He walks right past me to climb up to the lookout point and stand silhouetted by the sky as he lifts binoculars to his eyes to scan the land below him. I rise and walk to stand behind him, each of my steps as quiet as an eagle's feather falling to the earth.

I never say much out loud, but this is as good a time as any.

"Hello, Edwin," I say in a soft voice.

321

"Son of a . . . !"

Edwin whirls, the binoculars falling from his hands, their lenses shattering on the ground. He's trying to bring up the AK-47 which he'd slung so carelessly over his shoulder that his frantic hand cannot quite reach the stock.

I hold up my left hand and shake my head. He freezes. Wise move, seeing as how the .357 in my right hand is pointed at his head and is only a foot away from his nose.

I back up, motioning him to unsling the rifle, put it down, step away from it.

He's smart enough to do that. But then he turns to me with a wide-eyed, sincere expression on his face.

"Lozen," he says. "I . . . I was looking for you."

No duh?

He takes a few steps toward me, coming down off the lookout point. I wait until he's no longer visible to anyone below. Then I hold up my hand again, palm out. He stops.

"Listen," he says. "I was looking for you. I mean looking, not hunting."

Edwin's head is heavily bruised just above his right eye from the blow of something, probably a rifle butt. He also has a small bleeding wound on the back of his right wrist and his left pant leg is torn near the knee. Maybe a result of my little grenade serenade. Or maybe from what happened afterward when I left those barracks burning. Interesting.

Keep talking, I think. *Tell me more.*

322

He bites his lip and looks off slightly to the side as if hearing my thought. Then he moves half a foot toward me. "I'm, I'm leaving them. See."

Edwin grasps his right arm where the khaki fabric is less faded than elsewhere, the place where a red armband once encircled his bicep. "I gotta get out, see. It's gone crazy down there in Haven. They all started fighting with each other since you escaped. Diablita started it. She ordered us to attack Lady Time's barracks. She wants to run the whole place. But they fought back and then the Jester's guys joined in. It turned into a whole frigging civil war in no time. The only one who stayed out of it was the Dreamer. He and his men made themselves scarce."

Edwin gestures back over his shoulder toward Haven, taking another small step in my direction as he does so. He looks off to one side, his cheek twitching violently. Another symptom of the far-gone Chain user.

"When it was all done, the troops who survived had all gone over to Diablita. Then she ordered just about all of us who could still walk and carry a gun to find you. She even came along herself. She says she plans to drink your blood before the day is over. That's how hot she is for you, Lozen. That's what started it all. She was the only one of the four who wanted to go out and hunt you down right away and when the others didn't agree she ordered us to attack them."

Edwin has taken yet another step toward me. He is staring

right at me now, looking into my eyes to show how sincere he is in the story he's spinning for me.

Liar, liar, pants on fire.

People trying to deceive you will do that, stare you straight in the face with full eye contact. But they also look off to one side first as Edwin just did. He's probably not lying about the conflict that took place. I can believe that, just as I can believe that all of those troops out looking for me are now in the service of the craziest and most evil of the Ones. What I do not believe is that Edwin is jumping ship. Or that he wants to help me.

My disbelief in his sincerity is strengthened by the fact that I am picking up his thoughts now.

"You know I've always liked you, Lozen."

As much as I like a frigging rattlesnake.

"I want to help you."

Help you over the edge of that frigging cliff after I . . .

The rest of his sadistically pornographic thought is lost as he throws a lightning-fast kick at my gun. It's a nicely conceived move, an inside crescent intended to send the .357 spinning away to the side.

I can't help but admire his technique, despite the fact that my own quick backstep and half turn has resulted in his connecting with nothing but open air.

Hand bones tend to break when making percussive contact with the dense bones of the skull. Especially a skull as thick as his.

That's why I deliver a hard open-palm strike with my left hand to the side of Edwin's head. Hand cupped to blow out the ear drum.

It sends him staggering to the side and down to one knee. Not a knock-out blow, but enough to stun and discourage most attackers.

Edwin, though, is not smart enough to know when he should quit.

"Bitch!" he half-sobs.

Then, instead of raising his hands in defeat he hurls the rock he grasped as he went down.

I didn't expect that. And whether it is luck or skill on his part, that stone hits me in my right wrist. My .357 is sent spinning after all. It goes off as it lands.

BLAM!

I don't think that stray round has hit me. I don't know because Edwin's surprisingly fast bull rush at me has just taken me off my feet. We roll around on the ground and it takes all my training to react.

"AAARRHHH!"

Edwin is roaring, trying to bite me, clawing at my eyes. I get my hands up to protect my face, use my elbows to fend off his attack. It helps that my arms are as long as his. And my strength is still matching his, even with all the steroids he's injected and the adrenalin now rushing through his veins. I manage to get to my side, thrust one leg and then the other between us. I grasp his wrists, dig both feet into his hips. I roll to my back, pulling him toward me, launching him over my head to land on his back six feet behind me with a heavy thud.

I roll quickly to my feet and turn to face him. He's already on his feet. No surprise. I didn't expect that to stop him. I can smell the rank odor of Chain in his sweat. Chain really kicks in under stress.

I reach for my belt to try to slide out the hidden blade I have sheathed in there. But there's not time enough for that. His eyes blood red, Edwin is leaping at me like a tiger. He's pulled a long, razor-bladed knife from a calf sheath.

The objective of the gentle art of aikido, Uncle Chatto taught me, is to deflect the energy of an enemy's attack. You are at the center of a circle, and that which seeks to strike will flow past you even faster.

And that is what Edwin does as I grasp his wrist and shoulder, turn and throw. He flies past me.

Way past me.

Right over the cliff edge ten feet behind me.

It is a high enough drop for his final scream to last long enough for me to count. One and one pony, two and one pony, three and one pony . . .

And then the sickening sound like an egg dropped on concrete as his head meets the rocks below.

CHAPTER THIRTY-NINE

Another Trail

I don't look over the edge of the cliff to see what is all too visible in my mind's eye. He was a vicious creep the whole time I knew him and, until a few seconds ago, an enemy trying to take my life. But I am not happy to have caused his demise. And I can no longer say I've never killed another human being in hand-to-hand combat.

When Child of Water and Killer of Enemies finished destroying nearly all—but not all—of the monsters that threatened human life in that long ago time, they did not feel the thrill of victory. What they felt was sickness. Taking lives is a precarious job, one that can end up polluting your spirit and burning your heart. When you touch the enemy in battle, it unbalances you. The Hero Twins would have died if it had not been for the healing ceremonies that were used to restore their balance, to cool their interior, to soothe their spirits, to clean the dust of death from their vision.

I am going to need such a ceremony.

But not yet. Not yet.

I check myself for injuries. That stray round from the .357 seems to have missed me. I've suffered nothing more than a few bruises and scratches on my cheek from Edwin's nails. I walk over and pick up my gun, check it out. No dirt in the barrel, everything in working order.

I consider the direction of the main trail Edwin just ascended. Does that mean that somehow, even though I did not leave any tracks to reach this place—walking out of the heart of the mountain as I did, they still somehow knew to look for me up here? Maybe they are not totally like the Foolish People after all. Or maybe . . .

If I go down the trail about fifty yards, there's a place where I can edge out onto a lip of stone and get a good view of most of the eastern trail that leads up here. There's another, more precarious way off Place Where Birds Flew that involves maybe ten minutes of rock climbing, which wouldn't be that hard for me. But I'm not going to take that yet. Better to see what my enemies are doing. And see just where and who my enemies are.

I walk down the trail to the lookout.

The last few yards before the stone lip, I drop down and crawl on my stomach, flattening myself out as much as possible. I can see almost as far from here as on the higher lookout— but this time at the backside of this peak, looking east onto the Sonoran plain below. And there they are, the little army assembled to come after me.

They're a mile or more away. I take out my scope to get a clearer look. Right in the very middle of them is Ms. Evil herself, none other than Diablita Loca. She really does want to drink my blood. While it is still warm and flowing from my veins. Next to her are two tall, heavy-muscled men. I recognize Big Boy by the scars on his cheeks. The woodpecker crest of hair on the man next to him, along with the scarlet armband he's wearing, tells me that Red has jumped ship from Lady Time's crew to join what he sees as the winning team.

Everyone, including Diablita, is armed with rifles, the M-16s from Guy's armory. Some of the best guns ever made for human combat. So easy to take apart and clean that I was able to strip one down and reassemble it in total darkness by the time I was ten. Lightweight weapons, too, their straps easy on the shoulder. You can snap shots off one at a time or click it over to automatic and empty a thirty-round magazine in no time flat. And M-16s almost never jam.

But what catches my attention most are the tube-shaped objects carried by the three men fanned out in front. AT-4s.

Crap. I didn't know we had any of those. They were not in Guy's armory for sure. Must have been part of Diablita's private stash. Or maybe somebody just found them and brought them up from an armory down in what used to be old Mexico. My life has just gotten a bit harder.

An AT-4 is nothing to worry about unless getting blown up real good is one of your concerns. It's an .84 mm portable single-shot recoilless missile. Used in the old days as a tank killer or to destroy enemy fortifications. Especially when loaded with high explosive dual-purpose pounds, which have a heavy nose cap that allows the projective to penetrate a wall and then blow up or be skipped off the ground for an airburst.

It could be worse. It could be a Carl Gustav recoilless rifle, which can be reloaded. At least an AT-4 is only good for one shot before it's discarded.

They've brought those things along for more than just hunting me. They're to provide protection against a bulkier threat than just this one little Apache girl. Yet another monster lurks in that area, a huge one, somewhere out in the plain behind them. Its tracks had been seen there, not far at all from Haven, huge, deep footprints. It's the critter that I'd heard rumors about, the one I expected I was going to be sent after on my last mission. And it is one reason why our flight from Haven two nights ago had been in the opposite direction of where Diablita and her little army now are.

Be that as it may, with that many people and weapons such as those AT-4s, a frontal approach on Diablita's forces does not seem like such a good idea right now.

The image of that back trail down the mountain comes into my mind. I picture myself going down it, circling behind my enemies so I can either make an escape or start to pick them off. I hold up my hands. My palms are burning. More enemies coming up the trail that Edwin followed.

Which means they probably heard that gunshot.

Rock-climbing time.

"Don't just see the mountain," Uncle Chatto once said. "Be the mountain."

That is what I have to do now as I start my descent. It's harder with a pack on my back than it would be unburdened. But I make allowances for that weight as I feel my way from one toehold and fingerhold to the next.

I'm not just climbing this cliff, I'm part of it. It feels good as my palms move over its surface. Caressed by the touch of the sun, the old stone is as warm as the skin of a living being.

Reach out now. Touch the mountain. Feel what it feels.

And something begins to happen. I feel a sensation not of weight, but of immeasurable lightness, and I know that it is this mountain's spirit. I can't hold onto it long, this lightness that is heavier than anything I have ever known before, but as I hold it I begin to know some of what it knows, feel the life that shimmers all over it, every plant, every insect and small animal. It is a beautiful feeling, a feeling like being within a prayer.

And with the mountain's spirit helping me, I take a deep breath and move. The next thing I know I'm halfway down.

I take another deep breath. A feeling of flowing into the stones, of feeling the air embracing every part of this mountain, of roots of stone sinking deep beneath the surface of the earth.

331

And as if no time at all has passed, I find myself all the way down at the base. Off a mile to my left is where I saw the main body of Diablita's men. I can't see them now because of the rise and fall of the scrub that grows here and there, screening my view. I chart the path I need to follow to get close to them without being seen.

The sun has moved the width of a hand across the sky by the time I reach the point I've chosen. I am well concealed here, behind a thick tangle of hopseed and sage bush. But I can still peer through and see what is before me. Fifty yards to my left is the mouth of a very narrow and brushy arroyo. It's no more than twenty feet wide at its mouth. I've been through it before and I know all its twists and turns and choke points. That little valley was carved out of the living land by the many generations of flood waters that have come down every now and then after cloudbursts in the high country above here. It's the sort of place where one person might be able to hold off a small army of attackers, retreating step by step, making her attackers pay their toll in casualties. But to get there I have to cross open ground and pass the right flank of Diablita's men, including those with the three rocket launchers.

No need to try anything like that yet.

There, no more than a long stone's throw away, Diablita is standing. Her posture is as impassive as the mask that hides her face.

CHAPTER FORTY

The Walking Hill

I watch, my presence still unnoticed, as Diablita turns to Big Boy.

"Take two more men," she says. "See why the men we sent into that canyon over there haven't returned."

She's talking about the narrow arroyo where I was planning to take refuge and lure them in after me. The arroyo over past that smooth brown hill a hundred feet from them.

A hill? I do not remember a hill being there in the past. Nor did I see it when I was looking down with the scope from the lookout. Then I realize why.

"AWWWROOOO!"

With an ear-splitting roar, that hill rears up, revealing itself to be a huge, earth-brown creature with a gigantic horned head.

Time to run.

I rapidly retreat back up into the relative safety of the big tumbled stones on the slope behind me. From there I watch the chaotic scene unfolding below. I'm above the bushes that screened me, but no one is about to look my way.

The beast, that same one that I might have been sent out to dispatch, has charged into the mass of men who are scattering in every direction. I no longer see Diablita Loca, Big Boy, or Red. They were the furthest from the monster and may have retreated back into the saguaro forest to my left. But I do see lots of other bodies on the ground. Six, now seven, now eight men, crushed under the creature's feet. At least thirty feet tall at its massive front shoulders, it resembles an immense American buffalo. Except the sides of its body are covered with thick plates like an armadillo's.

Outside of viddies, I've never seen any living buffalo, those bison that once covered the plains of this continent like a great brown carpet, their thundering hooves raising dust clouds to the sky. They were all gone before I was alive. I heard that there were efforts to restore the herds from those that survived, but they carried some disease that killed domestic cattle. So a virus was bio-engineered to wipe out the buffalo a second time.

But some of their DNA was kept to create such unnatural beasts as the one wreaking havoc among Diablita's unfortunate crew right now. It's cutting through them like a scythe through weeds. Screaming men are being trampled by its wide hooves and tossed in the air by its huge sharp horns.

A bulky blond man who had been standing a few yards in

front of Diablita, Red, and Big Boy didn't retreat with them. He is holding his ground. Lars is his name. Another Chainer. He aims at the creature's side and empties his thirty-shot magazine. When the bolt locks on the empty chamber, with the dextrous moves of an expert killer, Lars ejects and inverts the magazine to jam in the second magazine he jungle-clipped onto the first. He raises the gun and presses the trigger again.

Ba-da-da-da-da-da-da-da-da-da-da-da-da-da!

I doubt that even one shot missed the mark, striking the creature's side exactly where the heart should be. I also doubt that any of those small caliber rounds had any more effect than a peashooter.

Those heavy plates on its body seems to be impervious to small arms fire. But those shots do have one effect. They draw the giant gemod's attention to Lars.

It sweeps its head to the side, piercing him in the belly with the sharp tip of one of its curved horns, tosses its head up, opens its mouth and . . . *gulp!* Bye-bye, Lars.

And although I am still running as fast as I can, I do notice that this monster's biological antecedents are not those of normal hooved animals. Not with those fangs and that appetite. Part wolverine, maybe.

I reach the mouth of the canyon and stop for a moment. One benefit of not being the object of this lethal critter's affection is that, for once, I have the opportunity to observe a monster's mode of attack without being the target. It charges with its head down, hooks and gores with its horns, tramples with its massive hooves. It's decimated about two-thirds of Diablita's little army in the time it has taken me to count to twenty.

And now it is pausing to graze—if you could call crunching down corpses grazing. Time for me to study it for any weaknesses. It's well protected in front by its heavy skull and its horns. Its side has that thick-plated skin. But as it turns away from me to pick up yet another body, I notice that its hindquarters look less protected. Maybe vulnerable to a high-explosive projectile.

I'd love to have one of those AT-4s in my hands right now. Like the three that lie discarded and unfired on the plain below, not far from the mouth of my rocky arroyo. The men carrying them were so panicked by that first charge that they lacked either the calmness or the time to deploy them. When one passing sweep of a deadly horn disemboweled the first AT-4 man and sent his weapon flying, the other two dropped their weapons and tried to run. But they didn't get far before being flattened under those splayed hooves.

I've counted now to forty and one pony. That is all the time it has taken for the giant buffalo to complete its task of wiping out an entire little army. Every man out there is either dead or about to be deceased. Those who are wounded and moaning from the pain are the ones attracting the monster's attention as it moves leisurely over the field of carnage.

It's still turned away from me. The wind is blowing from

its direction towards mine. Maybe a more cautious person would use this opportunity to escape further up the arroyo. But I have been given a task to fulfill in this life. It's not just to please those who have used me as a human weapon. To preserve life, you must protect life. And as long as unnatural monsters such as this one are able to walk about on the earth, it will not be safe for life. I am Killer of Enemies. It is my job to slay this monster.

Or at least try.

I take a little pollen out of the pouch on my belt, offer it. Then I begin to sing very softly under my breath. Singing, singing, I make my way through the rocks, through the brush, and out onto the plain.

Let my enemy not see me.

Let mist cover its eyes.

Let me succeed in my task.

Let me help the People.

I stay low on my belly as I crawl toward the first AT-4. I lift it, draw it back to me very slowly to avoid any sound of metal scraping against stone. It's the only one I can get to right now. The monster is between me and the other two rocket launchers.

I start to move back. The buffalo stays where it is. Wait! It is starting to shift its head in my direction.

"No! I don't want to die," someone moans.

The monster turns toward the bleeding and delirious man who's just pushed himself up to his knees fifty yards away. The monster takes three big stalking steps.

"Noooooo! Aghhh!"

As the man's cries are cut short, I start to crawl. Ten feet, twenty feet, fifty.

I continue back until I am again out of sight from the plain behind me. I scan my surroundings, the old sedimentary stones carved into pillars by wind and water over the long passing of time. There's a spot deeper into the arroyo that looks perfect. It's just a little above the floor of the small valley among the roots of an old pinon pine. I walk back in, climb up, move aside a few broken branches, shift a stone. Perfect. I remove the safety pin at the end of the tube, position the weapon where I can pick it up and aim it easily when I'm ready to fire it.

But one shot may not be enough. So I venture back out a second time. I leave the arroyo, softly chanting my song.

Let my enemy not see me.
Let mist cover its eyes.
Let me succeed in my task.
Let me help the People.

Once again the wind stays in my face. The giant buffalo is continuing its gruesome grazing. It's moved away from the second AT-4. I lift the heavy weapon with its lethal rocket. It seems untouched. I retreat to the arroyo again, this time to a second spot I've picked out. It's a hundred paces closer to the little canyon's mouth and though on the same side of the canyon, at a forty-five degree angle to the first one. And I can reach the first AT-4 I placed near the pinon pine by scrambling through and under a jumble of stones that form something like a narrow tunnel.

I take out the safety pin from the second rocket launcher, position it.

That was the easy part. I take three deep breaths and return to the arroyo's mouth. My careful movements, my song—and my luck—have worked thus far to avoid my being seen, but now I have to do just the opposite.

The third AT-4 is the one that was being carried by the man hooked by the giant buffalo's horn. It's the furthest from the arroyo. Fifty feet further. An eternity further. I stay as low to the ground as a sidewinder, move no more than a finger's width at a time. I don't bother to count.

Let my enemy not see me.
Let mist cover its eyes.
Let me succeed in my task.
Let me help the People.

Aside from my song I try to avoid any thought. The sun beats down on me. It makes my mouth dry, beads my forehead with sweat. The small breeze that was blowing has stopped. As I crawl, the sand beneath me is sticky from spilled blood. The stench of death is all around me. Spilled organs, voided bladders and bowels. It's so quiet that I can hear every crunch of bone and flesh as the monster buffalo continues to feed on the bodies. It's more than forty yards from me.

And then my hands are grasping the metal tube, so hot from the blazing sun that it burns my fingertips. I pull the AT-4 to me, pull out the firing pin. It makes a small click as I do so and I think I see one of the giant buffalo's ears move. I make sure that I am lying on my stomach with my legs well to the side so I won't burn myself with the back blast—a mistake people sometimes make that is almost as bad as frying an unwary comrade behind you.

No worries about that, Lozen. You are on your own here, girl.

I move back the front and rear sight covers. With an all-too-audible click, the sights pop up in the firing positions. I remove the first safety by moving the firing rod cock lever on the left. Forward, then over the top to the right. Another click and another movement of that ear, back in my direction.

The giant buffalo starts to turn as I hold down the red safety lever in front of the cocking lever, my aim on its huge left hip. I press the firing button with my left thumb.

FWOOOOSH!

As the fin-stabilized projectile explodes from the front, a giant rooster tail of fire bursts out of the back of the firing tube over my back and I feel it searing the side of my right calf, despite the fact that my legs are off to the side.

WHOMP!

It hits the monster halfway through its turn, but more in its flank and less in the more vulnerable hindquarters than I'd hoped. The explosion staggers the creature but doesn't knock it down.

Not enough.

I toss the empty tube, leap to my feet and sprint toward the arroyo.

"AWROOOO!"

The enraged bellow and the irregular thudding of hooves coming up from behind me is enough to chill my blood, but not enough to slow me down at all.

Dad once said that with my long limbs, my big lungs, and my fast-twitch reflexes I was built to be a world-class sprinter, and if they still had Olympic Games I could have been a gold medal winner. The only prize I want to win right now is the right to keep breathing.

I can hear the giant buffalo's feet pounding behind me, feel its hot breath on my neck as I reach the arroyo's mouth and veer down into it. That mouth is wide enough for me to pass through without pausing, but the big stones that choke its entrance are enough, I hope, to slow my pursuer.

The sounds behind me of angry bellowing, horns clacking against stones, rocks being rolled aside, tell me that thus far

341

my plan is working. The giant gemod isn't giving up, but it's been held back long enough for me to round another turn, run deeper into the canyon to the place where I put the second AT-4 at the front of the arroyo. I flatten myself, raise the tube, ready it for firing down into the little canyon . . . and then wait.

But not for long. The monster buffalo pushes its way around the narrow turn in the arroyo, scattering red dirt and pebbles with its shoulders as it thrusts forward below me and, yes, past me. One of its back legs is lame and its flank is blackened from the blast of a missile designed to pierce through sixteen inches of armor. But it is far from mortally wounded. It hasn't seen me or caught my scent, even though it's so close as it passes my place of concealment that I could hit it with a rock.

I wait, my heart pounding. Just a little further, a little more. Now!

WHOMP-POW!

The strike of the missile—which can travel over two hundred yards in less than a second—and the thudding explosion are almost simultaneous with the whooshing sound of its brief flight. The back blast sets fire to the tipi of brush and branches I've piled behind me, a fire that will be as visible to the wounded beast as I will be invisible.

No waiting this time to see the results of my shot and admire my work. I've discarded the tube as soon as I fired it, turned, and ducked down into the tunnel that will lead to my final position up by the pinon pine.

The sound of the beast's bellows tell me that, once again, my shot wasn't fatal. But there's a different tone to its ear-shattering roars. Pain is mixed in with the rage. And when I raise my head to look back up the canyon, I see that my aim was much truer this time. The monster has managed to turn and force its way up the side of the arroyo to the place where I shot at it. It is tearing with its horns at the bonfire ignited by the backblast, scattering burning brush in every direction. And that is starting more fires in the dry grass and bushes. With the wind blowing down from the mountainside, this arroyo is going to turn into an inferno. That fire is going to reach me in a matter of seconds.

Flames are also licking up from the thick hair on the beast's shoulders. It's practically bathed in flame. As it drags itself along, blood spurting from the deep gash inflicted by the rocket, it's setting even more fires around it. It's not giving up, despite the fact that it's ablaze and crippled by the blast that shattered its pelvis and tore the scales from its side. I can feel its pain washing through my mind.

I also feel a twinge of my own regret. Terrible as this creature may be, there's a kind of awful beauty about it. But it's wrong for this world.

The fire is getting closer to me. I need to get out of here, but I need to end this beast's suffering. I raise the third and last rocket launcher, stand up, and take aim.

Look at me.

The giant buffalo stops bellowing. It raises its head above

the flames, shifts itself in my direction. The no-longer shielded side of its immense body is open to the shot that will penetrate into its heart.

I press the firing button.

CHAPTER FORTY-ONE

Just a Second

The arroyo is a rolling inferno of flame as I scramble out of it. My face and hands are blackened by soot. The pack on my back is smoking. The tips of my long hair that shook free from my braids are burned. I was almost killed by that monster after all—albeit indirectly. Behind me there's the scent of burning wood and cooking flesh. The world's biggest buffalo burger now being grilled for the buzzards and coyotes.

I kneel down in the shade of a huge flat-topped boulder far enough to the side of the arroyo's mouth to be away from the fire, which is now burning itself out. I take the top off my canteen, half fill my mouth with water, and swish it around. The thirstier you are, the slower you should drink.

Thank you, Life Giver.

I put the top back on the canteen, settle down with my

back against the boulder. I'm exhausted by the exertion of outrunning the flames, but I am also elated at having defeated another monster. The thought of having succeeded, of being reunited with my family, wills me with so much emotion I feel as if I am about to overflow.

And what will we do now? Go back to Haven and trust that the Dreamer will be an ally? Turn instead to the mountains and return to that little valley where we were so happy before Diablita's men found us?

My mind is tired, filled with so many thoughts and contradictory emotions. Maybe that is why I am, just for a second, unwary. Maybe that is why, just for a second, I don't respond to the touch of my power, to its warning of danger. Just a second.

But a second is way too long. A second in which it comes to me that among all those killed by the giant buffalo beast there were three people that I never saw among them. Three who disappeared when it began.

Snick.

It's the sound of the safety being clicked off on an M-16. A sound that comes from the top of the boulder I'm leaning against.

"Don't move or I'll shoot you," a voice as harsh as a handful of gravel scraped across a windshield growls. "Hands up."

Now there's an interesting paradox. How nice to know that the enemy who has a drop on me is logically challenged. There are advantages to not talking much. Numero Uno is that you avoid sounding like the one who has just given me those two contradictory commands. Don't move and hands up. It's not often a little Apache girl gets a straight man like Big Boy, whose voice is as easy to recognize as his limited mental prowess.

"Which?" I ask, trying not to laugh.

"Huh?"

"Shut up, idiot," another voice says. Diablita steps out from behind the boulder and positions herself in front of me. But not close. She is not as stupid as her head surviving henchman. She's staying at least twenty feet away. Red is standing to her left, his M-16 to his shoulder, squinting down the sights at me. Things are not looking good.

However, the fact that Diablita hasn't told Big Boy or Red to punch my ticket pronto or shot me herself yet–which I would have done if I were her—indicates several things.

Numero Uno, she wants to keep me alive for a little while.

Numero Dos, she thinks she has me where she wants me.

Numero Tres, she is planning on getting much more enjoyment out of my dying than simply plugging me with a volley of bullets from the M-16 she is holding would provide.

Numero Quatro, she has a little speech she wants to deliver to me, just like every dastardly evil doer in every grade-B viddy that Dad and I used to watch. Gloating over a defenseless enemy seems to be built into the DNA of villains.

Keeping her gun pointed dead center at me, she motions

for Big Boy to come down from his perch. He leaps down to land on his feet. He may be half-crazed and terminally violent after all those years on Chain, but he's still as graceful as a big cat—and just as lethal. I can tell from the look on his face that he'd like nothing better than to be given the opportunity to do what he wants with me. The way he's eyeing me from head to toe sends a little shiver down my spine. As well as what he's thinking, which I'd rather not be hearing in my head right now.

My mind is picking up the thoughts of all three of my enemies. Their vile ideas are buzzing like poisonous wasps through my brain. Somehow, I keep my face impassive.

Diablita's mask quivers as she lets out a slow exhalation of breath and adjusts her long, perfect hands on the rifle she is holding.

"So," she says, "my little killer, what shall I do with you?"

As if she didn't already have the whole scenario worked out in her twisted brain.

First skin her hands. Yes. Then her feet and make her run.

I don't say anything. After all, it wasn't really a question.

Diablita laughs. It's a little too high and too long of a laugh for it to sound as if it is coming from someone entirely—or even partly—sane. Even Big Boy takes half a step back and away from her. Then she coughs, reaches up one hand to wipe the scarred mouth hidden beneath the mask that covers her facial deformity.

"Do you think I was always this way?" she says. "Do you think I was always so ruthless in my pursuit of power, in my desire to destroy anyone foolish enough to get in my way?" She pauses again, waiting this time for an answer that I am not about to give her. Saying nothing is to my advantage. It keeps her attention, as well as Red's and Big Boy's eyes, focused on me. She hasn't realized—as I did just a few seconds ago—that I'm actually not alone.

Diablita takes a step toward me. It looks as if she plans to prod me with her gun barrel. Then she thinks better of it and stops. Too bad. But I can wait. And she's only ten feet away now.

"I want to tell you a story," Diablita says. Her voice has changed. It is softer now, almost wistful. "It is a story about a little girl, a girl as sweet and innocent as the dawn of a day in spring. That golden-haired little girl was always kind to everyone. She believed that life was good and that if she did good to others, then happiness would be hers. She wasn't engaged in the wearying struggle of trying to maintain her power from day to day. She wasn't bitter, she knew nothing of injustice. She was the sort of child who would pick up a baby bird and gently put it back into its nest."

Diablita pauses, reaches out a hand toward me. "And do you know who that little girl was, what that little girl's name was?"

Her mask does not cover her left eye, so I can see her raise the eyebrow on that side of her face. A clear sign that she is waiting for me to answer before giving me the punch line.

"No," I say.

"Neither do I. I just killed her and drank her blood. Just as I am going to do with you. Although I may wait until we find your mother and your sister and your brother so I can make you watch as I kill them inch by inch!"

Diablita's laugh—that follows her undoubtedly true little anecdote and her equally sincere statement of intent—is even more maniacal than her first one. The events of the last hour or so, which have decimated her forces and, thus far, thwarted her plans, have driven her off the deep end. If the door of her sanity was slightly unhinged before, it has now been blown off the hinges. Her laughing is bringing her close to me. Less than six feet away now.

It's time, I think.

It's not polite to use your hand to point. That's what we Apaches believe. But we also know how non-Indians think. So when I raise my right hand to point behind them, my three adversaries take immediate notice.

Diablita stops laughing and raises her gun to point it at my chest.

"Hold it," Big Boy growls. Red's finger tightens on his trigger.

"Look," I say.

I move my index finger slightly, jabbing it forward and

indicating a spot just behind and to the left of them. Of course, none of them turn to look.

"That is the oldest trick in the book," Diablita giggles, shaking her head.

"How stupid you think we are?" Big Boy snarls.

Just stupid enough. I drop my index finger down.

Now.

A tall shape steps out from the other side of the giant saguaro twenty feet behind them. Two very large, hirsute hands reach down and around Big Boy, pinning his gun to his side and lifting him off the ground.

Red starts to swing his gun in the direction where Big Boy has just been pulled back behind the giant saguaro that hid Hally's bulk. But he never completes his turn, stopped by the crossbow bolt that is suddenly jutting from the center of the skull tattoo on his heavy right shoulder. He drops his gun to grab at the short arrow and pull it free. He's still yanking at it as Hussein comes leaping in and cracks him across the jaw with an elbow strike. They grapple together and fall out of sight behind a clump of ocotillos.

Diablita sees all this out of the corner of her eye. It briefly takes her attention off me. Just long enough for me to step in and swing my leg up in a crescent kick that tears the M-16 from her grasp and sends it spinning. I follow up with a back kick from my other leg at her chin. My aim is to take her head off. But all I hit is the edge of her mask, knocking it from her face. She's dodged out of the way. Her reflexes are so incredibly fast that it takes my breath away.

There's no time to see what is happening with my two allies, though I can hear the struggle between Hussein and Red still going on.

Diablita has already spun back toward me. Crouched down, she resembles a leopard. It's not just her hands, held out like claws, that make her look more like a beast than a human. It's also her exposed face. She was, I can now see, far more "improved" than the Dreamer was before the Silver Cloud brought an end to the Age of Edison. Her implants were so much deeper that much of the flesh on one side of her face is not merely scarred, it is gone. There is nothing but bone from just above her chin to her hairline. Some of that bone is blackened and pitted from the burning components that were ripped out. A normal person would have died from infection with those wounds. But Diablita must have been saved by the bio enhancements flowing through the bloodstream of One who was made nearly immortal. The mask she donned is gone. The one she wears beneath it is that of death embodied.

In less than a heartbeat, barely time enough to think this, she is leaping at me with a scream.

"AYYYYYYYYY!"

I grasp her clawed hands and fall backward, bending my knees, placing my feet between her hips and waist, then roll and thrust upward. She goes flying over me.

She should have landed on her back, knocking the wind out of her. Instead she twisted in midair and ended up on her feet. I barely have time to regain my balance before she's attacking again, this time with a sharp-edged rock that she has grabbed from the ground. I lean back, block her blow past me at the same time as I sweep her feet out from under her. She lands on her stomach. Well, not quite on her stomach.

The ground around here isn't smooth. It's stony desert soil and there are desert plants growing here and there around us. Ocotillo, creosote bushes, cactuses. Not just giant saguaros such as the one that hid Hally's silent approach, but also barrel cactuses.

Diablita has just fallen belly down on one of those. Its spines dig deeply into her as she rolls to pull herself free.

That takes long enough for me to notice that my least favorite desert plant, the cholla "jumping cactus," is also a prevalent part of the ecosystem here. Cholla got its nickname from the fact that its fat, modified leaves so easily detach from the main plant that it seems to leap up to stick into you.

The follow-through on my block ended up with my left hand in a clump of cholla. I don't feel the pain yet, but I'm wearing a piece of heavily thorned cholla on my palm like a fat green mitten.

Her struggle to escape from the embrace of that barrel cactus seems to have given Diablita enough time to return to whatever passes for rational thought in her brain. When she turns toward me, plucking cactus spines from her body and her hands and arms, she doesn't just attack. She reaches back to her waist and unsheathes a long, thin blade. Then she drops into the stance of a well-trained knife fighter and begins to make the figure eight moves that suggest her points of attack. Either side of the throat, the inner thighs where the femoral arteries might be cut . . .

"I am going to kill you," she hisses as she circles me. "Skin you!"

Whatever.

I stand there, one foot slightly in front of the other, my hands at shoulder height. I still have my own hidden knife inside my belt. But the time it would take to reach down, twist, and pull it free might take too long. Plus I have this piece of cholla clamped on my hand. So, as she circles me, I just concentrate on keeping her in sight.

Suddenly, quick as a cat, she feints right, then slashes at my throat.

Perhaps if she had two eyes and not just the one, her attack might have been more successful. She might have seen my left hand coming at her face as my right hand parried her knife strike past me. Her rattlesnake-swift slash comes closer than I expected. The warmth I feel flowing down my neck tells me that she's managed to slice my cheek.

But I've done worse to her. The slap of my cholla-gloved hand dislodged the sharp-needled piece of cactus from my palm and fastened itself to her face. I've blinded her one remaining eye.

"ARRRRRHHHHHHEEEEE!"

Screaming like a banshee, she slashes her blade back and forth. Tearing the air with her anguish, she stumbles backward, trips over the skeleton of a fallen saguaro branch, twists, falls. And goes silent.

Plucking cholla thorns from my palm, I walk over to her, kick her limp body over with my foot. As she fell, her knife ended up in her own belly, thrust deep by her own weight. My enemy is dead, a victim of her own bloodlust.

But what about my two allies?

Hussein?

I am here, Lozen.

And there he is. He's starting to push himself up to his feet a few yards to my left. Below him is the body of Red. Though Red freed that crossbow bolt from his shoulder, it's now thrust deep into his throat. The bandage has been torn from Hussein's wounded hand by the struggle just ended. He's covered with blood.

Most of it is his, Hussein thinks to me.

And there is no pain in my forehead as I catch his thoughts. Instead, it just feels . . . right.

He walks over to me.

Are you all right? he thinks.

He starts to reach his left hand to touch the cut on my

cheek. I push his hand aside, step in and put my arms around him. I lean my head down for a moment onto his shoulder. I can feel his warm breath on my neck.

We're all right, he thinks to me. ***All three of us.***

Hally?

Here.

He's standing right next to us. I didn't feel him coming up.

Hussein and I let go of each other—aside from his left hand and my right one, which remain linked together. We look up at our Bigfoot friend.

Hally starts humming. No, singing. But it is in a language that sounds so strange I have no words to describe it. Yet somehow, strange as it is, I understand it in a way beyond words. I understand what he is doing, what he is saying. I can see—no, more than see, I can *feel* a glow around him. It's a living presence that touches everything living around us. Every plant, every animal, every insect, every stone, every molecule in the air seems to be responding to it.

Then there is a silence, a silence that must have been here when the whole world was about to come into being. I've been holding my breath. I let it out and as I do so I feel my breath come.

I look up at Hally.

I thought this was my world now, and that you were done helping me.

He spreads his arms out, shrugs, and holds his palms up in front of him.

So sue me.

I look behind him toward the big saguaro.

Where did Big Boy, that other bad guy, go?

To a better place.

Hally rubs his stomach.

No.

Hally burps and I notice as he opens his mouth just how long those canine teeth of his really are. Hussein laughs out loud.

Oh, never mind. But where are Mom and Ana and Victor?

Sleeping in a cave. Safe. They'll wake up when you get to them.

Where?

Just over there.

Hally points with his chin toward a part of the cliff face a hundred yards or so beyond the place where I climbed down.

Both Hussein and I look in that direction. Only for a second, but when we turn back we see just what I expected. No one there. Hally has vanished again.

his is not a once upon a time story. It's not ending with everyone living happily ever after. It's only pausing after a few victories for yours truly and with some uncertainty. I have no idea what is going to happen next other than that I am going to rejoin my family and together we are going to face whatever is ahead of us. And that "us" includes one slightly maimed musical gardener.

Will we go back to Haven? And will the Dreamer welcome us if we do?

Will we go to Valley Where First Light Paints the Cliffs, to live there quietly in peace?

Or will it be necessary for me to keep playing this role that some strange destiny seems to have laid on me, to be a killer of enemies? Do more monsters lie ahead of me on my path?

I can't say. All I can do is put one foot in front of the other and see where it leads me. After all, as Uncle Chatto always said, step by step is the only way to climb a mountain.

AUTHOR'S NOTE

Killer of Enemies is, first and foremost, a work of speculative fiction. Aside from its several references to Chiricahua Apache history and culture, it's a product of my imagination. And I had fun writing it.

The most important connection, perhaps, between this novel and Native American people in the years to come is that it asserts, as I believe, that Indians will be a part of whatever future this continent holds—post-apocalyptic or not. American Indians, and especially the Tinneh (Apache) Nations have shown incredible resiliency throughout five centuries of cultural genocide and colonialism by majority cultures throughout the Americas. Lozen might be seen as an incarnation of that sort of spirit.

Thinking of spirit, as my main character knows, she's lightly based on the historical figure of Lozen. That first Lozen was a true warrior woman of the Chiricahuas. She used her mystical power to find enemies as she fought beside her brother Victorio during the long Apache resistance against Mexico and the United States. Born around 1840, the first Lozen never married and died in 1890 in Alabama where the entire Chiricahua nation had been sent into exile by the United States government. Today, her memory is deeply honored and I know of several contemporary Native women who bear her name. My main character's toughness and determination echo her namesake.

My Lozen is also a sort of reincarnation of another important being in Tinneh traditions, one whose mission in life—back in the beginning times—was to kill the monsters that threatened human life. Called Killer of Enemies or Child of Water among the Apache nations, this being and his twin brother were born to Changing Woman at a time when terrible giant beings roamed the land. Some of the gemods Lozen terminates, such as the Monster Birds, are based on those awful creatures.

If you'd like to know more about the Chiricahuas, take a look at a historical novel I spent years writing and researching called *Geronimo* (Scholastic, 2006). (And let me take this opportunity again to thank the many Apache tradition bearers who were so generous to me over the years with their knowledge and helpful suggestions: Swift Eagle, Michael Lacapa, Michael Darrow, and Harry Mithlo in particular.)

On the following page is a brief bibliography to provide further insight into the rich oral traditions and histories of the Tinneh nations.

Ball, Eve. *In the Days of Victorio.* Tucson: University of Arizona,1970.

Basso, Keith H. *Wisdom Sits in Places.* Albuquerque: University of New Mexico, 1996.

Bray, Dorothy, ed. *Western Apache-English Dictionary.* Tempe: Bilingual Press, 1998.

Clarke, Laverne Harrell. *They Sang for Horses.* Tucson: University of Arizona, 1966.

Cremony, John. *Life Among the Apaches.* Lincoln: University of Nebraska, 1983 (1868).

Farrer, Claire R. *Living Life's Circle: Mescalero Apache Cosmovision.* Albuquerque: University of New Mexico, 1991.

Goddard, Pliny Earle. *Myths and Tales from the San Carlos Apache.* New York: 1918.

Golston, Sydele E. *Changing Woman of the Apache.* New York: Franklin Watts, 1996.

Goodwin, Grenville. *Myths and Tale of the White Mountain Apache.* Tucson: University of Arizona, 1994.

Melody, Michael E. *The Apache.* New York: Chelsea House, 1989.

Opler, Morris Edward. *An Apache Life-Way.* Lincoln: University of Nebraska, 1966 (1941).

--------. *Myths and Tales of the Chiricahua Apache Indians.* Lincoln: University of Nebraska, 1994 (1942).

--------. *Myths and Tales of the Jicarilla Apache Indians.* Mineola: Dover, 1994 (1938).

Roberts, David. *Once They Moved like the Wind.* New York: Touchstone, 1994.

Ortiz, Alfonso, ed. *Handbook of North American Indians: Southwest.* Washington: Smithsonian Institution, 1983.